SAVE
THE
ENEMY

SAVE THE ENEMY

arin greenwood

Published in the United States by Soho Teen
an imprint of
Soho Press, Inc.
853 Broadway
New York, NY 10003

Library of Congress Cataloging-in-Publication Data

Greenwood, Arin.
Save the enemy / Arin Greenwood.
p. cm
ISBN 978-1-61695-259-4
eISBN 978-1-61695-260-0
1. Survival—Fiction. 2. Families—Fiction. 3. Kidnapping—Fiction.
4. Enemies—Fiction. I. Title.
PZ7.G85286Sav 2013
[Fic]—dc23   2013028073

Interior design by Janine Agro, Soho Press, Inc.

Printed in the United States of America

10 9 8 7 6 5 4 3 2 1

For Ray, Murray, and Derrick

FALSE DICHOTOMY

Prologue

Do I believe in ghosts? I didn't used to.

About six years before my mom was randomly murdered, she said that she believed in "spirituality." She couldn't define what that meant. Dad didn't tell her that she was being stupid. No, he gave her his worst: she was being irrational.

"Spirits are inherently irrational," Mom replied. She kissed my little brother Ben on the head as he read the *Wall Street Journal*. He was, like, seven at the time and seemed to know more about the Federal Reserve's goings-on than Dad (or Mom or I) did.

"They're raising interest rates," Ben announced. "The economy is probably improving."

Mom kissed him again, half motherly affection and half showing off. Even then she was the only one who could touch Ben. He would fidget away from Dad and me. Ben and Mom were in their own weird little bubble together sometimes. And still are, as it turns out.

"You're inherently irrational, Julia," Dad said. Then he

got all pissy and went into the kitchen to make a sandwich and a mess.

I was always Dad's good little student, as much as I could be. When he told me that paper money would sink the American economy, I'd repeat this theory back to perfect strangers while they were trying to buy an ice cream. When Dad tried to teach me his own made-up version of jiu-jitsu—yes, Dad's special nonsense jiu-jitsu, Jesus Christ, I called it jiu-Dadsu for the love of everything—I tried to learn; Dad said that in this day and age a girl should be able to flip a potential enemy onto his back. This girl never quite could, but she surely tried. And it really seemed to irritate Mom that I preferred Dad's hobbies (flipping enemies, eating sandwiches) to the ones she tried to steer me toward, like group athletics, playing an instrument, or washing my hair. And so, when Dad said that ghosts were irrational and therefore didn't exist, I took his side against Mom's.

What's funny about that? My name means "spiritual life," if you spell it without the "y," which is only on there because Mom thought it was cuter that way. Dad likes to tell me that he didn't know that's what Zoey, or "Zoe," meant when he named me. He likes to say that he only knew about a book he liked with that name in the title, and a French nuclear reactor that also shares my name. The first nuclear reactor in France, in fact. Dad is into both books and nuclear power and says it's a "crying shame" and a "travesty" that the "no-goodnick environmentalists" are standing in the way of human progress.

About a month after Mom was murdered, I woke up desperately sad, realizing I'd never find out what she really thought of the universe's mysterious and ethereal ways. We'd never argue over the violin or the piano. We'd never share a private laugh over Dad's overbearing ridiculousness. I wished, *wish*, that instead of taking the opportunity to be on Dad's side—to follow him into the kitchen and steal a little bit of his PB&J—I'd stayed with her and Ben.

I'm not sure if Dad's right about paper money either, for that matter.

The point is, that same day I woke up so sad, it started looking like I would have the chance to know Mom's beliefs on the afterlife. Better yet, it seemed as if I might glimpse her experience of the afterlife, so long as my little brother asked her the right questions in his dreams. Ben announced at breakfast that he and Mom communicated while he was asleep.

It's worth mentioning that he made this proclamation in the same dull monotone that he says everything, including his commentary on the economy.

Apparently Mom and Ben have kept up a dialogue since. Either that or my little brother is crazy. I say this like it's either/or, but I suppose it's really not. It's what my dad would say is a "false dichotomy." It's probably not fair to suggest that little Ben is crazy. The doctors prefer terms like "autistic spectrum." Or worse: "Neurodiverse," as Dad would argue.

Or he would have argued, before he got himself kidnapped.

WHERE IS JOHN GALT?

Chapter One

I'm sitting next to Brian Keegan in English class, trying to make a chair levitate.

"The book said you should try to make it vibrate first," I say to Brian. "Then, once it's vibrating, you can lift it off the ground. With your thoughts." I show him a peek of *You Can Levitate*, a book I found at the new age bookstore up the street from my house.

Brian nods. The chair is motionless.

Kids at The Shenandoah School are a lot more tolerant of almost everything than kids at my old school were. Up until this year (my senior year, no less), I went to a huge public school in Warwick, Rhode Island. You had to be careful to wear the right brand of jeans there. You could not speak openly about your levitation goals. Or else—and, really, this is just conjecture, but I think I'm right—the school's meanest and prettiest girls would say, very loudly, something along the lines of "How's your levitating going? Are you levitating very much these days? Are you feeling wicked psychic right now?"

At The Shenandoah School in Alexandria, Virginia? We all wear uniforms, so the jeans issue is nil. Nobody uses "wicked" as an adverb. And the kids here have mostly been going to school together since kindergarten. Mostly, they just seem frigging psyched that some new girl—me, that is—turned up, giving them someone new to talk to. About psychic phenomena. What I still haven't figured out is if these kids' politeness means that they like me or not. The rich are different, that's all I know. At least these ones are.

"I don't think I believe in levitation," I whisper to Brian after a few more minutes of brow-furrowed concentration.

"Me neither," Brian says back. "I had a theory that ghosts and other purely 'psychical' phenomenon could exist in a manner of speaking—" he makes air-quotes "—due to the conservation of energy principle. But my uncle runs the history of the universe lab at Georgetown. He told me that there is no 'missing energy—'" again, with the fingers "—that would have to be accounted for with something like a ghost."

This is how Shenandoah kids are. They are willing to contemplate the existence of ghosts up until their history-of-the-universe-studying uncles tell them that there is no missing energy to account for. Then they are still willing to experiment, to see if the chair will in fact levitate anyway. There is a weird, worldly earnestness that I am still trying to get used to. Also: the money. My family doesn't have tons of money—not like these kids—though I'm guessing we have more since we moved to Alexandria, Virginia. And it's always been enough that I can buy a couple of pairs of decent jeans every year. My dad is, or was, a corporate auditor. I do not know what this means exactly, except that I want to go to sleep whenever he starts talking about work.

My mom used to do a little "consulting" (never clear

about what), but she mostly stayed at home, hovering from a quiet distance over me and my special little brother, Ben, the genius who can't stand anyone touching him now that she is dead and Roscoe is missing.

Mom was killed in January. She'd been out one night with Roscoe in Georgetown. Mom liked to drive to different neighborhoods, especially across the river in DC, to take Roscoe for walks. She said it was like being on a little vacation, going for a walk somewhere new. And what do you know? She walked right into a random mugging that got out of control. The police caught the guy; he was convicted; now he's rotting in prison somewhere. I ignored the court proceedings—I can barely remember what the guy looked like. Fortunately all of that ugly legal aftermath stuff went very quickly.

And during that time, honestly, I focused on Roscoe. He ran away during the attack and was never found. I am an atheist, just like Dad taught me to be, but I still pray, in the most atheistic way possible, that Roscoe is alive somewhere. We're still looking for him. He may have been taken in by a Georgetown family, in which case he is better off than he was when he was our dog. Or maybe he's lost in Rock Creek Park, or down by the Potomac, or along the Canal . . . Ben keeps me posted on the staggeringly low odds of lost dog recovery. "Fewer than one in one thousand. And the odds get worse when the dog goes missing in the context of a murder." When I failed to react appreciatively to this information— Who doesn't love *information*?—he finally said, "Don't you want to know the truth?"

"There's always the one in a thousand," I replied.

"I said fewer than one in a thousand."

Now I feel myself starting to cry again. I thought I was

numb enough not to cry in school anymore, but once more I realize that I will never see Roscoe again, just like I will never see Mom again. It would be a great time for the chair to fly away because that would certainly take my mind off these things. I'd take even a little jiggle.

Nothing. Stupid effing book. You cannot levitate.

"Excuse me," I say to Brian.

I exit the classroom as calmly as I can. A girl named Anne touches my hand as I pass. My private school classmates all came to my mom's funeral, even though I barely know them. Some of their parents are diplomats, so they know from propriety. Others are lawyers and they know from arguments and legal rights and estate planning and stuff. Point is that they all managed to turn up at the funeral and say things that were meant, I believe, to be comforting and correct. In the hall, I hurry past the headmaster's office, point to my tearing eyes, then finally dash into the girls bathroom to heave for a bit before splashing water on my face.

I still don't believe in ghosts. But I wish I did. Then I could be haunted by Mom the way Ben is. Maybe our relationship could still develop.

People—mostly teachers or other grown-ups who think they are being therapeutic—ask me what Mom was like. I give them the basics: she was taller than me, more elegant. She was in her forties but looked younger. She has a younger brother, my uncle Henry, who lives with his wife on an alpaca farm in Rhode Island. Then they inevitably ask, "But what was she *like*?"

There's a story I like to tell those people. They usually stop asking questions about her, or about anyone else in my family, once they've heard it.

When I was about six and my brother was about three,

my father brought home a golden retriever puppy he named Galt. At the time, my dad thought that "galt" meant gold in German. (It doesn't.) No, it's the name of one of the characters in my dad's favorite book, *Atlas Shrugged*. As it turns out, my dad loves dogs and freedom and certain weirdo books but is not so terrific with languages.

Your dad probably read you books like *The Giving Tree* when you were a kid. My dad did read me *The Giving Tree* once, calling it "evil" in that it "promotes the immoral destruction of the self." (I was four.) He preferred *Atlas Shrugged*, which is basically about how rich people shouldn't pay taxes. He has explained to me a lot over the course of my seventeen years that taxes are "slavery." People are only "free when they act as they want to act." Perfect for toddlers—Is my sarcasm coming through?—*Atlas Shrugged* is also the novelized explanation of the writer Ayn Rand's "objectivist" philosophy of "rational self-interest." In other words: extreme selfishness.

Try to get your mind around that a minute. Try to imagine your father preaching the virtues of extreme selfishness. Now imagine being four, the most selfish age in the world. Imagine trying to understand objectivism. Imagine trying to understand *anything* other than wanting to play and eat ice cream. (So I guess I was a good objectivist even without knowing it.) Over the years Dad tried to explain objectivism in less abstract terms. He said that people should be able to buy what they want and act how they want without the government or other people getting in their way. Interestingly, for all this, I still wasn't allowed to set my own bedtime.

Anyway, John Galt is the mysterious hero of *Atlas Shrugged*. Most of the book's other characters know his name but don't know who he is. They spend a lot of time asking "Who is John Galt?" One day I came home from first grade and heard a real-life spin-off of this. It was my dad yelling: "Galt! Galt! Where is Galt? Where is Galt?"

My mom came out of the kitchen, where she had been preparing an intricate meal that no one would appreciate. The kitchen was her sanctuary, her refuge: a place to cook for people who couldn't have cared less about food's subtleties. She wiped her hands on her elegant pants and said, "Galt is living on a farm in Scituate now."

"What? What? Scituate? My dog is in Scituate?"

"Where's Scituate?" I asked.

"It's really far from here!" Dad said.

"Near Boston," Mom explained.

"Jesus!" Dad said.

Calmly, my mom explained—once again—that she did not have time to deal with a puppy while also raising two children, one of whom was already showing signs of being able to recite the phone book while completely lacking interpersonal or consistent potty skills.

"So you just gave away my dog?" Dad protested, his voice rising. "You gave away my Galt? And now he's near goddamn Boston?"

"Jacob, I didn't give Galt away," she said, exasperated. "He's purebred." She handed my father a check. Dad, when he tells the story, likes to say that it was for fifty dollars. I don't remember how much it was for. I was six.

"This really takes selfishness to a whole new level," Dad muttered. "Even Ayn Rand wouldn't go this far." Then he turned to me. "Zoey, put on your shoes, we're going for a walk."

He attached the check to Galt's leash, which had not been

sent to Scituate, and made me take the check for a walk with him around the neighborhood. Mom went back into the kitchen to craft the perfect meal no one would want to eat. Ben rearranged the refrigerator magnets into geometric shapes.

Like I said, once people hear that story, they generally keep quiet on the subject of what my mom was really *like*.

On that walk, Dad talked about capitalism and pets. "Yes, they are unproductive. But they are very soothing. And they are primarily interested in themselves. Ayn Rand kept cats, you know." (I did not. At that time, I honestly still thought Ayn Rand was a family friend, just one I'd never met in person.) Of course, we did later get Roscoe when we moved to Alexandria. Roscoe, the husky, named for no one in particular. Dad and I were finally able to convince Mom that it was the right time, right place—dog walkers being a "thing" (they weren't back when we got Galt) and me big and responsible enough to help out, at least in theory. And Mom ended up loving Roscoe. Loved taking him for walks not just across the river, but all around Old Town, where she studied our neighborhood's pre-colonial architecture and mused about the Civil War's lingering presence. (The first deaths of the Civil War happened right near our townhouse, in a place that is now a luxury hotel.) Loved brushing him, buying him treats. She kissed and cuddled him in a way that she never did with the rest of us, not even Ben.

There's another story about my mom, one that I never tell: when I got my first period, she asked me if I needed her to take me to the doctor to be fitted for an IUD. I was eleven. I was an underdeveloped, shy girl who liked horses and books about girl detectives. Who hated to practice kicking and punching and backflips with my dad but still worshipped him enough to do those things anyway. I did not need an IUD. What I needed was a hug, a lesson in how to use pads, and a conversation about how to tell Dad, gently but firmly, that I was never going to be able to flip a grown man over my puny back.

At least Mom was a little better with Ben. She doted on him in a weird, distant, micromanaging sort of way. For example, she wouldn't care what he was doing for hours on end, and then suddenly she would become very concerned that he eat some kale. It fell on my weak and baffled shoulders to try to mother him in matters not having to do with bitter greens: homework, laundry, doctors, wearing shoes on the correct feet, and so on. But he still wouldn't let me touch him. Just Mom. The older I got, the worse things got between Mom and me, especially in the year before she died. (Died, meaning: was randomly killed. The word "died" somehow helps, like it was cancer or something, a slow and inevitable burn.) We yelled at each other about everything. If I talked too much. If I didn't talk enough. If was spending too much time practicing how to tie a rope into thirty different knots at Dad's bizarre insistence. Thankfully Dad seemed to approve of the way I lived my life, so long as I pretended to agree with 95 percent of what he said, but then gave 5 percent selfish "objectivist" pushback.

I figured we'd work it out. Once I went to college and Mom and I saw each other just a few weeks a year, we'd have a routine. We'd settle into one of those healthy and enjoyable mom/daughter relationships that involve a lot of shopping and silent knowing smiles over tea together. But unless there are ghosts, and she is one—and ghosts can shop—that's not going to happen. Not even Ben believes that.

So, one more splash of water in the bathroom mirror. One

more brave face for my new schoolmates. One more attempt to make sense of the life I never really understood to begin with. At times like these (and I hate myself for it), I wonder if Ben actually has it easier than I do.

SURELY YOU JOUST

Chapter Two

One of Maryland's state sports is jousting. I think I could have been happy as a jouster, if only my parents had moved us a little farther north and gave me access to a horse. (Did you know that milk is Maryland's state beverage? I really got fixated on Maryland for a while there.) But this is Virginia, and after school I have lacrosse practice.

It's hard for me to emphasize just how much I hate this sport. In Rhode Island I'd never really been aware of the existence of lacrosse. These Virginia kids seem to have been handed long sticks with nets shortly after birth. I'd understand using one to catch a butterfly. But to throw a very hard ball from one person to another, ultimately flinging it at some poor schlub standing in front of a goal? The strange part is that the nicest kids at my new school really *love* lacrosse. (Even the super-smart girl who's already gotten into Harvard and is likely to become a cardiac surgeon.) All these Shenandoah School girls: they are polite and persuasive, sporty yet bookish. That's how they convinced me. They said lacrosse would be easy. They said that it'd be a great way to meet people. And so fun, especially the away games. Time off from afternoon classes! Special treatment! A bus ride to a new place!

Mom agreed. It would be a first for her otherwise blank Zoey checklist: *check, my disappointing daughter is participating in team sports for once.* Never mind that I'm terrible at athletics, except for occasionally thriving when performing Dad's martial arts, which I'm certain he made up along the way. And that's not due to any natural ability. It's just all the years with him in the backyard. He once taught me how to use a *sword*, for Christ's sake, using a big black-smithed thing I could barely lift, that we got at a Renaissance Faire. *"In this dangerous world, it is important to know how to outwit and immobilize a foe with a weapon."* Granted, I refused to train anymore with him right around the time Mom suggested I get fitted for an IUD. Swinging swords and kicking an invisible enemy's ass no longer held the same appeal. Still, my muscles probably remember something. Maybe.

Dad was right, though, I guess. To his credit, he doesn't bring it up. I wonder if he wishes (as I do) that he or I had been with Mom during the attack so we could have fought back. That we could have pulled out our sword, which I believe is still somewhere in the house. Or in a perfect world, Mom had joined in with Dad and me when I was a kid. That she had known and practiced jiu-Dadsu and clumsy sword-fighting herself.

But, no. And now, lacrosse.

I'm the girl who always comes home with a clean uniform. This is a big no-no in group sports. I want to quit the team. Naturally, the Shenandoah headmaster won't let me. (Mr. Standiford is one of the well-meaning grown-ups who first asked me what mom was really *like*.)

Today, for instance, I spend the two-hour practice—two hours!—throwing the ball down the field, then racing to pick it up and dribbling back to where I started. It's a lot like being a dog, playing fetch with myself, except that Roscoe and Galt enjoyed fetch. The other girls interact with each other and learn plays. At least I think they do; I am not a hundred percent sure what a "play" is, and when it's all over I wait in the parking lot for Dad to pick me up, wishing I could curl up and melt into the asphalt.

One by one, the girls leave. All offer me a comic "Good practice!" as they hop into their cars or are picked up by their own parents. They mean well; they really do. They feel sorry for me. I am both New Girl and Tragic Figure. I feel sorry for me, too.

Half an hour later I am alone.

As discussed, Dad tries to be devoted but is absentminded. You'd think that an Objectivist would be full of the fire of life or something.

I try calling his cell phone. Straight to voice mail. I doubt he's charged it this week. Best-case scenario: he's at a shelter picking up Roscoe. Most likely: he's forgotten he has children and is at home on the Internet studying compelling new arguments on the wisdom of returning to the gold standard. Ben has actually tried to explain to Dad why returning to the gold standard is not, in fact, wise—especially if the United States wishes to keep participating in the global economy. Dad doesn't care if the United States drops out of the global economy, not if it means we no longer have a "fiat currency."

They've had this conversation many times. Maybe they're having it now.

I pick up my schoolbag, which weighs sixteen tons, and

start walking home. We live about a mile and a half from Shenandoah. It's not an impossible walk. Half an hour, very picturesque. But my legs are tired from all that fetching. My brain is tired from all that trying-to-hold-my-shit-together. As I shamble down the street, I hear someone call my name.

"Zoey!"

This guy, Pete, is right at the edge of the parking lot, beeping from the driver's seat of an old brown Volvo. His mom gave it to him. It's actually one of the few things I know about him, because at Shenandoah, having an old brown Volvo is laughable. (Not in a mean way; nothing is done in a mean way here. People just find the old brown Volvo amusing. I don't quite get the joke.) Pete and his twin sister, Abby, are in my class. Both of them are boarders. Abby is nice. I thought she was going to be the goofy sort of person I could become close with, especially after she told me—apropos only of sitting beside me at the same lunch table—that she was on the competitive roller-skating circuit. *Yes!* Weird, like my jiu-Dadsu. A competitive roller skater would be exactly the sort of person I could really let loose with.

Then I started asking about Pete, at which point she got sort of deflated. I also found out she was planning to get a PhD in biology after studying foreign relations at Georgetown. I'm still hoping, despite my up-and-down grades (some As, mostly in English, some C-minuses, mostly in anything that requires memorization or equations, then a bunch of B-pluses), to get into Berkeley. I think I'm the last kid in my class not to have heard back from the good colleges. I'd feel so much more connected with Shenandoah if I met even one person here who cared about jeans, aspired to be on reality TV, and was likely to become a mid-level state government employee. Pete wants to be a singer-songwriter, which may sound promising on the mediocrity front, but he already gets paid to perform.

"Hey, need a ride?" he asks. The passenger-side window is rolled down.

I lean in. I probably don't smell fantastic.

"I'm okay," I say. "I can walk."

"You live in Old Town, right?" Pete says. "I'm on my way to a gig there anyway. At Lee's. You should come by. It's a cool place."

Lee's is a Civil War-themed restaurant and bar in Old Town Alexandria, a few blocks from the small townhouse where I live. Dad has forbidden me to eat there because Confederate General Robert E. Lee, who is from Alexandria, was obviously "on the wrong side of the war." (Though I'll note there are a number of Virginians who don't think that's so obvious.) I'll add that my dad actually had to explain to me his reasons for thinking Lee was on the wrong side. In general, Dad fully supports states' rights, which would ordinarily mean he'd be on Lee's side. "If the slaves themselves, who are people, are unable to participate in the decision-making process about their own fates, then it's hard to understand the Confederacy's demands as being a true exercise of states' rights. Politics and personhood must coalesce. Understood?"

"So what about dinner?" was my response.

As I climb into Pete's brown Volvo, he gives me a once-over. "What position are you?"

I don't have an answer to this question. I'm not sure what he's asking. "Democrat?" I offer. "But with a libertarian twist. Small 'l' libertarian. Mostly, though, I like to think more abstractly, like, outside the two-party political system."

He smiles. "I meant lacrosse. You're actually on the team?"

"Oh!" My face gets hot and I stare out the window. "I

guess so. Technically. They won't let me quit." There's a lot of traffic, but I enjoy looking at the big houses. I don't mind sitting for a bit. "Are you nervous about your gig?" I ask, mostly to fill the silence at a red light. "Does it bother you playing at a place named for a hero of the Confederacy?"

"What do you mean?"

"Playing at a place named for Robert E. Lee?"

He starts laughing. "The owner's name is Lee. She's from Guam. Seriously, come check out the gig. I'm playing some new songs."

My face starts to burn again. No way will I look at him. After an eternity of start-and-stopping through Old Town, Pete finally reaches our townhouse. My brother is sitting out front.

"Nice place," Pete says.

"Thanks," I say with a mumble. His parents probably live in a castle or something. I slam the passenger door and hurry up the walk, fumbling with my keys. Pete stays there in his car, waiting for me to get safely inside, I guess. No doubt he knows about my Mom's murder and my Tragic Figure status, like everyone else. Ben asks in a really loud, matter-of-fact voice, "Is that your boyfriend?" I can only imagine how red my face is as Pete honks and zooms off to his gig at Not-Confederate Lee's. I push the door open, then turn and wave goodbye like a spaz.

The lights inside are off.

"Dad? Dad?" I call. I walk to the kitchen. No Dad. I walk to his computer room. No Dad. I go upstairs. He's not in his bedroom. When I come back down, Ben is in the kitchen, scribbling in one of his notebooks.

"Where is he?" I ask.

"He was supposed to pick you up," Ben says.

I frown. Once more, I try calling Dad's cell phone, but there's still no answer. "Were you outside for long?" I ask Ben as I hang up.

"I don't process time very well without benchmarks. I've told you that."

Fair enough, I think. I guess I should make us dinner. I know *I'm* starving, at least. Usually Dad has whipped something together or ordered takeout in advance of picking me up. I'm hoping Ben says peanut butter and jelly since it's all I really know how to make. We had a really old gas stove in Rhode Island. That's another reason the kitchen was my Mom's private place: whenever she was going to cook dinner, she'd make me leave in case the stove blew up. My best friend in Rhode Island once asked me how my mom thought it was possible that the stove might blow up, and yet Mom never bought a new one. I still have no answer. I asked my dad about it once, but he denied that Mom ever claimed such a thing, or if she did she was just pissed off. I point to my lack of cooking skills as evidence.

Ben is okay with PB&J. I think about slipping some kale into the sandwich, but I think we're out. I'm supposed to mind his veggie intake; there are a lot of things I'm supposed to do. I go into the bathroom to wash my hands before I fix our food. Then I notice something.

There's a cigarette butt in the toilet.

Dad doesn't smoke. Neither do I. I'm pretty sure my fourteen-year-old, autistic-spectrum brother isn't smoking. Mom always said Ben wouldn't smoke because he wouldn't betray her in that way. Dad said he wouldn't because the science literature shows a low incidence of smoking among the Neurodiverse. So I'm staring into the toilet trying to figure out how freaked out *I* should be. Is it possible that a Con Ed man or solicitor was in the house during the day? Smoking? Not likely. Is it possible Dad is dating a woman who comes over when Ben and I are at school, and she drops cigarettes in the toilet? Even less likely. According to Dad, Ayn Rand says that cigarettes are a wonderful human achievement, and we should celebrate them as an important work product. But he also says he can't participate in this facet of human achievement because of Mom's allergies. And he's even used that line since Mom died, so I don't think he'd date a smoker, even if he were capable of dating anyone but Ayn Rand now that Mom is gone. Plus, Ayn Rand is gone, too.

I call Ben in. "Can you look in there and tell me what you see?" I point at the toilet.

He peers into the bowl. "Urine," he says. "No feces."

"Do you see the cigarette butt?" I ask.

Ben peers into the bowl again. He says he sees it; it's floated under the rim where it's not so obvious, but he can see a bit of it. I ask him if he can conceive of any possible scenario in which there would be a cigarette butt in the toilet of the house. He tells me that he is not imaginative in that way. There's a lot of this kind of back-and-forth, and just when I am about to scream, he tilts his head.

"I have a solution. You come up with possibilities and ask me about them one by one."

There is no humor in his voice. If he were a friend, like I thought Abby would be (or maybe Brian Keegan could be, or better yet, Pete could be, and maybe more?) we'd probably be laughing to hide our anxiety. But this is Ben. Smiles and laughs are rare, and when they do come, the contexts can be baffling.

"Girlfriend who smokes. Worker in the house during the day. Our pipes are somehow connected with a neighbor's ashtray . . ."

Ben rejects the various scenarios. I take a photo of the toilet with my cell phone, then flush, wash my hands again, and go back into the kitchen where I try Dad's cell again. Nothing. Ben and I eat our kale-free sandwiches. I try to do some homework. We watch a little television. No Dad. All I can think about is Mom and how much she hated smokers. Not smoking. *Smokers.* Her parents smoked. Her father died of lung cancer in his fifties. Her mother died not long after that, while riding a motorcycle on a two-lane highway in rural Massachusetts. She'd taken up bikes as a hobby after her husband died. Mom blamed both their deaths on cigarettes.

By ten o'clock I can't sit still. I used to call the police on my parents when I was a kid if they were out too late—which they were quite often, which only made me more anxious. Mom once said I should try St. John's Wort. Then she was randomly murdered. There is no root that cures justifiable paranoia. For all I know, Dad is at the library (which closes at ten), or attending a meeting of Libertarians Anonymous, or doing any number of the Dad-like things he does when he bothers leaving the house.

"Should we call the police?" I ask Ben.

"Dad thinks that the police are an unwelcome use of tax dollars," Ben says.

"Brush your teeth. Go to bed."

Ben brushes his teeth. He refuses to floss. He will need a lot of dental work one day. I go into his room, decorated in *Star Wars* paraphernalia that Dad bought on eBay after Mom died, and pat his head. He flinches. I shove my hand in my pocket.

"I still keep dreaming about Mom," Ben says.

"It must be nice to see her every night," I say to him.

"She's telling me that it isn't Dad's fault she got killed," Ben says.

"Did we ever think it was?"

"I haven't come to a determination," he says. "I'm going to sleep now."

I squeeze my eyes shut, trembling. "Say hi to Mom for me if you see her," I say, quietly, so Ben won't really hear. Then, louder, while turning out the light on the way out: "See if you can find out where Dad is."

HELLO
PM COLUMBUS

Chapter Three

The next morning I oversleep. I know even before I get up that my dad isn't home. He's the one who nags me out of bed in the morning.

I scramble out from under the covers, heart pounding, and check on my brother. His room is empty. He's been an early riser all his life, like Mom always was. Dad claims he was once like me, prone to laziness. It's through sheer act of will that he became a Responsible Adult. Or so he likes to remind me over and over. He also claims that he doesn't tell me these things to be annoying or preachy. I think he wants to let me know what's in store for me when I grow up. If I grow up.

I race downstairs. My brother is sitting in the kitchen, reading *The Wall Street Journal* on his iPad and jotting things in a notebook.

"Did you eat?" I ask.

"I had some ice cream," Ben says.

"'The cornerstone of any nutritious breakfast,'" I quote from a movie, but Ben doesn't get the reference or the humor and my memory is so god-awful I can't remember which movie I'm quoting. I'm more certain about breakfast: cereal and coffee. Mom and Dad let me start drinking coffee young. It stuck. We learned I have an addictive personality. Self-awareness and honest insight about oneself are other important keys to survival, as I've also learned from You-know-who.

"Ice cream contains vital calories, sugars, and nutrients," Ben says.

"Dad's not home," I say. It's not a question.

That still does not mean that there is a crisis on our hands. This is Dad. One time, a few years before Mom was killed, he vanished for two days. Just took off to go hike some old train line that got turned into a walking trail. He wanted to see it because, he said, it had been transformed using only private funds, no government money, and also it was supposed to be very pretty. Pretty, but not well-marked; he apparently got lost, and then, once he realized where he was, discovered it was only one more day's hike to the execution spot of a famous abolitionist. So he stopped at a little store to buy water and food and kept walking, spending a tentless couple of nights at campgrounds along the way. Mom got a call at the end of it, asking for a ride back to his car.

When I asked him what he could have possibly been thinking with such an idiotic move, he said he was sorry; he hadn't realized he was going to be out so long. Then he said sometimes a person's best ideas come to him (or her) in a flash. And then he said, "All good ideas come while walking. Nietzsche said that." Then he said that the goal in life is to develop the wisdom to know which of these ideas to pursue, and then to muster the resources to pursue them.

"Self-awareness and honest insight"—I think that came from the same speech, now that I remember.

I would like both of the above right now to know if I need to be panicking. Or calling the police. I really have no idea.

On top of that, I keep having this terrible feeling that if I call the police, the police will realize that a seventeen-year-old girl and her overly literal fourteen-year-old brother are living unsupervised, and will dispatch us somewhere. Possibly somewhere unpleasant. I guess conceivably we could stay with my Mom's brother, Uncle Henry, and his wife, on their remote Rhode Island alpaca farm, if they would have us. Or with Molly, my former best friend, who has not spoken to me since Mom was killed, if she's finally forgiven me for sleeping with her boyfriend. (The boyfriend she'd broken up with when it happened, in my defense.) These are possibilities, maybe? None ideal. None even really possible. We have school. We can't just go and *leave Dad*. What if Roscoe comes home?

"We should go to school," I say to Ben.

He looks up from his ice cream and *The Wall Street Journal*. "Okay," he says.

"Or maybe we'll skip school today. Go look for Dad and the doggie."

"Okay," he repeats. Same tone, same everything. I appreciate his unexpected flexibilty in our schedule.

"No, school is better." I run upstairs, shower, put on my school uniform. I then remember that we have an away game today. I strip off my uniform and fling it on the floor and wriggle into my lacrosse clothes.

In a daze, I'm aware of Ben and me as we enter the world: heading over to King Street to take the trolley up the hill, and then catching another bus over to Shenandoah. It's nearly noon by the time we get there. I want to be talking to Ben about Dad—*that we haven't seen him in over 24 hours*—but I don't want to worry him if I don't have to. Plus, he's my little brother. I need to protect the little freak as best I can. Okay, "freak" is harsh. But love and anger are all tied up together: another valuable lesson I learned from Dad, apropos of god-knows-what.

"Bye," I say to Ben.

"Bye," he repeats. He turns and marches off to the middle school. I'm impressed by how calm he is. My knees are actually trembling. I head over to the upper school and into the lunchroom. Just as I walk in, with movie-set timing, the girls from the lacrosse team are finishing leading the other students in a big cheer: "Gooooo Librarians!"

Librarians. That's right. That's our team. No wonder Dad chose Shenandoah for me.

On the bus to the game, and on the bench at the game itself, I have some good thinking time. Nobody asks why I was three hours late for school; I am the Tragic Figure. For once, I am relieved that I own this identity. I come up with what might be the best plan for dealing with this Missing-Dad problem: if he is not there when Ben and I get home, I will call Uncle Henry and ask him what to do. He is next in line as an authority figure in my life, after Dad, which is not ideal—but his wife, Aunt Lisa, is very smart and would probably know the right thing to do. I'm worried they think we should be homeschooled, though. Uncle Henry, born and raised a Jew, got wicked into Jesus at some point along the way. And the alpaca farm isn't close to any public schools, I'm pretty sure.

Shenandoah wins the game. I don't know the score. *Good for them! I mean us! The Librarians!*

I picture the scene on the bus ride back to school: Dad is there in the parking lot, waiting for me. Roscoe is in the car with him. Dad explains that he spent the night tracking down our long-lost dog, and he is so sorry.

That's not what happens.

I hurry into the locker room and don't bother showering. I haven't even gotten a little bit dirty, though I am sweating because it's getting warm out, and I'm nervous as hell. I grab my books from my locker, mumble goodbye to my teammates and walk home. The whole way I try Dad's cell phone, over and over. My back aches from carrying my heavy books; my brain and my chest hurt from being too scared. I grip my cell phone tightly, willing it to ring or vibrate. As with the (un)levitating chair, my mental exertions, strenuous and powerful as they feel, result in fucking nothing.

As I pass Lee's, I see Pete standing in the window, playing his guitar, just sort of warming up or something. He sees me and nods his head, like "C'mon in." I shrug my shoulders in a way that he couldn't possibly understand. I try to communicate, in short: *I'd love to come in because you're very cute but my dad is missing and I'm really scared and are you sure this place isn't named after a pro-slavery guy and call me later and I hope my dad is at home now.*

Ben is waiting outside, same as yesterday.

I forgot to tell him I'd be late because of lacrosse. I've got my answer about Dad, though. Ben shoves his notebook into his messenger bag and we head inside together. I would love to hug him right now. But I don't. I can't. Who knows what he'd do? I just say to him, "I'm going to call the police."

He nods.

I open my mouth again, but my phone vibrates—a text.

"It's from Dad's phone!" I whisper. There is a flash of

crazed relief; Dad is probably texting to say he has bought a horse farm for us in Montana, where we're going to live until I leave for college (assuming I leave for college). Or that he was put in jail over an existential taxpayer matter last night, but it's been cleared up and he'll be home soon.

The text reads:

RETURN J-FILE AND YOUR FATHER WILL BE RELEASED. DO NOT INVOLVE THE AUTHORITIES. LEAVE AT PM COLUMBUS AT MIDNIGHT. WE ARE WATCHING.

IN YOUR DREAMS

Chapter Four

I reread the text. I have no idea what it means. J-File? PM Columbus? What are these things? WTF? How am I going to get anywhere at midnight and then back home again when the subway around here shuts down at midnight? Should I really not call the police?

Google says that a "j-file" is either a kind of computer file or else a band from Japan. (I accidentally hear one of their songs. Catchy.) Neither lets me know what I have to bring to the meeting at PM Columbus, whatever that is. I'm trying to imagine the "we" watching this scene. I imagine a lot of shaking heads, maybe even a slapped forehead. It feels hopeless.

I can't even fathom, even a little bit, that my parents have ever been in possession of something so significant that Dad would get kidnapped over it. *Jesus*. Did Dad stumble onto something while working as an auditor? Is that why he quit his job—not just to spend time with his motherless kids? This theory doesn't make a huge amount of sense—why wouldn't

I have been kidnapped then, or Ben, so that Dad, the only person in this family who presumably knows what the J-File is, could have gotten it to the proper authorities, or kidnappers, or whomever?

But what do I know—maybe the kidnappers think Dad wouldn't give up this precious file for kids. Maybe he'd have thought that the homespun self-defense training he gave me, or Ben's magnificent brain, would have gotten us out without him having to turn over the file. Maybe the kidnappers understood the lay of the land. How should I know? What should I know?

"Ben?" I say. "I'm going to ask you something now."

He's quiet. "Okay, Ben?"

"I'm waiting for you to ask me," he says.

"Do you have any idea what a J-File is? Or a PM Columbus?"

"I don't know what they are," he says. But something about his expression makes me ask him another question.

"Have you ever heard of them?"

"Yes," he says. He doesn't go on.

"AND?"

"Mom told me the J-File has been destroyed," he says. Again, that's it.

"That's it?" I shout. "When did Mom say this? What was she talking about?"

"Mom comes to me in my dreams and tells me things," he says.

"Ben, work with me," I respond.

"On what?" he says.

"BEN! What is Mom telling you?" This conversation is insane.

"I've written it down," he says. He gets the black and

white, cardboard-covered notebook out of his bag and opens it, flipping through pages. One page after another is covered in his chicken-scratch handwriting. His handwriting looks so much like Dad's. Initials. Addresses. Dates. Ben points me to one; if I squint, like I'm looking at one of those 3-D posters, I can sort of make it out: M.R., 467 Pennyfield Road, San Francisco, CA, 2/14/1999.

"Mom and Dad were in San Francisco then, for their anniversary," he says, his index finger touching the letters and numbers. "They left us with Uncle Henry."

"What is this?" I ask him. "How do you fricking remember this stuff?" I don't ask. I know the answer. It's because his brain is like a sponge for information. If only he could remember to look both ways while crossing the street!

"My dream diary," he says to me. "I told you I dream about Mom."

"That she's telling you to forgive Dad."

"Other things, too. She tells me to write down the information. I don't know what it means, but I've been doing it. It's important."

My little brother. From the outside, he appears normal. He is a little on the hefty side, like Dad, with Mom's attractive olive skin. (I got Dad's pink skin; luckily, even though I didn't get Mom's height, I did inherit her not-super-hefty build.) Mom used to dress him in strangely overly-formal clothes—clothes that were a little too perfect for an adolescent boy and that were made even a little odder because he'd spill food on the perfect clothes every day, and made a little odder still because *she* did not dress formally, and where did she get this idea that little boys need briefcases? Ben mostly shares T-shirts with Dad now. Those come pre-stained.

"I don't understand, Ben," I say. "Mom tells you things

like 'J-File' in your dreams?" I make the quote-unquote signs with my fingers. "She's giving you initials and addresses to write down? When? Every night? Does she tell you why you have to write it down? Why didn't you tell me this before?"

"Not every night," Ben says. "A couple of times a week. Not usually on the weekends. She might take Shabbat off? I don't know why I have to write it down. But Mom asked me to do it. So I do. She told me not to tell you. She said it was dangerous."

He wheezes a little as he says it. My hefty brother, in his T-shirt with Dad's coffee stains on it, has never breathed very well. His thick, dark hair needs to be cut. His eyes always look sure and certain. He never says things he's not one hundred percent about. He always looks like he has authority, even with that hair and that shirt.

And what I feel, in response to this news and this certainty, is an unspeakably degrading sensation: jealousy. That even after she died, my mother is favoring Ben. Sharing her life—no, her death—with him. But this is not the time for such feelings. I don't actually believe in ghosts, for one thing. For another, maybe my brother has some useful insights.

"Ben, did she tell you what these things are? What they mean? What is a J-File?"

"I don't know," he says.

"Did she tell you anything about it?"

"Just that it's gone," he says. "Destroyed."

"Oh shit," I say. "Shit. Shit. Shit." I look at my brother. "Sorry." After another second I ask him how he knows that this J-File thingie-whatsit has been destroyed.

"Mom told me," he explains again. "In my dreams."

Holy moly, this is ridiculous and amazing and terrible and scary and everything all at once. What is this J-File and how does Mom even know what it is? And how is Mom talking to Ben in his dreams? And how come she never visits me?

"What about PM Columbus?" I ask.

"Mom took me there once," he says.

"In your dreams?

"No," he says, like I'm a moron. "She took me there one day when I didn't go to school. PM stands for Postal Museum. On Columbus, near Union Station."

Mom used to do that sometimes. When it was time to walk out the door in the morning, she'd ask if we'd rather go to school or go have an adventure. It was rare. At least with me. I think she may have done it more with Ben. Usually she was very concerned that we go to school and do well in school and make friends who would help advance our careers, when the time came.

Now Ben begins telling me facts about the Postal Museum.

"It has the largest stamp collection in the world. I know that from when Mom and I went there. And it's where Dad goes to make drop-offs and pickups. That part Mom told me in a dream."

I shiver, not knowing why. "What is Dad dropping off and picking up?"

"I don't know," Ben says. "Mom never said. She just said that none of this is Dad's fault and he is doing his best. He wants to help."

"Help what?" I say.

"Mom never said," says Ben.

I spend I'm-not-sure-how-long reading Ben's notebook. If I squint a little, I can sort of figure out what's written there, and it's mysterious. Initials, dates, addresses (some complete, with street names and numbers, city names; others are just city names or even just the name of what I'd guess is just a building). Nothing else. There are about twenty or so listings, one per page.

Are they notes for some kind of screenplay or something Mom was working on? She used to say sometimes that she had the "soul of an artist but not the talent." She said in a better world she "would have been a rock and roll star or a movie director." I ignored her when she said this. I found it embarrassing. She had a terrible singing voice but would inflict that voice on us all the time, when she was cooking, or driving, or doing anything. Sometimes we'd meet someone out on the street and Mom would say they were "just like a character in a book." I guess it's not impossible that she was involved in some creative endeavor. I never saw any evidence of it. But maybe I just wasn't looking?

"What are these?" I ask Ben.

"They're what Mom tells me to write down," he says. He stares at me as if I've recently been lobotomized. "I told you that."

"You don't have any *context* for the information?" I ask.

He takes the notebook from me. He licks his finger before turning each page. Which is gross. He points his licked finger at one of the entries.

"R.S.," he says. "In Charleston, South Carolina. As I recall, the dates match up when our family took our Christmas trip to Charleston. An Australian businessman named Rob Smallneck died while we were visiting. On the Saturday. I believe he was found naked in the kitchen of an upscale barbeque restaurant under what the newspaper described as 'mysterious circumstances.'"

I shiver again. "That's weird," I say, rather obviously. I sometimes wish I could have Ben's brain for a day or two, instead of my brain, which works like this: I remember we took a horse-drawn carriage tour through the city and my father got into a fight with the carriage driver about whether the Civil War was really about states' rights or slavery. I couldn't even tell you what year that was, though, let alone specific dates, let alone specific details about Bob Smallneck turning up naked and dead in a fancy barbeque joint.

I do remember that Dad wanted to go eat barbeque while we were there, though. He wanted to eat it on Christmas Day. He got a real bee in his bonnet about that. And it had to be the sort of barbeque cooked at a restaurant with no table service. Out in the country, in a shack: that's what he was looking for. But the only place we could find open that day was this pricey place, on account of it probably not being infested with rats . . .

Oh, Dad, what have you done? Oh, holy Christ. I try to think about what Dad would do here. I make another PB&J (still, obviously, no kale). My stomach is in knots. My fists are clenched. Dead Mom told sleeping Ben that this all isn't Dad's fault. Whose fault is it?

"Are you okay, honey?" I ask Ben.

"I'm not sure how to answer that question," Ben says. My poor brother. He looks like he needs to shave; dark hairs are sprouting on his upper lip. Dad always liked to say that we Jews are a hairy people. Being half-Jewish doesn't make us half as hairy, Mom would interject. My little brother needs his father to teach him how to tame what will become an inevitably overgrown upper lip; he needs his mother to teach him not to wear Dad's filthy T-shirts. At the moment, he's stuck with me. I reach out to touch his shoulder. He moves away.

"I'm fine," he says.

"I'm not," I say, instantly wishing I could take it back, even though it's true.

I try to get onto my dad's computer. But it's password protected, and his passwords aren't anything obvious—not Mom's name or ours, or our birthdays. Or his birthday. Or Roscoe's birthday. I text Dad's phone to ask for the password to his computer. No response. I text the same question eight or ten more times, followed by "PLEASE" in all caps. No answer.

I have what feel like four more heart attacks before around eleven, which I try quelling by engaging in deep breathing that will enhance my "Qi" or "life force," which my dad says is bullshit and is also an important aspect to successful martial arts practice (thanks, Dad, for those clear guidelines). Once my life force seems about as prime as it's going to get on this terrible evening, I figure we should go to the Postal Museum. It is a few miles from the house, across the Potomac and in DC. We don't know what the J-File is, but if we go maybe we can explain to the nice kidnappers that Mom told Ben in a dream that it's no longer with us. I'm so bereft of solutions, and so exhausted from being so bereft of solutions.

Nor do I know how to get us to the Postal Museum, for that matter. I don't have a car; I don't know where Dad's car is. If I did, I'd still have to find his keys. The subway will shut down at midnight, so if we can get there, we still probably can't get home. I don't even have money for a stupid damn taxi.

This is all so impossible. I feel tears start. I've always cried easily, and often. Weirdly Dad used to tell me my "extreme vulnerability" would somehow make me a "better warrior" (??!!) if I needed to be one, because "stifling emotions leads to repression, which leads to delayed reactions" or something.

But I will my tears back, and it almost kind of works. Ben

doesn't need me to fall apart. For Pete's sake, I don't need me to fall apart. Wait: an idea.

Ben and I walk to Lee's. I see Pete through the window. He waves. Ben and I go in. Pete steps down from the small stage. He seems really happy to see us. I am trying not to cry again.

"This is Pete," I tell my brother as we lurk by the door.

"Pete Ashburn," Pete says, holding out his hand. What teenager shakes hands? Not my brother, that's for sure, I think, until Ben holds out his chubby, dirty, moist palm.

He says in this bizarrely assured voice, "Ben Trask. I believe we met outside my house this afternoon."

Pete walks us to the back of the restaurant, which is cheerful and plain, with yellow walls and wood tables. There he introduces us to Lee, who looks nothing like a Confederate soldier, so far as my ideas of what Confederate soldiers look like. She's about five feet tall with a muumuu and greyish blondish hair. When Pete introduces us, she hugs me and tries to hug my brother, who ducks.

"You kids want food?" she asks.

"Yes," my brother says as I'm explaining, nervously and apologetically, that we came to ask a favor.

"Sure," says Pete. "Sure, Zoey."

I take Pete aside and tell him I need a ride to the city but he shouldn't ask why. I'm hoping he asks why so I can unburden myself. But he doesn't. He smiles at me with this sort of loopy-looking smile. "Okay," he says, and goes to pack up his guitar as my brother eats a hamburger. Lee sits with him.

I stand back and watch for a moment. It looks like Lee's doing all the right things to make someone comfortable, which are all the things that make my brother uncomfortable. She's trying to make eye contact, she's talking a lot, most likely asking him to tell her about how he's *feeling* about the hamburger or whatnot. I walk over and sit down with them while Pete is off doing whatever he needs to do before we get going.

"Are you from the South?" I ask Lee.

"Guam," she says.

I'm trying to remember if Guam had any role in the Civil War—trying to think of how in the hell I am going to save my father tonight—when Pete returns.

"Let's go," he says, putting his hand on my shoulder and keeping it there as we walk a couple of blocks toward the waterfront on King Street, past the new age bookstore, past the store that sells homemade dog treats, past the restaurant that sells $15 peanut butter, jelly, and bacon sandwiches. The peanut butter, of course, is churned in-house.

We get in the brown Volvo and drive into the city. I don't know where by the museum we are supposed to meet, other than on Columbus.

Pete stops near Union Station. I ask him to wait for me in the circle just in front of the train station and tell my brother to wait in the car, but he hops out and comes with me anyway. I'm glad he's there, even though I'm not.

DC is a big city in some ways (high crime rate; expensive) but it's empty at this time of night near the Postal Museum, which for all I know may also be empty during the day. Are people so into postage that they'd go to a museum about it?

"The Pony Express was originally a private mail service," my brother says. It just makes me think of Dad and how much he would love a return to an all-private mail service.

The museum is a huge white marble building, with ornate columns and inspiring inscriptions engraved along the roof (they're lit up so as to be visible at night), like this one:

"It is said that as many days as there are in the whole

journey, so many are the men and horses that stand along the road, each horse and man at the interval of a day's journey; and these are stayed neither by snow nor rain nor heat nor darkness from accomplishing their appointed course with all speed."—Herodotus, *Histories*

I wish I had a horse, I catch myself thinking, for a moment, distracted.

The large-scale architecture and inspiring quotations suggest *someone* cares about philately—a lot of someones if this big building means anything about a nation's enthusiasm for stamps. But there's no one here now. My brother and I walk around the building once, the whole time my hands positioned into a "knife" so I can execute an open-hand strike if I need to. Please note that I've never used an open-hand strike in the wild, as it were—just against Dad, about forty gazillion times, before I hit puberty. I hope that my open hands remember how to strike after so many years lying fallow. But, thinking about it, I seem to recall Dad said I should always try to kick someone in the knee before even attempting the open-hand strike, though . . . Or maybe below the knee. Or behind it.

I move my hands back into my jacket pockets.

"You don't know *where* exactly the drop-off spot is?" I ask Ben. He says he doesn't. I tell him it would be great if he could get Mom to be more precise from now on. He says he will try, very seriously, my literal little brother, in one of Dad's old V-necks and a pair of dress pants with a streak of something on the leg.

On our second go-around, as we've turned the corner off North Capitol Street around to the poorly lit backside of the building, I hear a voice right behind me, a somewhat high-pitched, nasally voice—like the speaker is congested—and something poking into my back.

"You have the J-File?"

I start to turn around. "Don't move," the voice warns. This would not be a scary-sounding voice without the circumstances. With the circumstances, it's freaking terrifying. My heart starts beating two million beats per minute. This time, maybe literally.

"Where is my father?" I ask. I can feel adrenaline pumping through me. I might pee my pants. I finger the handle of my tote bag, with my wallet and keys and a book—I always have a book with me, but did I really think I'd have some time to enjoy a little *The Sun Also Rises* tonight?—inside of it. "Is he here?"

"Where is the J-File?"

"It's been destroyed," I say. "Please, where is my Dad? If you let me talk to him, I might be able to help you."

There is a hesitation. The man is likely trying to decide what he should do next. He has no way of knowing if the J-File has been destroyed. For that matter, I have no way of knowing if it has been destroyed. My brother telling me that my dead mother told him so in a dream is not really admissible in court, from what I understand of the American legal system. And how do we know Mom even really knows, for that matter? She is, after all, dead. Oh, Mom. Mom. Moms should be alive, protecting their brilliant children. Their naughty and useless ones, too, I hope.

"You have one week to make this right," the man says in my ear. I still can't see what he looks like. I haven't turned around, out of boot-quaking fear. But then he makes a sudden move and grabs my brother's arm. Whatever was shoved into my back is gone.

"We'll hold onto him until we have the file," the man says.

"Don't touch him!" I say, whipping around and looking straight at the man who's gripping my brother's upper arm.

The man does not look like a kidnapper. He looks like a lob-byist, a somewhat overweight white guy in his forties, in a khaki suit. *This* is the guy they sent to deal with us? "They"?

My father's jiu-Dadsu training does not kick in, at least not in the way I expect. I don't flip the guy over my shoulder and onto his back. (Frankly that move would have been a stretch.) But *something* kicks in. Literally. It's my foot, smashing into the man's knee, and as it happens I slip into a nearly medita-tive state. My heart slows. My breathing calms. My mind calms. Time stands still. I haven't felt like this since I was a kid, practicing the same moves over and over and over until I stopped having to think; my body just knew what to do.

The guy with the gun doesn't stand still, though. He tries to move away. Without having to decide to do it, I become aware of myself kicking him in the other knee, then the first knee again. My tote bag is thwapping on my side. Again, without being conscious that I am about to do it, I yank the tote off my shoulder, and spin it into the guy's face. This I become aware of: my hardback copy of *The Sun Also Rises* has come in handy.

"Ow!" The man yelps.

He lets go of my brother and bends forward a little, wincing. I kick him again, this time in the crotch. Dad told me that the crotch isn't such a great place to go for while engaging in self-defense, because while it's sensitive, it's also fairly well-protected (when I was young enough to be get-ting this instruction, I wasn't even scandalized by Dad saying things like "the crotch is sensitive, but don't go for it while you're trying to take a man down").

In this case I see a clear shot, even with the baggy pants. Then, when this lobbyist attacker leans forward, dropping something—I can't see what—I elbow him in the head. It's like I'm watching a movie of myself doing this; I cheer myself on in my head, using enthusiastic rah-rah language I'd never use in real life. "Go Zoey! Kick his ass!"

He backs up, trips over a step, and falls down, cracking his skull loud enough for me to hear. *I* wince. Then I kick him in the neck, hard, then scoot around to kick him in the crotch for good measure. He lies on the marble, barely moaning, not moving.

"Who are you?" I shout at him. "Where is my father? What is the J-File, you asshole? Who is *we*?"

The man doesn't respond. He keeps moaning a little bit but is otherwise still. His pants have torn in the crotch. I can see his red shorts underneath the khakis. This makes me almost pity him. Almost.

"Answer me! Answer me! Who are you and where is my father? What is the J-File? WHO ARE YOU?" I shout. I also keep kicking him. Probably not smart. The man stops moaning. He stops moving, except for his chest rising and falling a little bit. I can hear police sirens. Someone may have heard me shouting. They may have seen the man grab my brother—or me kick the man.

"We have to go," I tell my brother.

"Check his pockets first," my brother says.

He wheezes a little, despite not having exerted himself much. Ben never had to undergo prepubescent warrior training with Dad. We all figured he'd be able to *reason* his way out of any dangerous situation. He's the least animalistic of all of us. The most human: rationality being the mark of humanity. And completely without physical skills.

I try to reach into the lobbyist's pants pocket, where I assume his wallet will be. Nothing in his front pockets. I can't get into his back pockets the way he's lying, and he's too heavy to move. One of the blazer pockets yields an electronic cigarette. One of my teachers puffs on one all through class so I've come to be familiar with this new, and not yet FDA-approved, technology. I reach into the other pocket. There's a business card. For a P.F. Greenawalt, "Political Consultant," with an address in Georgetown.

"Let's go," I say to my brother, who is bending down on the ground, near. He stands up, holding something. He lifts it up and shows me.

"We might need his gun," Ben says. I go to snatch it from him, but I don't know how to safely snatch a gun.

"Give it to me," I say, holding out my hand. He hands it over. I put the cold, black piece of machinery in my tote bag and grab Ben's hand, then drop it when he pulls away. We run back to the brown Volvo. My heart goes back to pounding.

WAFFLE TIME

Chapter Five

"You guys okay?" Pete asks when my brother and I get back into the car.

I don't wait for my brother to respond. I'm shaking and nearly in tears, and am also the tiniest bit exhilarated. And still not quite ready to share all *this* with Pete.

"We're fine," I say.

"You guys want some waffles?" He turns around to look my brother in the eye. "My treat."

We drive off back toward Virginia. We go to an all-night diner in Del Ray, a cute neighborhood about a mile from Old Town. There is a good custard shop there that Dad and I walked Roscoe to a few times. On our walk we'd run into a cat named Harold, whose owner walks him on a leash. Harold loves dogs. He sniffed Roscoe. The custard was delicious.

This time we don't run into Harold the cat. It's about one in the morning. I realize it's a school night, but worrying about getting enough sleep seems kind of plebeian at the moment.

I just beat someone up. There's a momentary nausea. *I just beat someone up.*

Ben, Pete, and I sit at the Formica countertop. Ben gets waffles and fried chicken. Pete gets waffles, fried chicken, and a chocolate milkshake. I have pancakes with goopy strawberry slop on top. I don't think I'm hungry, but then I eat the whole stack. The sugar rush + coming down from the whole PM Columbus incident + having a *gun* with me + not knowing where my dad is + not knowing what Ben's notebook is + finding Pete exceptionally adorable = me a little frazzled.

I obsess about these various things while Pete asks Ben about school and life and the Federal Reserve. Ben tells Pete that Del Ray was one of the DC area's first "commuting suburbs," built in the early 1900s, and that waffles originated in ancient Greece. After we eat, Pete drives us back to the house.

"Your dad won't mind your getting home so late?" Pete asks, tapping the steering wheel as we idle out front. He looks nervous. "You can blame me if you want."

"Dad's not here," I say. I look down at my hands. Dad's not here. Dad's not here. Where is Dad? Not here.

If Pete asks me about Dad's whereabouts, I might tell him about the text, the cause of our evening's misadventures, but he doesn't, even as I am trying to transmit the question from my head into his. I suppose Pete's parents probably travel all the time for work. It seems like that's common around here.

I should invite him in. Or shouldn't. I imagine him inside our house, looking at the paintings—mostly ocean scenes my mother picked up at seaside art festivals—and the books, which are mostly German philosophers (like collections of Nietzsche's mysterious aphorisms, underlined, with a lot of question marks and exclamation points beside them), Ayn Rand novels (also underlined, with markings in the margins that say things like TRUE! and SO TRUE!), a collection of new age and psychic phenomena books (useless thus far), my brother's economics collection (most with dog-eared pages but no markings), some self-help treatises (*Self-Healing for Atheist Widowers* and its ilk, largely unread), and then hundreds of random paperbacks that Dad or I brought home over the years (like *Dog Care for Dummies*, *Understanding Goethe in a New World*, and a very small book called *An Illustrated Guide to Alexandria's Jewish Civil War Heroes*).

Our furniture is not Old Town style—not that I've been inside so many Old Town houses, which I haven't, because our neighbors are mostly kind of standoffish. But I can see in people's first-floor windows. So I know they have a lot of carved wood and dusty-pink upholstery. Their paintings tend toward the dark portraits of severe-looking men in military costumes. Our furniture is eclectic. Mom took a lot of pleasure going to yard sales and antique shops, assembling an upscale-flea-market style for our living quarters. She called it "tiki chic," and always made those annoying scare quotes when she said that, a couple of times a year, usually apropos of nothing.

With Mom gone, dead, the house looks more straight-up flea market. We might even have actual fleas. I'm not what you might call a neat freak, but compared with Dad or Ben I'm obsessive-compulsive about dust, clutter, mess, pillows askew on the yellow velvet couch, and the two velvet chairs which don't match the one leather recliner that Dad insisted we get. (Mom objected on the grounds that those recliners "read lower class"; Dad called her a "pretentious twit" and kept the recliner.) Our lamps have burned-out bulbs. There are dead flies on the windowsills. Dog hair still creeps out from underneath all the furniture, even though we haven't had a dog here in months. I need to get on top of taking over the domestic arts in *chez nous* or else we're going to become the sorts of people you see on TV, on the shows about people who really, really don't have their shit together.

And, as I imagine Pete's eyes moving from one object to another, my mind's eye (it probably needs glasses) fixes on the big smear of dust across the shabby white wicker coffee table Mom thought was so "witty" when she brought it home from some trip she'd taken to Fort Lauderdale. I've been meaning to dust the table for weeks but haven't felt up to it.

"I had a good time tonight," Pete says before Ben and I get out of the car. He gets close to my face. His breath smells syrupy.

"Me, too," I say. I immediately regret saying it. *A good time?*

But for all that, I'm extremely grateful that Pete and his brown Volvo were there with us. The night would have been worse without them. I've never contemplated syrupy breath before.

Pete looks at me, with these big brown eyes and thick eyebrows. He's got on some battered flannel shirt and attractive jeans. I can't tell if his hair is due for a cut or if he's had it cut to appear to be overdue for a cut. Either way, it's appealing. Me, I'm just a nervous girl with bad bangs, bad clothes, a missing father, a highly developed anxious instinct, and a stolen gun in her tote bag.

"Are you dating my sister?" Ben asks.

Right, all that and a brother.

"It's time for bed," I say to Ben. "Say goodnight to Pete."

"I'm not five," Ben says, getting out of the car.

"Don't forget to brush your teeth," I call after him. This is theatrical and bossy for no good reason. Ben doesn't have a key and can't get into the house without me.

And indeed, Ben is standing at the front door waiting for me, like Roscoe used to do. "I don't want to brush my teeth," he shouts. I don't want Ben throwing a temper tantrum now. He does that occasionally. It usually happens when his schedule has been disrupted, he hasn't had enough sleep, and he's had a lot of sugar. I can't imagine that an encounter with a diabolical, armed lobbyist helped. So, this really would be the time.

I shrug toward Pete. "He doesn't want to brush his teeth," I say.

"You don't have a nanny who makes him?" Pete asks.

I can't tell if he's joking to lighten the mood. "Just me."

Pete leans in toward me. I want to explain about my dad being missing and thank him for not asking why we had to go to the Postal Museum in the middle of the night. I want to kiss him. I want to cry. I also want to go examine the gun—I've never had one in my hands before; Dad's special self-reliance training didn't extend to firearms. He's afraid of them. Seems reasonable, I guess, unless you believe that might makes right or that the Second Amendment is worth preserving. Or that you might actually need to defend yourself one day.

Pete reaches out, touches my left hand. I realize my hands are clenched in fists again. Or maybe still.

He rubs my hand and says, "Goodnight, Zoey."

I get out of the car and go inside. Ben goes up to his room without brushing his teeth.

In my own room, I want to examine the gun, but it scares me too much. What if I accidentally shoot it? What if I accidentally do it on purpose?

So I don't even take it out of the tote bag—just remove my book, keys, wallet, and lip gloss, then put the bag-wrapped gun in my newsstand. I turn on this stupid, cheesy little lamp my mom and dad gave me for my twelfth birthday, that's next to my bed. It's one of those "motion lamps" where the heat of the light makes a paper cylinder spin. My cylinder has pictures of fish and dolphins on it. The fish and dolphins look like they are swimming. I wanted to be a marine biologist back then, which made my dad happy because—stay with me—we lived in Rhode Island and the University of Rhode Island has a good marine biology program, which meant I could be educated for in-state tuition.

Dad also thinks that education shouldn't be publicly financed, so he is opposed to state universities on principle, but he's not going to turn away a good bargain. Mom thought marine biology wasn't a good profession for me. It would mean too much time in boats, which would make having a family hard. I wasn't thinking about having a family. I wasn't concerned about my education. I just liked dolphins. They are ancient descendants of land-walking mammals, you know. I like that animals can evolve back into the ocean. And that dolphins are remarkably, stunningly good at recovering from injuries. They can be bitten by a shark and survive. I like that, too. And their permanent smiles. Are they as happy as they look? They must be happy to be able to survive shark bites so readily.

I watch the swimmy creatures move around my room for a few minutes, saying "Goodnight, Mom. Goodnight, Dad" quietly. Then I look at the tote bag with its gun snuggled inside. And in case there's more from Dad or his abductors, I look at my cell phone. But nothing, goddamn nothing. I look at the photo of the cigarette in the toilet. Then flip through some that are less alarming. When I get back to one of Mom wearing a holiday-themed sweater at Christmas—we had no tree, since "Jews don't decorate shrubbery, but Catholics like themed knitwear" (Dad's words)—I turn the phone off. It's time for sleep.

I wake up in the morning to find Ben standing over me, staring.

"Pete made breakfast," he says to me, as I try to control my startle.

"Pete?"

"He's downstairs."

"Why?" I ask.

"He's making breakfast," Ben repeats. I'm not going to get satisfactory answers here.

"Did you . . . sleep well?" I ask him as I start getting out of bed. The lamp is still spinning around. I turn it off, and the fishes and dolphins disappear. They've died is one way to look at it. They are just lights on the wall that have been turned off is another.

"Yes," he says.

"Did you . . . see Mom?"

"She told me some more information," he says.

"Did she say if Dad is okay?"

"No," he says. "I don't think she's omniscient. She might not *know* how Dad is."

Ben leaves my room. I check my phone—still nothing—then pad downstairs, groggy, already in a somewhat anxious state. I don't know what time it is. I have a vague recollection of some exciting, thrilling, terrible events from the evening before. I have a vague recollection that *school* is where I'm supposed to be going.

Pete has scrambled eggs and toast.

"Coffee?" I ask him.

"Just tea," he says, pouring a cup from a pot.

"Nietzsche would like that," I say to him. Yes, Zoey at—I

check the clock on the microwave—6:45 in the morning is full of random allusions to the German philosophers. "No meals between meals, no coffee, coffee breeds darkness," I mumble. "*Tea* is wholesome only in the morning. A little, but strong. It's from *Ecce Homo*. My dad read it to me when I was a kid. But I still like coffee . . ."

Pete turns back to the food. "You can have a lot of tea if you want. It's pretty strong."

"Thanks," I say. This boy is so chipper so early in the morning. It is a relief to see my brother eating eggs, not ice cream. "So . . . what are you doing here?" I ask.

"Cooking breakfast," he says.

"Why are you here cooking breakfast?"

"I slept in the car last night. We got done in DC after curfew," he says. "Figured I'd stay outside your house, make sure you and Benster are okay, with your father out of town and no nanny."

Jesus. This guy is looking out for me and Ben. He slept in the car and is here making breakfast. I can feel a tiny drop in my anxiety. For a moment, my heart rate seems very nearly normal. My head isn't completely buzzy. Adrenaline isn't giving me the sensation of EVERYTHING BEING AWFUL AND SCARY AND UNMANAGEABLE AND COMPLETELY UNFATH-OMABLE. Do all rich kids stand guard outside some girl's house all night when the father isn't home, only to swoop in and man the griddle first thing in the morning?

"Do you find yourself sleeping in your car outside your classmates' houses a lot?" I ask him. "Is this something normal for your cohort?"

"Heh," Pete says. "I don't know about my 'cohort' but I've slept in my car a few times. When I go play gigs, some-times I'll sleep in the car if I'm missing curfew. Or when I stay at my mom's house, if she *happens* to be in the country, I'll sometimes sleep in the car rather than coming in and having to deal with her. Moms can be really crazy."

"Yeah, I know," I say. But then I get sad. My mom was crazy, but now I really miss her. I didn't have my own car or maybe I'd have slept outside rather than deal with her, too. We won't get to see. "What about your dad?" I ask.

"He died when I was little," Pete says. "He drowned."

"Oh, that's terrible," I say.

"Thanks," Pete says.

Pete serves me up one last piece of buttered toast, drinks another swig of tea, then says he has to get going to school soon, so he can change clothes before classes. He asks if we want to ride in with him.

"Sure," I say. "We'll just go get dressed."

By 7:30 we are out the door, back in the Volvo, on our way to school, where I quickly realize that my homework is not done, my reading isn't completed, and—since I seem unable to read people's minds, despite reading several books on the topic—I am not going to pass the pop quiz in chemistry. My dream of going to Berkeley—it's always been a long shot, given my wildly erratic transcript, but I have good SATs and my *mother is dead*, which should count for something— seems ever-farther away. As far away as California.

I run into Pete in the hall between miserable, unfathomable chemistry and English, which I am pretty good at, though distracted by trying to employ psychic phenomenon. He smiles. "Hey," he says. "How are you feeling today?"

How honest an answer should I give?

"Thanks for driving us," I say. "Thanks for cooking breakfast."

"No problem," he says. He pauses. "There's a party tonight. Want to come with?"

Oh boy. My pulse quickens. Little Zoey, getting asked on a date. Little Zoey, who can't leave little Ben by himself, lest he turn on the stove and forget to turn it off.

"Can my brother come?" I ask.

"Ben? Sure, of course," Pete says. "Ben's the best."

A voice inside of me says, "This is not the time to develop a frivolous social life. Now is the time to find Dad." Another, louder, less sophisticated voice inside of me says, "Squee! Pete wants to take me to a party!"

Ben is waiting for me by the field house after lacrosse practice. I notice that instead of his uniform, Ben is wearing suspenders with a pair of Dad's pants and what may be one of Mom's T-shirts. His shoes don't match, but at least he is wearing two of them. How did I miss this outfit when we were going to school today? Did Pete notice it?

"Want to go to a party tonight?" I ask him as we start walking toward home.

"Not really," he says. "Not at all." Then he starts to breathe quickly. "Please don't make me go to a party. We need to go find Dad."

"How about we go to the party for fifteen minutes, then go to P.F. Greenawalt's house?"

"Okay," Ben says.

I'll find a way to make this work.

Pete comes to pick us up at 8:30. I've agonized over what to wear—what indeed is the appropriate outfit for an evening that includes romance, socializing with wealthy classmates, and then hunting for one's mysteriously kidnapped father? I have no idea. In Rhode Island, I'd have worn tight jeans, old clogs, and an acrylic sweater. Then I would have regretted what I was wearing when I saw what the other kids were wearing. But mostly those are just the sorts of things I owned. Mom had great clothes; I have acrylic sweaters and spritzed bangs.

For all I know, kids wear, like, suits to private school parties. Or floral dresses. A lot of girls wear exceedingly prim floral dresses on our few "dress-up days" at school. I finally put on a floral dress that I found at an Old Town consignment shop with tights and my clogs. This is what I now usually wear to dress-up day. It is a soft teal with lilac flowers on it, and it's made of a very fine corduroy.

I used to wear a different outfit to dress-up day—a navy blue skirt with a nice orange T-shirt—but then one day that kid Brian Keegan asked me why I always wore the same outfit and why it didn't look like what the other girls wore. He didn't ask it meanly. He seemed genuinely curious. I don't know how or why he noticed my attire, but I went out after that and hunted down a floral dress I wore to three subsequent dress-up days. It is an alarmingly repellent dress, according to some people—Mom, who was raised semi-Catholic, told me that only backwards Protestants wear dresses like that—but I hope I will fit in.

I've asked my brother to change his clothes, but he refuses. He says he won't leave the house at all if I keep talking about clothes.

"You look like you're going to church," he says to me. Then he says that people who care about clothes are bad people, immoral people. I don't think this. I usually believe that people's outward appearance is somehow a manifestation of what's going on inside. So if my brother is wearing an odd, stained T-shirt with dress pants, it's because inside he is a strange man-boy who doesn't give two hoots about how he's viewed by others. Meanwhile, when I wear weird prim floral dresses, it's because inside I'm a Quaker. Or something. Until Pete arrives, I internally debate changing my shirt. The orange T-shirt is clean. I could just go put that on . . .

Pete has come in a taxi, not in the brown Volvo. He is wearing a jacket that looks like it is made of very expensive leather; it fits him in this sort of perfect, *insouciant* sort of way. Mom used to enjoy insouciant clothing, she always said. She meant casual and free-spirited-looking but expensive, which is how she thought of herself. My clothes tend to be the opposite of that. Uptight and cheap.

"Nice dress," Pete says to me.

I smooth the floral fabric. It is a little bit Amish-looking, really, and I guess it's fair to say that the Amish are not known as an especially free-spirited-looking or fashionable people. Might be more insouciant if I were wearing an expensive leather jacket over the dress. And then maybe a garbage bag over that.

"Where are we going?" I ask, trying not to blush or smile at his compliment.

"To Megan's," Pete says, like I have any idea what that means. I realize as the car starts that I forgot to check on the gun before we left, but it's too late. I'm not used to checking on guns before going out the door, like making sure the stove is off. Speaking of, I didn't check the stove, either. Shit. I don't remember Ben cooking anything. But he's "baked" non-food items in the oven before.

The taxi drives down the George Washington Memorial Parkway and over the 14th Street Bridge, up through the National Mall, through downtown. Ben, sitting between me and Pete in the backseat, reads the book *Economics In One*

Lesson while we head west and end up at a two-story brick house near Dupont Circle, where Pete pays the driver before I can even reach for my wallet. We get out, walk through an artsy-looking iron gate that blocks a flower-filled front lawn. There are some kids from school sitting in chairs on the front porch. We stop to say hi. None look as if they come from an isolated religious community, and I regret the floral dress. I regret my little brother's big briefcase.

Inside, the house has big vibrant art on the walls. The couches are tufted leather. Girls wear cutoff shorts with tank tops or button-down shirts. Some of them have on canvas sneakers or boat shoes. Some wear flip-flops, despite the somewhat chilly evening. Why did I wear this stupid *floral* dress? With thick Amish tights? And clogs? (Which I don't know if Amish people wear. What shoes *do* the Amish wear?) Pete's sister, Abby, has on silver wedge shoes, gold pants, a black embroidered shirt, and is drinking something out of a plastic cup. She is the very epitome of insouciant dressing. I'd look preposterous in that getup. I look like I should be churning her butter.

"Heyyyyy, Zoey," she says to me, coming over and bending down to give me a hug. "And hey there, Ben," she says. She nods at her brother. "Pete," she says.

"Doctor," he says back. Then he says to me, "Let's get a drink." He puts his arm around my shoulder and steers me toward the back of the house.

I turn to look and make sure that Ben's following, but I don't see him. Intellectually, I feel like thirty seconds after getting to a party, he's probably fine. Probably sitting in a quiet corner reading. Or maybe being social by giving a lecture on the natural history of Inuit architecture to some drunk seniors. But I can feel the anxiety re-bubbling up inside of me, pushing out the excitement of the date (is that what this even is?) and the regret about the floral dress.

Out on the back patio, some kids are standing around a keg. Others are on the tiny yard playing bocce ball. *Hey Zoey, Hey Zoey,* they say, then talk to Pete about whatever—music or friends or something. I hardly even hear them; mostly my thoughts veer between wondering where Ben is, hating my dress, and trying desperately to imagine what a girl detective would do to save her father. (Likely get her two closest friends to help gather evidence, identify suspects and make observations. Unfortunately, my best friend isn't speaking with me. And observations aren't my strong suit. As for suspects? I mean, seriously. No idea.)

Other courses of action are easier. Someone hands me a cup. I drink what's in it. It's coconutty. I haven't had any alcohol since moving to this area. The last time I'd gotten drunk was that time at the movies, when I slept with my best friend's ex. And *that* did not improve my life much. I feel that pleasant driftiness starting after half a cup, then the whole thing.

"Where did this come from?" I ask someone standing nearby. A boy from my class named David pours some more from a blender. I drink it. The drift, the fuzz, is welcome.

A girl named Muffy—it's her real name—is saying how she's looking for a condo in Georgetown now, since she'll be going to college there next year, but that she's "super angry" that her parents are going to make her get a two-bedroom in case her sister stays in town for college, too.

"I need my independence," Muffy says. "Why can't my parents understand this?"

"Totally," someone else says.

Then David says, "But aren't your parents buying you the condo?"

"Oh, shut up!" Muffy says. "Like your parents aren't buying you a place in New York!"

"Are you going to New York for college?" I ask him.

"NYU for film school," he says. "I'm gonna make documentaries. Shine a light on reality. How do you like your drink?"

"Tasty," I say. "Strong, I think. Have you seen Ben?"

David leans toward me and whispers, "There's no alcohol in it. I like to see people make themselves drunk through the sheer power of suggestion." He brushes his lips on my ear. These kids, these kids, I don't understand these kids. I still feel drunk. I do not know where I will be going to college in the fall, if I will be going.

If Dad doesn't come back, I couldn't go anyway . . . I couldn't leave my brother. We'd have to go somewhere, though. The house is paid off, I think, but how would we even pay for, like, electricity? How would I pay for Ben's school? His doctors? Where is he? *Where is he?*

"I'm going to find Ben," I say to Pete, who is tossing a bocce ball into the middle of someone else's game. If I were him I'd be worried about tearing my jacket while tossing those heavy balls around. The leather looks so supple and delicate. We've only been at the party a short time, maybe fifteen minutes, maybe twenty, and I know I have to leave once I find my brother, so that he and I can embark on our next steps in the effort to save our fucked family.

"I'll help," Pete says.

We walk back into the perfect house, filled with the rich and friendly. My brother isn't in the kitchen, he's not in the living room. I could call him if he'd carry a cell phone, but he won't, on the grounds that given the lack of study, he's not yet convinced that long-term exposure to the radiation won't cause cancer, and, he says, he has no one to call and can't think of anyone he'd want to hear from.

Pete goes off upstairs to look. I stay on the bottom floor. Ben is not in the den, where I thought I might find him watching something on the gigantic television, amidst the many books. A girl named Lucille from the lacrosse team is in there with some guy from the class below us.

"You're here with *Pete*?" she asks me. "I didn't know you knew him."

"Kind of," I say.

"You know Anne's liked him since second grade," she says, which of course I didn't know. I also don't know how girls at this school react to interlopers. Probably politely.

I walk upstairs, toward a large black and white photograph of a glamorous woman smoking. I open a closed bedroom door, startling some *in flagrante delicto* classmates (Brian Keegan from English class, who says, "Hey Zoey, how're your psychic powers?" when he sees me—he's fooling around with a girl I've seen around but don't think I know) but I don't find my brother. Shit shit shit shit. I run into Pete coming out of the bathroom. Or restroom. Or latrine. Or whatever stupid word rich people use in expensive houses.

"No luck," he says. He takes my hand as we walk down the stairs and start asking people if they've seen Ben.

People ask, "Who?"

"My brother," I say. "He's wearing suspenders."

I'm feeling more and more on the verge of tears. As always, these days—but this time it's my own fault. I'm so upset about losing my brother I've forgotten to be humiliated by wearing stupid clothing.

Why did I bring him here? Why did I even want to be here myself? I don't get these kids. This is not my world.

My father is missing, my dog is missing, I'm wearing Amish clothing, I probably won't get into college, my mother is dead, my brother—where is my brother?

Pete's sister finds me. She says that Ben walked out the door some ten minutes earlier, telling her to tell me that he was leaving, going to . . .

"Georgetown? I think he said Georgetown," Abby says, shifting in her big silver shoes. She has her hair tied up in a knot on top of her head. "He said there was some lobbyist's house he had to go to or something. P.F. Chang's? No, wait, that's that crappy Chinese restaurant . . ."

"P.F. Greenawalt," I say. "Of course."

"Maybe," she says. "I don't really know lobbyists. Just the ones my parents are friends with. MAN, I'm so wasted! Are you so wasted?"

How could I not have known, just immediately, that's where my brother had gone? All these years of living with Ben and having my deductive logic skills honed via Dad's constant lectures, and still, I'm a fucking moron. A moron in a bad dress. I go back to find Pete again. He's in the kitchen, talking to Muffy and Anne.

"You find Ben?" he asks me when I come over.

"He left," I say to him. "I have to go find him. I really have to go find him. This is a disaster."

"We'll go get him. But I'm sure Ben's fine," Pete says. "He's fourteen, right?"

What a comforting thought. No one's ever talked about my brother before as if he could just be "fine." I contemplate the idea of it. Then I realize that, like me, he's got no money with him. He's got a better sense of direction than I do, at least. If he had to, he could probably walk home. Though he forgets to look both ways when he's crossing the street, so . . .

"I think I know where he is." To get the address, I dig the business card out of my tote bag—a different one from the other night, the one that holds the gun, and which I believe and hope is still in my nightstand.

"I'll come," Pete says.

Pete puts his hand on my shoulder and steers me out the front door. We walk out onto the tree-lined residential street. It's gotten chilly and I'm shivering. Pete takes off the leather jacket and hands it to me. I put it on. It is softer than silk, softer than velvet. I have that feeling again, of panic and elation and anxiety and family and the possibility of sex and the possibility of growing up and the possibility of losing— maybe even already having lost—everything I care about, all mixed into an alienating cocktail of a head-state.

Pete is in the here and now. He asks where we're going.

"Georgetown," I say.

"Then we should get a cab," he says, raising his arm. And magically, one appears.

SCRAMBLED

Chapter Six

The cab driver is from Ethiopia and listens to NPR. He tells us that DC has the second-largest Ethiopian population in the world.

"Outside, of course, of Ethiopia," he says.

Pete has been to Ethiopia. His mom, he says, used to be in the State Department. She was some sort of attaché. When he was a kid, she took him and his sister along on a lot of trips. He says he doesn't remember much about the trip—he was young—but does recall eating raw beef by hand with a bunch of mid-level diplomats in Addis Ababa. Pete and the driver share information about a certain Ethiopian jazz musician who'd recently turned up in a club on U Street after being missing for some twenty years. They make tentative plans to go see him play together sometime soon. I half-listen. Pete takes my hand, keeps talking. Eavesdropping on this worldly conversation takes my mind off what we're doing in this cab hardly at all.

I watch out the window as the city passes, from yuppie Dupont through somewhat sterile Foggy Bottom into

Georgetown. We drive along M Street for a little bit. The gorgeous girls with glossy hair and leather boots have shopping bags, even near eleven at night. They do not wear flowered dresses. The boys have popped collars. They look like assholes. "Date-rapey," Mom would have said. She liked to point out guys who she thought would carry roofies. She told me never to accept a drink from one of them, but that it could, in some circumstances, be acceptable to have them pay for dinner. Helpful life lessons were Mom's forte. Oh, Mom. Were you joking? Did you mean it? Did you teach me what to look out for well enough? Did Dad teach me how to get myself out of the fixes you didn't teach me to avoid? I look for more assholes; I look for Roscoe. I miss my parents. I have this crazy feeling of wanting to make babies with Pete.

The cab takes us up to O Street and along the street of beautiful houses. The houses here look like the ones in Old Town but somehow, without any clear visual difference (to me), they look even more expensive. The cab stops in front of a large stone house. The meter reads $14.75. I look at Pete. He pulls out his wallet.

"I'm sorry," I say to him.

"You're very cute," he says, as we get out of the car, and I realize, with a sick stab in my stomach, that this is the very spot where my mother was killed. I haven't been back to this spot since the week after she was found there, shot on the sidewalk. We kept going back to look for Roscoe. Dad made me knock on all the doors on the block to see if anyone had seen our dog, because he doesn't like talking to strangers. No one had seen a dog. Several people invited me in to have cups of tea, though. They saw the crying and cold girl asking about the dog that went missing when her mother was killed outside on the sidewalk. I declined, since Dad didn't want me leaving him alone outside.

I don't know how I could not have realized we were coming back now to that same place. I suppose the world goes on, reusing the same settings. Or else that my mother being killed here, and P.F. Greenawalt's business card sending us here, is something other than just a weird coincidence.

"Okay," I say, taking in a deep breath. I want Pete to ask what we are doing, coming to this odd house in Georgetown late at night. He puts his hand on my shoulder.

I can see in the front window, as I stand ringing the doorbell. Leather couches. Rows and rows of books. Dark portraits of severe men in military uniforms. No sign of my brother.

"Whose house is this?" Pete asks as the door starts to open. I wish I knew. No one answered the door here when I came by looking for Roscoe.

Before me is a short guy, about five four, with dark hair gelled into rows of crispy waves and wire-rim glasses. He appears to be in his mid-thirties, maybe. It's hard to tell given his clothes: schlumpy white button-down shirt, wrinkled khaki pants with pleating at the hips that makes it look like he's got hips made for birthing. If the guy at the Postal Museum looked nerdy, this guy looks like the dude that guy would call a nerd.

"Is my brother here?" I ask the guy. I am still feeling slightly woozy. I may ask this more loudly than intended.

"You must be Zoey," he says in a nasal voice. "I'm P.F. Greenawalt. Political Consultant. Come in. Please. I'm anxious to speak with you. I knew your mother."

"I'm Pete," says Pete in his easy way, following. "Should I call you P.F.?"

P.F. Greenawalt pauses for a second and looks Pete over. "Mhm," he then says, nodding and leading us toward the back of the house, into a big kitchen.

My mother. How does this guy know my mother? Why is he anxious to talk to me? My brother is sitting at a farm table. I feel a surge of the sweetest relief I think I've ever felt. Just as quickly, it's gone. The gun is in the middle of the table. Perhaps not *the* gun. Maybe it's just *a* gun.

"Sit down," P.F. says, pointing at the table. "I was making your brother some eggs."

I sit next to Ben. I whisper to him, "Are you okay?" He shrugs and pulls away.

"So," says P.F. "How do you like your eggs?"

"Scrambled," says Pete.

"How do you know my mother?" I ask.

"We met when your family moved here," he says, as if that somehow explains anything at all. My mind whirls. Ben stares. P.F. cooks. Pete asks him questions about being a Political Consultant—who does he do it for, how long has he been doing it, etc. P.F. says he's got his own small firm. He has a variety of clients. He does some consulting on elections. And some other things, which is how he met my mom.

"Do you spend a lot of time on the road?" Pete asks. "My mom used to do that. Hard on the family."

"I enjoy most of the travel," P.F. says.

"Have you ever come across something called a 'J-File' in your work?" I ask. My brother gives me a look.

"Zoey, can you help me carry something in from the other room?" P.F. asks, putting three plates of scrambled eggs on the table.

I follow him up a flight of stairs. We go into a room with a harpsichord in it.

"I've always been interested in the Renaissance," he says by way of explanation. Then he points to a well-worn leather chair in a corner, underneath a framed Harvard diploma. I sit down.

"J-File," P.F. begins. "What do you know about a J-File?"

"What do *you* know about it?" I ask him.

He closes his eyes a moment, then pulls the bench from underneath the harpsichord and sits on it.

"Your brother came to my house tonight asking why my business card was in the pocket of a man who accosted you the other night," P.F. says. "I didn't tell him. Though when he pulled out a gun . . ."

"Why was it there? The business card, why was it in that man's pocket?"

"How old are you?" he asks.

"Seventeen," I say.

"You are too young," he says, "to have to be hearing any of this—"

"I haven't heard anything yet," I interrupt.

"Your mom," he begins, "was coming to see me when she got . . . murdered. She was bringing me a, a, a . . . a record. A record of . . . of bad things. It's called a J-File."

"What kind of bad things? Why was my mother bringing this to you?"

P.F. Greenawalt, Political Consultant, looks exceedingly uncomfortable. He pulls a piece of paper out of a pocket and fidgets with it, twisting it into a string, then untwisting it. I grab him by the wrist and dig my nails in a little bit. Dad called this move "the human handcuffs." It was very effective when he, a grown man, used it against me as a small eleven-year-old.

"Just tell me," I say, quaking. "My father is being held hostage. His kidnappers say that I have to bring them the J-File. I don't know what it is or where it is, and I can't get him back without it."

"Oh, hell," P.F. Greenawalt says. He twists his wrists out of my hands, using a deft move that Dad didn't know or neglected to teach me. My nail catches on his skin and rips, which hurts. Now I have a hangnail. I try to bite it off. It starts to bleed. I watch the blood bubble on my cuticle. The pain of it is odd because I don't really feel it in my finger. I feel it in my stomach. I feel nauseated. (Not *nauseous*. Nauseated. Mom was a stickler for correct usage.)

"Do you have a Band-Aid?" I ask. I don't want to suck on the blood because it's gross and I think it might undermine my authority here.

P.F. Greenawalt sighs and leaves the room. I sit there, trying not to wipe my finger on one of the leather chairs. But then I do anyway. I don't want to get blood on my dress. My gross dress would be even more gross. More punk rock, though. The blood leaves a mark on the leather. I lick my finger and try to wipe it out, but the spot just gets darker and more damp.

Finally P.F. comes back with some damp, generic-brand Band-Aids. He holds them out to me. He doesn't seem to notice the blood on the chair. I take the bandages from his hand, then grab his wrist again, smearing some blood on his hand.

"Please tell me," I say.

He extracts his wrist again, frowning, then wiping his hand onto his pants. He seems ruffled. Then again, I have no idea what is running through his mind or how he's feeling. He made my brother eggs after my brother pulled a gun on him.

"Your mother was bringing me the J-File," he says, avoiding my eyes. "She was killed on the sidewalk outside my house. I believe by someone from the group whose nefarious activities would have been exposed by this list . . . This is all speculation, of course."

"And you don't think that the person who killed her also took the J-File?"

"I don't think so. If she had it on her, then why would your father have been kidnapped?"

"I don't know. Maybe someone other than the kidnappers got the J-File. And why did my mother have the list at all?" I ask.

"I really can't say," says P.F.

"Was it my dad?" I say. "Is my dad . . . ?" It sounds too preposterous to contemplate. But all of this is preposterous. "Is my dad a spy of some sort? A *murderer*?" He's such a goofy libertarian, I think. Did he take Ayn Rand to some crazy logical extreme for real? Is he responsible for my mother's death? My mother's murder? I know Mom says no when she comes to visit Ben in his dreams. But on the other hand, he is responsible for trying to teach me martial arts. And he's such a goddamn weirdo. And he's my dad. And I miss him. And I don't know what to think.

Neither, apparently, does anyone else.

"I really don't know," P.F. says. "I would just encourage you to find the list. And bring it to me."

"But my dad," I say. "My dad."

"If my clients have the file, they can save your father," he says.

"Why can't they save him without the list then?" I ask.

"They don't have a bargaining chip without the J-File," he says.

"But if *I* have the J-File, then why shouldn't I just give it to them directly to get my father back?"

"Look, Zoey," P.F. says. "This is how it has to work. You have to trust me."

He has a smear of my blood on his trousers now, and I

have so many questions. I don't know if this is the time to push . . . My judgment feels impaired. This also feels like a situation for which I don't have a body of experience to guide my intuition.

I reach out to grab his wrist once more for good measure. Perhaps I should have tried a different move. He doesn't seem surprised, or even annoyed, and definitely not scared. He just moves his arms out of reach, then comes back to pat my own.

"Your eggs are cold," P.F. says. He isn't so much cold as he is cool. As a cucumber. An incredibly dorky cucumber. "Zoey, you have to trust me," he says again. "Does your hand hurt? I'm sorry you got cut."

The fuzzy boldness gives way to P.F. Greenawalt's certainty. I touch my hangnail.

"I'm okay," I say loudly, like I'm objecting.

We go back downstairs. Ben and Pete have finished their eggs and are spinning the gun around on the table. It slows and stops, pointing right at me as I approach the table.

"That seems unsafe," I say.

Pete opens his hand. He's taken out the bullets, a small cluster of shiny, brass-colored things. I pick one up. It's cold and lighter than I thought it would be. I give it back. Pete puts all the bullets in his front pocket.

"They're just pieces of metal," he says, trying to make me feel safe, I think.

"Let's go home," I say.

"Do you need a ride?" P.F. Greenawalt asks. "I can drive you."

This saves me the problem of needing to expect Pete to pay. But I don't think that I want P.F. Greenawalt, Political Consultant, knowing where I live. On the other hand, he probably knows already. He knew Mom. He knew who I was when I appeared at his doorstep.

"I'm tired," Ben says.

"There probably won't be any cabs nearby," Pete says.

I stare at P.F. Greenawalt.

"It's no trouble," he says in his nasally voice. "I couldn't live with myself if something happened to you kids and I hadn't made sure you got home safe."

I'm tired, too, I realize. I pick up the gun and put it in my tote bag. It's about as heavy as a hardback volume of *The Sun Also Rises*. With the two of these objects, the tote has gotten uncomfortably heavy on my shoulder. It would really be terrible if I got, like, scoliosis from walking all the way home to Virginia with *The Sun Also Rises* and a *gun* in my tote bag. I finally nod, surrendering.

We walk a few blocks and find his black Lincoln sedan. I get in the front seat and P.F. explains his car-buying philosophy, as if this were a natural conversation to have. "I always buy a luxury car that isn't trendy," he says. "I can get more car for the money that way." He shows me a panel that lets each front-seat passenger control their own air temperature.

"That mattered more when I was married."

Now he has my attention. "Oh yeah?" I ask. "So how did you and Mom meet?"

"Through mutual acquaintances," he says, waving his left hand a little bit. He's still got a thin gold band on his ring finger. Did he and my mom have an *affair*? That is the *most* preposterous idea yet, I think. I stare out the window as we drive over the Key Bridge, look at the few boats enjoying this spring Saturday night on the Potomac. Through Rosslyn, which is a grim and militaristic-looking place, then through some of the other Virginia suburbs, which are grim without seeming *especially* militaristic.

Pete tries to make conversation, asking if anyone's seen

any good movies lately. P.F. Greenawalt describes a Hallmark movie he saw on television that weekend.

"It turns out that Hallmark films pack a surprising emotional punch," he concludes.

He and Pete get to talking about what makes for a good film, and if a good film has to have any meaningful intellectual content or if it's sufficient for the viewer merely to be emotionally engaged. Pete argues that art has to have *some* intellectual content to be good, and that he always makes sure his songs are more than just cheap tearjerkers. P.F. says he thinks artists who over-rely on intellectual content are lazy.

"I truly can't believe I'm hearing you say this," Pete keeps repeating. "You're saying that Hallmark moviemakers are the *most* honest artists?"

"That's what I'm saying," P.F. says back, spiritedly, nasally, this odd man who likes the Renaissance and has my blood on his pants, and is driving us home in his old-man car.

I actually have mixed opinions on this topic, but I keep them to myself. Part of me wonders if P.F. is trying to get us to lower our collective guards so he can kill us all and bury us in our backyard. Joke's on him; we don't have a backyard. We drive through Crystal City, which has a revolving restaurant/bar that we all went to when we first moved to the area, so we could see the monuments "in the round." Mom's words, uttered after having gotten a little tipsy on pink cocktails as the bar was going around and around and around. We spent hours there, looking out over the Reagan National Airport (which Mom refused to call the "Reagan National Airport"; she'd only call it "National Airport"), the Jefferson Memorial, the Pentagon, time and time again.

Dad made a big deal about the Pentagon, pointing out the

part of it still black and ruined from where a plane hit it on 9/11. He said that there shouldn't be a Pentagon, shouldn't be a state-sponsored military.

"Do you know why houses are so ungodly expensive in this area?" he asked me.

"Because they're nice?" I said.

He had only been drinking coffee with whipped cream on it and had become a little bit agitated from the caffeine and sugar and views of government expansion.

"Because of defense contractors," he said. "That big Pentagon spends billions of dollars per year buying airplanes and missiles and tanks. The people around here make millions persuading the Pentagon to buy their airplanes instead of the other guys'. It's a racket."

As the restaurant rotated, the Jefferson Memorial came into view. This thing of glowing white marble, with columns and a round roof, built to honor the primary author of the Declaration of Independence, which I'd been reading as part of my American History class.

"It's so pretty," I remarked, mostly to change the subject "When can we go see it in person?"

"Never. There shouldn't be a Lincoln Memorial, either," Dad said. "Don't get me started on Lincoln. The only thing he was good for was his strategy when it comes to enemies. It's wrong to create worshipful white marble shrines for politicians, as if they're Roman gods."

"And getting rid of slavery."

"Well, yes, of course that, too," said Dad, before embarking into a new tirade about Jefferson and his monument and its political-slash-economic implications. "The monument was built by FDR."

"But it's Thomas Jefferson."

"He's a power-monger who'd enslave a country of freedom-lovers to advance his own political aims," said my Dad. "And the monument was built by FDR. You'll notice that all the quotations inside the Jefferson Memorial sound like Jefferson would have supported FDR's political agenda." He snorted in an annoyed and jauntily self-righteous manner. "The New Deal never should have happened!"

P.F. Greenawalt doesn't give us any lectures about the New Deal on our drive along the George Washington Memorial Parkway. He drops us outside the house. He does not pull a gun or knife on us. He smiles, a sad and tired smile, and says goodnight. I open the door, wave goodbye. Ben and Pete come inside with me. I feel another strange surge of relief, even though I shouldn't.

"Brush your teeth," I say to Ben. He starts to go up the stairs.

"Wait," I say to Pete. "I'll be right back."

I follow Ben upstairs and plant myself in front of him. "Ben. Ben. You can't do that. You can't leave without telling me where you are going. You can't walk to Georgetown. You can't carry a *gun*. You can't leave without telling me."

"I told that girl to tell you," he says. "By the transitive property that is telling you."

"Ben," I say. I want to hug him and slap him. I don't do either. "Were you scared?"

"I didn't like the party," he says. "There were too many drunk people. None of them said anything interesting."

"Ben, please, if you see Mom tonight. Ask her where we can find the J-File."

"Okay," he says.

"I love you, honey," I say. I try to hug him. He pulls away and bows. That's friendlier than it could have been.

I change into my orange T-shirt and some shorts and go

back downstairs. Pete is sitting on the couch. He is strumming a ukulele—a little toy instrument that Mom collected from somewhere and put on display. I didn't even know it could be played.

"You're just a little girl trapped in a kooky whirl," he's singing. "You've got a little brother, kind of strange but not a bother. You are mysterious. Sometimes so serious. Other times imperious. Still other times so nervous."

He stops and looks at me. "It's true, you know."

"Yeah," I say. "Hey, thanks for . . . you know. Thanks."

"Of course," he says. "I know what it's like when your parents are gone a lot."

"Is that why you're being . . . so nice?" I ask. I feel shy. I feel depleted.

"That's one reason," he says. Then he asks if he can stay on the couch tonight, instead of out in the car.

"Okay," I say. I tug on my shirt.

"Sit down," he says. "Come hang out with me."

I sit on the couch shyly, like it's not my house. He keeps playing the ukulele. I watch a little, then get up, get a book, sit back down again. It's one of the new age books. This one is about palm reading. I find the section about "lifelines" and try to find mine on my left palm. It seems awfully short . . .

Pete takes my hand and looks at it. "I met a palm reader in India who taught me how to do some basic readings," he says.

"Is my lifeline too short?" I ask, trying to make out as if it's funny that I might have a really, really short lifeline, like it might not mean that I'm going to die.

Pete moves his face in to examine my hand more closely. He traces his index finger along my palm. It makes me feel all a-quivery, on high alert.

"What happened here?" he asks, ever so gently tapping the Band-Aid.

"Hangnail," I say, not very loudly.

He goes back to examining the other parts of my hand for what feels like a very, very long time. Like, if the broken lifeline means what I think it means, then I might be dead by the time he's done even looking at it.

But I'm not. He says, "I'm trying to remember. I was in India a few years ago now. But I think when it's broken like that, it means that things are about to change."

"Oh," I say. I'm still feeling lost in this moment. But I also can't quite tell what kind of moment we're having here exactly. It's feeling like a very soft and tender moment.

"Don't be scared of change," he says. "Life is change."

"I'm scared of life," I say quietly, then laugh, but not in a "Ha ha!" kind of way. More like a "What the fuck am I going to do?" kind of way.

"You seem to be doing okay," he says. "You're going to be okay."

He's smiling. I'm dying inside. In two scary days, I've come to depend on him. It scares me to be attached to anyone— best friends ditch you when you bed their exes; parents die, get kidnapped—and it seems especially stupid to get attached to someone I don't actually know. Who doesn't actually know me. I have no way to predict what he will do. If he will stay even when he asks if he can stay. Or anything else. About anyone.

"I'll get you some sheets," I say, breaking up whatever it is that's happening here. I go upstairs, get the sheets, blankets, pillows. A towel for the morning. He gets up off the couch. I make it into a bed.

"Goodnight," he says to me as I go up to my own bed. "Don't be scared."

FIRE

Chapter Seven

I dream of my mother. It's the dream I had a lot when I was a kid. I'm running through a dark path in the woods. My mother is chasing me. I keep falling. She's getting closer. I am terrified. I wake up remembering that Pete is downstairs. I look at my lifeline, which is still broken, and get up to go check on my brother.

He's not there. I feel the dread rising—is he off with the gun having another adventure?—but he's downstairs in the den, watching CNN and scribbling in his notebook.

I sit down next to him on the yellow velvet couch. "Hey, hon," I say. "Sleep okay?"

He grunts and keeps writing.

"Did . . ." I look up to make sure Pete won't hear. Maybe he's still asleep. Or was never here to begin with. "Mom? You saw Mom last night?"

"Yeah," he says.

"What did she say?"

"I'm writing it down before I forget," he says. "Can you please stop talking?"

Pete bursts in and says, full of energy, "Buddy! Brunch?"

Ben lays down his pen. "This is useless," he says. "You people are impossible."

"So, brunch then?" Pete says. "It's only Saturday. You have two days to do your homework."

"We could go without you and leave you to get your . . . homework . . . done," I say. "If you swear to God you won't leave the house."

"You know that I don't believe in God," Ben says. "So you know that oath is meaningless."

"But you believe in promises," I say. "Remember? Dad told us that breaking promises is a violation of the categorical imperative?" I look at Pete. Our tender moment has evaporated. Back to pure awkward. "It's Kant," I say. "The German philosopher? He said that not breaking promises is a perfect duty toward others."

"You really like the Germans," Pete says. "Nietzsche, Kant. I thought you were Jewish."

"Culturally," I say. "And still only on my Dad's side."

"Ayn Rand said Kant was wrong," Ben says. "Dad only told us otherwise so we wouldn't lie to him."

"Pete and I are going to get some food," I say to him. "You can come with us and eat. Or if you want to work on your *homework* and you promise your sister that you won't leave the house or turn on the stove, then you can stay home."

"Buddy, you should come," Pete says. "Lee makes a great breakfast."

"I can make myself something here," Ben says. I glare at him, then remember that he does not pick up on facial cues.

"No turning on the stove," I tell him.

"I'll have cereal," he says.

I put on my orange T-shirt again, with some jeans. Squirt a little hairspray into my bangs, then fluff them up the tiniest bit. Is this an attractive look? It is not necessarily an attractive look. I don't quite know how to give myself a definitively attractive look, however. Maybe I will buy some new T-shirts, when I have access to money again. No more floral dresses, though.

We walk over to the restaurant. It is Saturday morning. No one is carrying a gun, though. Because this is an open-carry state, I have been given to understand that I might sometimes see regular people with holsters. I haven't noticed that so far, though.

People with baby strollers holding unbleached tote bags with green leaves and flowers poking out the top are walking up and down King Street, presumably to and from the farmers market that's held on the ground of Alexandria's City Hall. Where slaves were once sold, now preppy folks can pick up heirloom tomatoes and homemade jam. (Both of which are, incidentally, delicious.) I notice myself looking for smokers. Is Dad's kidnapper around? I'm on the lookout for smokers the way Roscoe used to be on the lookout for squirrels. What am I going to do if I see one? Point? Bark? Run up and ask, "DO YOU HAVE MY DAD?"

We get to Lee's. The restaurant is having a special Civil War brunch. We get a table right away. A waitress, wearing a long dress, a prim bonnet, and a pin that reads "My Name Is Britney" brings us coffee and plates of cornmeal pancakes and some fried meats. I drink the coffee. It is not coffee.

"What is this?" I ask Britney when she next appears.

"Chicory," she explains. "Coffee wasn't available during the war."

Lee comes over to the table. She is wearing a hoop skirt, with her hair parted in the middle, pulled into a low bun.

"Hello, children!" she says. Then she stops. "You, girl. Your aura is a mess. What is going on?"

"Oh, nothing," I say. I'm touched she noticed and asked. But I also think she might be a little stupid for believing in auras.

"*Nothing* my behind," she says. "Come back. I'm going to give you a reading."

I start getting up from the table. Pete, too. Lee tells Pete to sit back down.

"Readings aren't theater," she says.

Lee and I walk past the mostly empty tables to a small office at the back of the restaurant. Her office seems oddly sterile. Lee seems like such a warm person, and at least once she wore such a colorful muumuu, I thought that she'd have, like, kids' paintings in the office or some framed original pop art. Instead, there's just some framed, dusty black-and-white photos of what might be Robert E. Lee and company. And some fairly austere furniture.

She has me sit on a hard wooden chair at a round, tiled table. Shuffling a deck of cards, Lee asks me how things are going: school, family, health. "Love?"

At that, I blush.

"Cut the deck," she instructs me. I split it at what looks like the halfway point. Lee flips cards, places them into a sort of funky-looking H shape on the plain-wood, piney-smelling table, and looks at me with her eyebrows raised.

"Do you believe that the cards really connect with . . . the spiritual world?" I ask. "You think there is a spiritual world to connect with?"

"Honey, I have no idea. I can only tell you that the cards tell me things, and I tell those things to other people, and those people find what I have to say useful from time to time. And, this is not entirely related, but for some reason I am nearly certain I was a medium named Betty Cockburn in Georgetown in the eighteen sixties," she says. "An aide to the Lincolns."

"So you do support the North?" I ask.

"Let's see what the cards tell us," Lee says. She looks over the colorful, spooky array, pausing on a card that appears to show a man in a tunic carrying a satchel, accompanied by a small dog.

"The Fool," she says. "He symbolizes new beginnings. But he also tells you to watch your step before you walk over a cliff. And now here," she says, flipping over another card, "The *Lovers*. Well that seems obvious."

She looks at the cards, turning them over one by one. A woman who may be pregnant. A man with a sword. A skeleton riding a horse. Three swords going through a heart. I don't like the look on Lee's face. I do wish she'd say I'm about to take horseback-riding lessons.

"Honey, what is happening in your life right now? I am getting a serious sense of urgency from these cards," she says.

"Oh, it's nothing," I say, feeling a little well of panic and of wanting to talk. Lee has this earth-mother air about her, even with her Civil War dress and hairdo. I could easily unburden to her. Are tarot readers required to maintain confidentiality?

"Honey, these cards are telling me that there is big time shit going down. And that you need to deal with it," she says. "You don't have all the time in the world. People could die."

"Do you know what I should do?" I ask. My throat catches. I do not believe in tarot cards. But I truly need guidance. In general, I rely on either logic or authority to get me through situations. I figure out the right thing to do by thinking about it. Or Mom and Dad tell me what to do. I've got no way to know what I should do in this situation. And there's no one to tell me.

"Do I call the police?" I ask.

"I can't tell you how to proceed. I can only tell you that the time is now. You have to make choices. Understanding that this is a mixed message, I am saying you can't wait for other people to tell you what to do. You have to take action. You are angry, but don't let the anger stop you from doing what needs to be done."

"Can you see . . . is my dad to blame? Can you see . . . things . . . about him? About my mom?" I assume Lee knows about my mom's murder; everyone knows, I think.

Lee smiles. "I see a lot, honey. Not everything. But when I see something, I see it. Speaking of," she says, "if you want to work a shift or two, I can find something for you to do."

"Thank you," I say. "Yeah. I really could do that." Then, "What about the dog? On that one card. The one with the little dog on it."

"The dog usually represents loyalty. Faithfulness. Faith itself."

"Do you see anything in the cards about *my* dog? Roscoe. He's a husky. He's missing. He got lost the night my mom was killed."

"I'll be honest. I don't see anything about Roscoe in the cards, honey," Lee says. "But I hope you find your doggie."

We go back into the dining room.

Pete's drinking his chicory, reading a paperback. I glance at the restrooms—a heretofore unexpected downside to having a sudden and unplanned-for live-in boy is that one can never really poop—but Lee had been so insistent about taking action now. I do not think bowel action is what she had in mind. It pains me that there is this pressure in my gut, and also that I am so very susceptible to woo-woo types of stuff when my father is not there to suggest to me that only stupid people would take advice from some painted pieces of paper. *Mom* liked going to palm readers and tarot card readers. I think Mom would have liked Lee a lot. I think she'd have appreciated the austerity of the office, even, because it shows a real *commitment* to a particular vision.

And, you know, I think Mom would have liked Pete, too. I don't think Dad would like either of them, but he's not *here* to tell me not to listen to their advice or accept their help.

But I can still feel myself trying to disregard what Lee is saying to me. I'm still trying to imagine that Pete, with his "you've got changes coming, I can see it in your lifeline," is full of shit. I'm still thinking that Ben isn't really talking to Mom every night. Kid won't use a cell phone but has a direct line to our dead mother, eh? Nothing makes sense if these things are true. A spiritual world that *really exists* and isn't just a metaphor? Forget about all that being illogical—which it is, because, as Brian Keegan's physicist uncle says, there isn't any place in the universe for things like ghosts or gods to be hiding out.

And also, I mean, what if palms and cards really can be read? What do you even *do* with yourself then?

Back outside, the sun is shining. It is one of those spring days you only get this time of year, with the kind of sky that's light but not bright blue. A hint of flowers wafts—yes, it *wafts*, that's what it's doing—through the air, into my nose. I sniff the delicate hint of a scent. I sneeze.

"Bless you," Pete says. He asks if I've ever been to India. I tell him I have not. He tells me about that trip he took with his mom and twin sister there, when he met the palm readers. He went to a town called Kochi, a southern port city which is famous for its spice markets.

"I met this dude there. I don't even remember his name. It was at this gallery in Jew Town—yeah, that's what the neighborhood is called. No, it's not anti-Semitic or whatever. One of the oldest colonies of Jews in the world was there. Can you say colonies of Jews? Like bats? They've been there for almost two thousand years. Two groups of them. Well, there's hardly any left now. But I'm getting off track.

"I met this dude who told me he's an accidental guru. He had this amazing hair and was wearing a long, embroidered tunic of some sort. Different from the other tunics. But I can't really say what exactly made him different, just that he *was*. I knew it as soon as I saw him. And I'm not the only one. I had a cup of tea with him at the gallery and he got to telling me that all his life, people have met him and decided that he was their guru. He told me he tried to send all these people away. He wants to draw and run his gallery. But they kept coming. And they wouldn't leave. So finally he started giving them things to do. Hang paintings in the gallery. Do chores. When I met him he was having them build a whole encampment up in the hills, where the tea is grown. I wanted to go. He was going to hold Ayurvedic retreats there or something."

"Why didn't you go?"

"Eh, I was fifteen. I go to school. I'm not Hindu . . . But he took me to this amazing place where the people have a trance ritual. It goes on all night in this little village in the country. We stayed with his uncle in a big purple house that the uncle's son bought for him. The son's a lawyer. The house was almost as cool as the trance ritual. I'd love to have a purple house . . ."

"Me, too," I say.

"So the people in this village stay up all night for the ritual. They build a big bonfire. They wear costumes—these crazy costumes, some with straw—and dance and dance and dance. The idea is that eventually you become a deity yourself, with all the dancing. And then you throw yourself into the fire. People standing around watching pull you out. Then you throw yourself back in. They throw themselves in. I didn't do it. I don't know why they didn't burn up. I dunno. I think about it a lot. The world has all these rules. Don't jump into fire. And then here's a bunch of people who jump into fire. And they're okay. At least they were at the ritual I saw. What explains that?"

"What did your friend say?"

"He said that when you dance like that you go into a trance and then you're, um, impervious to sensations that ordinarily would be shocking. He said there are neuroscience explanations. That going into a trance releases endorphins. I like the religious explanation. You really *become* a god. But I wonder why gods don't burn."

"Where are you going to college next year?" I ask.

"I'm not," he says. "I'm going to Europe for the year. Going to bring my guitar and play. Write songs. Live some of my own life so I have my own things to write about."

"I'm still waiting to hear from Berkeley," I say. "I bet I don't get in. I probably won't be going to college."

"You should come to Europe!" Pete says. "I figure I'll start with Sweden. There's a fishing village all the way up north where they found a new Stonehenge. It might be in the south, actually."

"I don't have money," I say.

"Oh, me neither. I'm dipping into my trust. My mom is

totally not happy about it. But . . . I just feel like I can go to college any time. I have my whole life for that . . ." He's looks at me. "I sound like an asshole, don't I? I don't mean any of this in an assholey way. I just feel like there's a lot of things in the world that I don't know about, and I want to know about them. Don't you?"

I nod, but don't answer. Pete's world is much bigger than mine is. My world is small, and getting smaller, and there are no reluctant gurus (or trust funds) in it, and it's still full of mysteries. Not pleasant, interesting mysteries. Horrible, life-threatening mysteries.

We get back to the house and go inside. I check the stove first thing to make sure that nothing is on fire in it. Nothing is. So I don't need to solve the mystery of why my brother sometimes seems hell-bent on ruination.

"Ben? Ben?" I call out. I run upstairs. First stop: my night-stand. The gun is there. I've got to remember to ask Pete for the bullets back . . . Next stop: my brother's room to see if he is in there. He is. He is asleep. The notebook is lying next to him. I pick it up.

He's filled in more pages. "X.C.," an address in Montreal, a date from a few years ago. "K.S.," an address in Miami, a date from about nine years ago. "S.G.," an address in Cape Cod, a date from two years ago.

I scowl at the page. We went to Cape Cod two years ago as a family. On vacation. At first we'd tried going camping because Dad, for some reason, got all excited about the Great Outdoors. He bought, like, $700 worth of gear—tents and sleeping bags—on account of us not being an outdoorsy family already in possession of such things.

Then, when we were at the campsite in North Kingstown,

only a few miles from our actual house in Rhode Island, Mom saw a snake. And that was it. Camping over. We tried to pack up the tents and sleeping bags that were already halfway being set up, but we couldn't get them folded properly, so we just left them with some other campers.

We ended up driving from North Kingstown to Cape Cod. Ben got horribly antsy. He was in one of those moods of his, when he said, or rather screamed, no to everything—did he have to use the bathroom? Did he want ice cream? Did he think that Narragansett Bay looked pretty? It looked like the whole trip might fall apart, between Dad's sulking about Mom's snake and Ben's fidgety whininess—and me being me, both sullen and also trying to make everyone else get along. I tried to read in the car but got *nauseated*. (That was the trip I learned the difference between nauseated and nauseous. I'm puking by the side of the road, and Mom is giving me an English lesson.)

We got out by Hyannis, which wasn't where Mom wanted to go—she wanted to go to Provincetown, all the way at the tip of the island—and we settled into a bed and breakfast. It was on a strip mall. The B&B's chief attribute was having one vacant room. But what a room! Painted bright blue, the room was decorated entirely in paintings and other representations of dogs. Dog bedspreads, dog lamps, throw pillows with embroidered dogs on them. Many varieties: labs, Boston terriers, Chihuahuas, poodles. No golden retrievers, thank goodness, or Mom and Dad might have started fighting about John Galt being sent to Scituate again.

My parents both snore like crazy. Snored like crazy. Sharing a room with them meant no sleep. I stayed up all night reading *A Moveable Feast*, but that was nice, too; I imagined one day I would move to Paris and eat long, drunken dinners with writers, and maybe even be a writer, if I were not already being a marine biologist, an astronaut, or a bike messenger.

At some point during the night Mom got up, got dressed, and went out for a while. Another of her solo peregrinations. Maybe she got herself to Provincetown for a stroll. She got back around seven A.M., seeming happier and more relaxed than she had the night before. She rustled us all out of bed and woke us all up to enjoy the "breakfast" part of this establishment.

I replace the notebook and stand in the room for a moment, still lost in memories. I am also trying to think of how a person of action would act right now. By checking her cell phone for new texts, right? But there are no messages. Which means Dad is . . . what?

I go back downstairs. Pete's sitting on the couch again, strumming the ukulele.

"Does someone here smoke?" he asks when I join him. "There was a cigarette in the toilet."

MARRY THE
MED STUDENT

Chapter Eight

I am about to call the police when I get an all-caps, unpunctuated text on my cell phone.

DONT CALL THE POLICE YOU HAVE FIVE DAYS TO PRODUCE JFILE

OR WHAT? I text back. WHO ARE YOU? WHERE IS MY DAD? DO YOU MEAN FIVE DAYS INCLUDING TODAY, OR STARTING TOMORROW?

No response.

I don't even know who we are supposed to get the J-File *to* within five days. Shit. Shit. SHIT SHIT SHIT. How are we going to save Dad when we don't have the J-File? Should I tell the kidnappers that the J-File has been destroyed? But then what if they just decide to go and off Dad on account that he no longer makes for a worthwhile trade?

What do I do? What do *we* do?

I don't want to confide in Pete, for lots of reasons; among them, I don't want him to think I'm a freak. Not to mention that I don't think he'd really be able to help, being a teenage musician and not a super-detective with his finger on the pulse of crazy lobbyists who are kidnapping my father in an effort to gain control over this "J-File." (Yes, this thing that dead Mom told sleeping Ben no longer exists.)

I can think of someone who does appear to have his finger on that pulse. Someone who gives me the creeps—someone I know not to trust but who could possibly help. It's hard to see how it could *hurt* getting in touch with him, anyway. He already knows who we are and where we live and all of the relevant circumstances.

I call P.F. Greenawalt, Political Consultant.

Before he's even said hello, I've told him about the cigarette in the toilet bowl and the text message. He is quiet for a moment.

"Is the J-File still in the house?" he asks.

"P.F., I don't mean to be rude, but how the hell should I know? I don't know what it looks like or where it is. It might have been destroyed for all I know," I say, playing coy.

"I'd like to search your home. I'll be right over. Sit tight." He hangs up, preempting a reply.

I do not sit tight. I sit uptight.

Pete strums the ukulele, oddly oblivious, or pretending to be oblivious. (Maybe he's having second thoughts about me? Third or fourth thoughts about me?) My brother is still asleep. Then I stop sitting at all and go around ransacking the house, throwing books off the shelves, ripping clothes from drawers. Even if the J-File has been destroyed, pieces of this thing might still be around. I get distracted by access to Mom's things—Mom never let me wear her clothes (they were too delicate and I was too slovenly), and Dad kept respecting her wishes after she was no longer around to have wishes. I like this pink silk tank top of my mom's; too bad it's not my size. *Could I get away with wearing a gigantic tank top like this?* I wonder. But then I go back to work.

Dad's laptop sits on the messy desk. I hit a random key to wake it up from its lazy electronic snooze. This computer is a deep sleeper. Dad was always saying he was going to need a new computer soon. I hope it hasn't died quite yet . . . and there, it hasn't, here's the blue password screen.

I bang on the keys, trying to guess once again. My mom's name and birthday. My name and my brother's name. My dad's parents' names, Eliza and Moishe, both kids of Prussian immigrants who spoke Yiddish at home but didn't teach it to their own American offspring. They died in a car accident when Dad was twenty-one. Then I try some unlikely prospects: "I love horsies" (because I do) and "I hate lacrosse" (true, too) then "I miss Dad" (because also that's on my mind). Next up, the more promising "JohnGalt123." *Oy vey*; that gets me in.

A search for "J-File" reveals nothing.

A search for "file" reveals thousands of documents and emails. Oh, and a cache of photos of compromised starlets I really, really did not need to know my father finds appealing.

His e-correspondence seems mainly to consist of discussions among a group of internet friends calling themselves "The Individualists." These lovers of liberty have conversations about things like roads. Boring, you'd think, but the language is so odd and colorful and foul. One particularly explicit back-and-forth is on the topic of how the world would be better if all roads were privatized. Another vigorous debate concerns the government's right to outlaw child labor (most agree that the government has that right but shouldn't exercise it) or to mandate that kids go to school (no consensus on that one).

I try not to get consumed reading these emails, since I am trying to save my father's life, but it is hard not to linger on the long-winded messages he wrote himself. Like this one, from over the summer:

TO: INDIVIDUALISTS

FROM: ALMOST-FREE MAN 401

RE: ENSURING LAZY DAUGHTER WILL NOT EAT CAT FOOD IN OLD
    AGE?

DATE: AUGUST 21

I have children—two of them, a boy and a girl. Do I want them to work? Verily, I think that paid labor might benefit them more than school itself. At least in certain, possibly different ways. Let me explain.

The boy is neurodiverse. He is a brilliant autodidact. When he was a child, my wife and I worried that he would be severely autistic. Smearing feces on the walls, that kind of thing. It became clear as he got older, both through testing and personal observation, that he is certainly on the spectrum. Yet while he does have the occasional bout of . . . not rage exactly, but almost like a flash storm of anger from time to time . . . he is not, overall, so different from many of us. As we Individualists like to say, he should be free to experience his own life as it unfolds. This smidge of an issue will certainly impact his life in difficult ways. He does not make eye contact or like to be touched, except by my late wife and our dog, whom he adores. He loathes disruptions to his schedule. I doubt he will ever meet a partner with whom he can connect with on this *human* level; he will most likely live alone, forever.

On the other hand, he has a phenomenal memory, and while he is wrong about the gold standard (who raised him to think that paper money is a solid foundation on which to build an economy???), he will thrive. Professionally. He could even become rich. In which case, even if he can't make eye contact, some woman will, in all probability, make eye contact with him. I do not believe that my son needs school. He does not need his teachers to guide his studies. He is self-directed.

My daughter is a tougher case. *Oy vey*, as my parents would say. Seventeen now. Smart—very smart—but not ingenious like my son. Lazy about certain things. Like I was at her age. Indecisive. Nervous. I tried to teach her self-defense and survival techniques. I think all girls—all people—should know how to defend and care for themselves. She's a natural, more gifted than I am, at Shotokan, for instance. But she has no interest in the art or history of this discipline. She refused to practice further once I'd instructed.

Higher education will be more important for my daughter. Not because of the knowledge she will gain. It will serve as a signaling device to others that she is the sort of person who can be accepted into impressive institutions. But then for what purpose? How will she support herself? Would she be just as well-off working instead of studying? I believe that real-life experience could teach her to treasure her own gifts and to apply them.

Other times I think that she should go to a prestigious university in order to meet the sorts of people who will help her attain material comfort. She may meet a boy of high standing at a young age. Perhaps I should encourage her to settle down early, have children, and skip having a profession. Except I wouldn't want her to flounder and do some "consulting" like my late wife. She would regret that life. I know she would. I know it.

Individualists: What think you?

Despite the shock of reading my father's ungenerous, if true (true?) analysis of me and my personality disorders, I am curious what his online friends would suggest for me. (Though I am secretly relieved that he finds my brother's disorders not so horribly disorderly after all.)

Indeed, the fellow Individualists have some ideas. So many ideas.

One thinks I should join the military—the Marines, to be exact. Another thinks military service is an awful idea because it is wrong for the country to maintain tax-financed armed forces. "Only private militias should exist in these United States." Yet another thinks that I should go to college if and only if I get into a very "prestigious" school, in order to "enhance the signaling effect of the diploma." My favorite Individualist tells my dad that perhaps he should consider setting up a trust for me, so that in case none of the other options come to fruition, at least I will have lifelong dining options beyond the pet food aisle. A final emailer, my second favorite, has a son she thinks I might like. Twenty-five years old, about to enter medical school. She's attached a photo. Not bad . . .

The doorbell rings. I heave myself up from the desk and go downstairs, where Pete is standing in the doorway with P.F. Greenawalt.

Pete's back is to me, so I can't see his face. I can see P.F.'s, and he has a pretty intense look on it. He's huffing a little and seems a bit out of breath. I suppose he's an intense guy, anyway, in what anyone would understand to be a pretty intense situation. He's dressed sort of like Dad-going-to-work. (Which he used to do, once upon a time, looking both frumpy and disheveled, just like I often do.)

It's not warm, but there's a line of sweat at his hairline. He's wearing a dirty wool coat that looks like it's about three sizes too big. His khakis are worn on the edges. His metal glasses are smudged and quite a bit askew. Taking P.F.'s somewhat malodorous coat and draping it over a chair, I wonder how all this differs from his usual weekend afternoon.

Pete stares at him, an intense look on his own face ("pinched" is the best word) as P.F. and I head back into my Dad's office. I ponder the pinched-ness for a moment. Pete usually looks friendly and sleepy, not anxiously constipated. Is something wrong? Is he upset with me? Is he actually constipated? (Hey, at least we'd have that in common!) But then I remember why P.F. is here: the cigarette in the toilet bowl and who may have left it there.

"I was going to call the police, but I didn't," I tell him.

"Good, good . . ." Looking up, P.F. must realize that this is anything but double-good. "I mean, good that you didn't call the police. If the authorities become involved, it will compromise everything."

"You mean put my father in greater danger?" I ask.

P.F. blinks by way of response. He sort of reminds me of Ben right now. I kind of want to punch him, too, which is how I sometimes feel about Ben.

"Is anything missing from the house?" he asks after a moment, perhaps noticing what one might interpret as an unusual amount of chaos.

"Not that I can see. I assume that they've come looking for the J-File. I assume that they dropped the cigarette in the toilet to scare the shit out of us. Since I don't know what a J-File looks like or where it is, I can't say if it's missing. I assume it would be in here." I gesture around the cramped, musty office that—when not ransacked by a panicking Zoey—is organized in a way that makes sense to exactly one person. "If it were ever here at all," I add.

I consider telling P.F. about ghost Mom, about how she told Ben that the J-File was destroyed, but I'm worried that he'll stop helping us. We need him. I think we need him.

"I understand," says P.F. His lips turn downward as he surveys the room, wandering from spot to spot to spot. He rubs his finger along, but not—and I monitor this closely—*into* a nostril. Then he turns to his eyebrows, smoothing them, then fixing his glasses. He pokes an index finger into one ear, circling it, wiping the finger on his pants, then the same routine with the other ear. P.F. is gross. I did not know you could be this kind of gross and work in politics. *You must be really good at your job*, I think.

Tall stacks of paper teeter precariously on whatever flat space is available. Books are strewn across the room (thanks mostly to me); so are piles of dust and dog hair. Roscoe's cushioned bed still sits next to Dad's desk; there's still a circle of chewed-on bones and rawhides, along with Roscoe's favorite squeaky toy: a stuffed dreidel that Mom got him as a Hanukkah present last year. (Yes, those tops you use during Hanukkah to play the world's most boring holiday gambling game; the winner receives the world's least delicious chocolates.) It's apparently a huge hit with the canine crowd. Roscoe carried that stuffed, spit-soaked top around with him from room to room, shoving it at us, trying to make us throw it for him, even way past the holiday's eight nights. He'd sometimes take it out on walks, holding it in his mouth as we wandered the cobbled streets of our not-so-new neighborhood. The more worldly neighbors would wish him a Happy Festival of Lights and ask what the Hanukkah fairies left for him under the menorah. He must miss all that, I think. If he's still alive.

Shit. SHIT.

"Do you see anything . . . significant, or . . . promising in here?" I ask P.F. I bend down to pick up the dry stuffed dreidel and, hugging it to me, I sit on the dog bed. It's very comfortable. It's made of some special NASA-approved foam, according to the tag. I used to read here sometimes while snuggling with Roscoe, while Dad did what dads do at his computer. I guess my dad was doing dangerous, diabolical things. I had no idea that while Roscoe was snoring and I was digging into *Wuthering Heights* he was . . . what? I still don't know. Doing things that led to this, I guess.

P.F. blinks again. He opens drawers. Pulls out pens, checkbooks, delivery menus. Birth certificates and passports from another drawer. He flips through the passports, one by one. Mine, with a really, really gawky photo, but otherwise nearly empty—I've been to Paris, once, with my parents when I was fourteen. Ben's has a better photo but just the one stamp in it, too. My parents' are filled with colorful pages. Jacob Trask, born in Philadelphia, dorky and pink-cheeked but not hideously un-photogenic. Stamps from Australia. Bali. Some other warm places with pretty beaches. Mom's passport, which is much the same, except she was born in Rhode Island and possessed a flattering photo in which she wears a black linen V-neck and smiles warmly, her dark hair in long, loose waves.

"Sad," P.F. says, examining the photo a little longer. He

looks up at me and wins me over with three words. "You look alike."

"Can I see?"

P.F. hands me the passports. I glance through them, page by page, trying to remember our lives, their lives. My parents used to go on vacation a couple of times a year together— alone, just the two of them—when we lived in Rhode Island. That Hyannis vacation, come to think of it, was one of the few we ever took as a family. They would alternate between stupid, boring beach resorts and then more exotic beach resorts. I always wondered why they didn't include us. Were we that much of a hassle? ("Sixty four percent of parents in the United States vacation without their children," Ben once told me, ending another potential brother-sister heart-to-heart.)

Not that I *wanted* to go, either. Dad said he hated the more exotic places because he always ended up feeling like an "Orientalist" while he was there. He hated "exoti-cizing" the "local poverty and squalor." Mom said you could get a good bargain in that sort of a place. Their ridic-ulous commentary was enough to make me grateful to be left out.

Besides, Ben and I would always stay with Uncle Henry and Aunt Lisa. We'd go to our own decidedly unexotic Rhode Island beaches for clam cakes. Not to be underestimated: this is a Rhode Island specialty, with bits of clam fried into big balls of dough. We'd go to the movies. Movies *without sub-titles*, even. We'd have fun.

That stopped when we moved to Alexandria. And Mom died.

I push myself from the dog bed and put the passports back in the drawer. P.F. stays at the desk and presses a button on

Dad's computer. After a good long time, it chugs back to the blue screen again. I type the password, trying not to let P.F. see what it is, both to maintain the slightest bit of privacy and also because it just seems like an embarrassing window into our family quirks.

"You going to marry the med student?" he asks me.

I almost laugh. "I'll let you know."

"This is going to turn out okay," he says. He reaches out. I worry that he is going to place his hand on my arm—*ew, snot and earwax!*— but he doesn't. He just stretches and adds, as I've heard from someone else who doesn't seem in a position to make these assurances: "I promise. Listen, Zoey, I really promise. If we work together, it will be okay."

P.F. asks to look over the rest of the house. I trail him from room to room to room to room. Pretty much just the four rooms. We only have three bedrooms upstairs, and we skip Ben's because he's still asleep. Downstairs, there's the combo living room/ den/kitchen and Dad's already-pored-over office. As P.F. peers bloodlessly into each space once inhabited by our fractured family—now just with Pete on the couch, reading some dusty book, looking up from time to time with a somewhat lost, some-what impatient expression on that lovely, clear-skinned face, the ukulele again sitting in his lap—I recollect slivers of memories of what our family did here:

In front of the stove, Dad, exasperated, said to me that I had to do my homework if I wanted a hope of going to Berkeley. Then he made me practice tying fishing knots for an hour as punishment for getting a C on a calculus test.

In the den, Mom, who herself was no snazzy dancer, tried to teach my graceless brother how to do the box step. He refused. Then she danced with Roscoe. Then she danced with my dad. She tried to get me to dance with her, but I stormed off, angry about something; I don't even remember what. It may have had to do with being picked well after our dog.

In the living room, Dad and I fought about me not wanting to go see Wagner's *Ring* cycle at the Kennedy Center.

"I thought Wagner was a Nazi," I said at the time.

"This is a monumental work," Dad argued.

"Why can't we go to the Civil War-themed restaurant if our principles are that flexible?"

"Because hamburgers do not qualify as an individual and monumental work," Dad replied. "This does. And it's about Thor. You have to love an opera that's about Thor."

But in fact you do not have to love an opera that's about Thor. It was long and boring. And, as I later learned on the Internet, anti-Semitic. And I wanted a hamburger.

Still, there are not so many memories here. We haven't lived in the house for even a year, and Mom's been gone for a lot of it. Which leaves those two awful questions.

Is Dad a killer? Is Dad alive?

What the hell is going on here?

P.F. seems discouraged. "Is Ben awake now?" he says, looking at his watch. "It's past eleven. He should be up." He starts heading back to the stairs. I follow him, feeling anxious again. Pete comes up behind me. He puts his hand on my back.

"I'm here," he says.

"Stay downstairs," I respond without thinking.

A flash of some unpleasant emotion—hurt or anger or confusion—appears on his face, and then is gone. "Okay," he says quietly, turning around.

When I reach the top of the stairs, P.F. is knocking on my brother's door. He opens without waiting for a response.

"Don't do that," I say.

"C'mon, Zoey," P.F. says back. "Let's be partners here."

Ben is still in bed. But when P.F. gets into the room, he lurches upright, tossing his *Star Wars* comforter aside. He reaches immediately for that black-and-white notebook. He clutches it to his *Star Wars* pajama-ed chest. He needs new pajamas. These are far too small and far too wrong for a teenager. Does he even need pajamas at all?

"Get out," Ben says in a low voice.

My brother's voice is getting deeper. He will be a man at some point. If Dad were more conscientious, and believed in spiritual things, or wanted to be part of any kind of community and/or tradition, Ben would have been bar mitzvahed. In which case he would have gotten bar mitzvah money. In which case we'd have some money to keep us rich in things like, say, self-esteem. Or more practically, new clothes. Or groceries, which we are beginning to run low on. Or taxis, which we are coming to need more of.

"P.F. Greenawalt here is going to look around your room," I tell Ben in a gentle voice, "to see if the J-File is here. Okay?"

"No," Ben says. "I told you what Mom said."

"But P.F. wants to see if it's here," I repeat, trying to give Ben a look to tell him to shut the fuck up about the destruction of the J-File and that he should *perhaps* cooperate so we can try to get Dad back. But Ben isn't so hot at reading facial expressions. "P.F. wants to see for himself."

"I don't want him in here," my brother says. His voice is loud now. "Get out!"

I whirl to P.F. and see that Pete has joined us in the doorway.

"Everything okay in here?" Pete asks, those light eyes looking very dark, locked on P.F.'s face.

P.F. bristles. His sweaty brow is creased. We have a standoff. Wonderful.

In the meantime, Ben flips his notebook onto his mattress, opens to a blank page, and starts to write. I can see his loopy scrawl: the initials *W.L.* I can't make out the street address he's putting down, but I see it's in San Francisco. He puts down some dates, which I also can't make up, then looks up at me.

"These dates coincide with Mom and Dad's trip to San Francisco," he says.

P.F. and Pete are still glaring at each other.

"I have to get one more thing into the notebook," Ben says, flipping to the next page. It occurs to me that his too-tight and probably age-inappropriate pajamas haven't been washed in a month.

The three of us tiptoe forward. None of us breathe. We watch my brother write:

M.L., 19 Riverside Road, Missoula, Montana, 2/5/1997

P.F. turns his stare to me. The color seems to have drained from his face.

"Why is he doing this?" he asks in a stingily quiet way. "I mean . . . where is he getting this information?"

Oh, how to respond?

"Ben is having some . . . I dunno. Some delusions, I guess," I begin. "He thinks that Mom is . . ." I stop. These are words I never, ever, ever thought I'd utter to a nose-wiping Political Consultant—a stranger who is hanging around the house trying to figure out who is leaving cigarette butts in our toilet. *Jesus.* But he could help us. And we are running out of time. And are bereft of ideas. "He thinks Mom is telling him things that he should write in a notebook. Telling him those things while he's sleeping." I take in a deep breath. "She told him that the J-File was destroyed."

We're quiet.

Ben closes the book but doesn't look up.

"Do you believe in ghosts?" I ask P.F.

"No," he says, without surprise or shock. I might as well have asked him if he liked Wagner. He seems to be reacting very carefully, deliberately. He runs his left index finger along his left nostril again, ever so slowly, and stops. "I don't believe in ghosts."

"Me neither," I say.

I scratch my nose. Watching P.F. Greenawalt's various gross tics are making me feel itchy myself. They're like a virus spreading among those who are too sensitive to social cues. After what feels like a very long time, Ben lifts his head. He seems puzzled that Pete is there.

"I'll be downstairs if you need me," Pete says. I'm not sure if he's talking to Ben or to me. I hope both.

"May I?" P.F. asks Ben, once Pete is gone. Then he asks again, cajoling, wheedling, transparently trying to charm. "Please, fella? I think I recognize some of what you're writing. I am just trying to help your father. It may seem impossible . . . Hell, it seems impossible even to little old me. But this note-book may help me help your dad."

I'm not sure if I want Ben to give over the notebook or not. This P.F, he's cooking eggs and telling us about his car-buying philosophy one second; the next, he's promising to save our father, our goddamned father. Who might have killed people. Who might be responsible for Mom's death. Who might not have killed people and might not be respon-sible for Mom's death. Me, Dad's once-acolyte . . . I still can't get myself to imagine what Dad might or might not have done. I want an authority figure here to help me know what to think.

Maybe Ben, independent Ben, does, too. Because he does something I never would have expected: he hands P.F. the dingy little notebook.

And now P.F. is all business. He flips through the pages, each with its initials, its addresses, its dates written out.

A smile breaks on his face. He very nearly looks angelic, even with that gleam of oil across his forehead.

"I was wrong," he says. "Ghosts might exist after all."

DO GHOSTS HAVE HAIR SALONS?

Chapter Nine

So, kooky thing here: it turns out that the notes my brother has been writing down based on what our dead mother tells him in his dreams are what constitute a J-File. Or maybe they represent the *essence* of a J-File. Or maybe they *are* the J-File. P.F. won't confirm or deny, other than acknowledge that this is what everyone's been looking for, more or freaking less.

Right here. Right in Ben's stupid, mystical, incomprehensible, *sad* notebook.

"Ben, this is important," P.F. says. "How are you really getting this information?"

"My brother is constitutionally incapable of lying," I cut in. I sit next to Ben on the bed. He stiffens. In my eagerness to be protective, I've gotten too close again.

"Did your father tell you to write this down?" P.F. asks. "Did you hear your parents talking?"

Ben, apparently having resigned himself to a full confession, shakes his head. "Sometimes at night my mother comes to me in my dreams. She tells me what to write down. She says it is important information."

"Like how to talk to girls?" P.F. jokes.

Even Ben glares at him.

"Ha ha!" P.F. tries again. "Talk to girls!" He wipes his moist forehead with this sleeve, clutching the notebook tightly with his other hand. "No, really. What does she tell you? And what does she look like when she's there? Does she still have that long hair, like in the passport photo? Or is it shorter, like it was in real life?"

Ben looks at me. I hate to admit it, but I'm curious about these things, too, even though I am also slightly creeped out that P.F. is asking. And still not comfortable that I know, or want to know, the exact nature of their relationship.

"What *does* her hair look like?" I ask, surprised that I said it out loud.

In addition to wearing her hair a little shorter than she used to, Mom had been getting her hair colored these last few years, since sprouts of grey began appearing. I wonder if ghost Mom has access to ghost hair salons. With ghost colorists who sometimes don't use the right dye and who consequently get a small tip. Are there also ghost facialists? If not, how will she be getting all those nice-smelling lotions she used to keep her skin looking smooth? And who will teach me how to keep my skin looking smooth?

"I don't know what her hair looks like," Ben says. "I don't notice hair."

"Do you actually *see* her in your dreams?" I ask, suddenly as curious as P.F. and just as eager to get to the bottom of this.

"Not with my eyes," Ben says. "My eyes are closed because I am asleep."

P.F. hands the notebook back to me.

I flip through it as he did. My eyes flash across those unfathomable lines of initials, addresses, dates. Some ink smears make a few impossible to read; Ben is left-handed, and almost always has a dark, sticky smudge on the side of his hand and a corresponding wave of ink along any page he's used. I flip, flip, flip—again and again—hunting for any details that will spur memories of my own. I stare at Ben with an expectant expression, like, *Kid, help me out here.* But he just stares at P.F., who stares at me. I wonder what Pete is up to downstairs.

"This looks like the J-File," P.F. says, breaking the silence. "Or a piece of the J-File. I understood that the document your mother was bringing to me . . . that night"—his throat catches—"had about fifty pages in it. This one. . . ?" He reaches for the book again and I hand it to him. I'm on autopilot as he turns the pages once more. "This one has fewer. Maybe thirty. And because the purported origin of these pages is so . . . nontraditional . . . it's also hard for me to verify that this is, indeed, the J-File."

"But what *is* the J-File?" I demand. What are these initials? What are the dates?"

"Specifically?" P.F.'s eyes are more furtive. They dart between my brother and me. "Well, I would have to go back and cross-check various pieces of data in order to tell you that. And even then, I'm not sure how much I could tell you."

Maybe he's just yet another of these overly-literal males who just *sound* evasive.

"What *can* you tell me, P.F.?" I ask. "Please. Tell me something. What am I looking at? What is my brother writing?" I flex my hands. Think about grabbing his wrists again. We're establishing who's in control here. So far it looks like no one is in control.

P.F. sighs. "I believe that this is a record of various . . . assassinations."

"Of who?" I ask.

"Of *whom*," corrects P.F. Then: "Sorry. My wife always said I'm pedantic. Which does not rhyme with romantic."

"It does rhyme," says Ben. "Those two words are perfect rhymes."

"Yes," says P.F. He smiles. His shoulders slump a little. His smile is surprisingly endearing. It makes his sweaty face look open and friendly and warm. "My wife didn't see it that way."

"Who did my father kill?" I ask. Now is not the time to be charmed.

"I can't say," P.F. says. The smile turns into more of a pinch.

"You *can*."

"No," P.F. says. "I can't. I don't have the information you're looking for, Zoey. I know the meta-meaning of this notebook. It's . . ." He swallows. "It's a compendium of assassinations. But I don't know the identities of the victims, nor do I know why they were killed. I can almost guarantee you that these initials will not make immediate sense to us. This is why the J-File is so critical to my law enforcement sources." He pauses. "Am I making sense? My wife said that sometimes I could talk forever without ever really explaining what I meant to say."

"I understand," Ben says.

I frown at him. At them.

"Is my dad a murderer?" I ask P.F. "Is he a . . . a bad guy?"

"Zoey, I wish I knew what to tell you."

"So now what? Can we get this to your sources and get my dad back?"

"Not quite yet," P.F. says.

"Why?" I shout.

Ben hugs his knees and starts rocking back and forth on his mattress, so gently you might not notice, unless you knew that this is what sometimes precedes one of his manic fits. His eyes are wide, fixed on nothing.

I kick the wall. The wall is made of plaster and, even wearing shoes—the usual not-very-attractive wood-soled clogs—my foot throbs. Kicking the wall was a mistake, but I am so full of rage. I have nowhere to direct it. "Ow," I say. Tears start to flow. I wipe them on the sleeve of my ill-fitting, plaid button-down shirt, which I am wearing underneath Mom's pink tank top, which I'd forgotten I still had on. I'm staining the front with my tears. The silk becomes translucent in spots, then dries just as quickly. "Why can't we? Can't I just give this to my father's kidnappers, then? They want it. They will give me him back."

"It's not that simple," P.F. says. His tone is soothing now. "Zoey, please be careful. Don't hurt yourself. Tell me, what incentives are there for the kidnappers to release your father once they have the J-File? What incentives are there for the kidnappers not to dispose of you and Ben, too? Do we have to keep going over this? Do we? I can help you. I *will* help you, Zoey. The kidnappers can't. They won't."

My brain is getting that foggy racing feeling it gets when I've got too much information to take in. When I don't have enough experience to process it in any kind of reasonable way. This feeling has come to me during history tests I've neglected to study for (which is almost all of them). It came to me the night my mother was killed. I instantly remember the last thing I said to her as she was walking out the door with Roscoe. It was in response to a fight we'd been having, about why I refused to study for my history tests. She'd walked out saying she needed to cool off before we both said things we'd regret. And I shouted that I hated her. She said I shouldn't say that unless I really meant it. I shouted that I hated her again. And I *did* hate her right then. But then she died.

Now this.

"So what do we do?" I ask P.F. I wipe my eyes and sniff. "What do we do?"

"Well." He drums his damp fingers on the notebook. That all-important, completely useless notebook. Finally he sighs.

"I suppose we have a couple of options here. The one I'd recommend is that you and Ben go somewhere safe until Ben finishes making all his entries. Which he should do quickly. Time is running out."

Ben keeps not making eye contact, staying in his own bubble. Then he says "Yes, that's what Mom says, too. Time is running out."

Ben changes out of his tiny *Star Wars* pajamas and into one of Dad's gigantic, coffee-stained T-shirts. It hangs down to his thighs. And, of course, a pair of grey polyester pants. And sneakers that squeak below the hem. He carries his polished briefcase. *This* is the Trask sibling who is going to make it big.

I fetch P.F. his shabby coat and find Pete. He is still in the living room, the ukulele in his lap, though he isn't playing. His left hand fingers the frets, but he's glancing around, antsy. I have to admit: seeing him still here, not talking about ghosts or assassinations or kidnappings, I am so grateful that my eyes start to burn. My throat tightens. I tell him that we are going out for a little bit. I do not say that we are going to a local copy shop. I do not say that P.F.

wants his own edition of Ben's freakish scrawls—what I've come to think of as Ben's "dream diary": dictation from our dead mother, pertaining to reprehensible acts committed by our missing dad.

"Want me to come?" Pete asks.

He looks like he'd like to come. He looks a little like he's jumping out of his skin.

"Nah, you wait," I say.

"I'd rather not. I'll drive."

"Let's walk," says P.F. "I could use the fresh air. I agree with Zoey. Pete, you should stay. There should be someone in the house to scare off the smoker, in case the smoker tries to come back. You might even get a look . . ." His voice trails off.

Why would the smoker be scared of us? I wonder. But then it occurs to me that the kidnappers can only scare us in our absence. They can only scare us by leaving something threatening. They certainly wouldn't want to reveal their identities.

Pete, perhaps getting it too, nods and picks up the ukulele.

Minus Pete, we head over to the copy shop. How amazing that in this day and age there are still copy shops. Every time I spot a cigarette smoker on the way, I feel my stomach knot up more tightly. That dude pushing the baby carriage, he could be the kidnapper. (Who smokes in front of an infant except the truly evil?) That old homeless-looking lady who's always walking up and down the street muttering to herself, it could be her. I keep glancing over at P.F. to see if he is responding to any of these people, but he's not. He's just humming to himself, too quietly for me to make out the tune. We probably look like an awkward little family here, just out for a stroll: me, my brother, and P.F.

Inside, fluorescent lighting makes everyone look a little wearier. We ask the middle-aged guy at the counter to make a copy of the notebook. He seems too old for this kind of job. Maybe it's his store; maybe he's not just the clerk. I hope he doesn't ask what the notebook is. Or maybe I hope that he *does* ask, so I can unload. Which is not a good idea.

"You want a copy of the cover, too, or just what's inside?" the guy asks.

I look to P.F. to answer.

"Just what's inside," he says.

While we wait, I ask P.F. if he's religious.

"I grew up culturally Jewish, but secular," he answers.

"We grew up culturally half-Jewish," I tell him.

"Your mom mentioned that, I think."

"So you don't believe in . . . life after death?" I ask. "I mean, not just when it comes to ghosts. You think when it's over it's over?"

P.F. is drumming his fingers on the counter. He stops then starts again.

"It's hard to say," he says. "I've called myself agnostic for most of my life. But then things like *this* happen, and wouldn't it be nice to believe in divine justice . . . ? What about you?"

"Oh, I don't have a well-developed worldview on this issue," I say. "Dad does. He says that gods are for idiots."

"What do you think, Ben?" P.F. asks.

Ben is busy examining the inside of his nose with an extended index finger. He removes the finger and examines it, then wipes his finger on the counter. Again, I remind myself that *this* is the Trask kid headed for greatness. *This. This one.* P.F. really could be like our new dad.

"I don't think it matters," Ben says.

"You think Mom's ghost telling you to write down these weird details is unrelated to life after death?" I sound angry. Maybe I am. "Or God? Or religion? Or any of it?"

"You think Mom is God?" Ben asks. "I haven't seen anything suggesting Mom is God."

P.F. laughs. "You're a good kid," he says to Ben. "Smart."

"Were you in love with my mom?" I ask. "Were you . . . having an affair?"

P.F. laughs again. "I think everyone was a little in love with your mom," he says. "It was hard not to be. But, no, we were not having an affair. Never. Your mother was very much in love with your father. You should know that," he says. "Every couple has trying times, of course."

"But how did you know her?" I ask. "We didn't have any friends here." I feel so small and sad saying that.

"Your parents have friends. You don't know them?" he says.

"No," I say.

The middle-aged guy comes back with our copy. The papers are in a manila envelope, collated with a silver paperclip, the notebook rubber-banded to the envelope.

"Seventeen twenty-five," he says, handing me the package. I give P.F. the copies and hand the original back to Ben, who slips it into his briefcase.

P.F. pays. He hands me the change. Then he opens his large leather wallet and hands me more cash: some twenties, a few fives, two hundred dollar bills. I see that there is more cash inside that lush pouch. He must see me see this, because he opens the wallet again and hands me the rest. The Political Consultant business must be a good one. P.F. should buy himself a new coat. As he puts the wallet away I also catch a little peek at some photos in cracked plastic.

"Pictures of your kids?" I ask.

"I don't have kids," he says. "My wife and I tried for a couple of years. Her womb didn't like my sperm."

Ben nods, as if this makes perfect sense to him.

On the short walk home, P.F. tells us that he needs us to get the rest of the information together quickly. If the kidnappers are giving us until Friday, he says, that means we need to have everything ready long before that deadline.

"It's not up to me," Ben says.

"Do your best, kid," says P.F. He pauses at his sedan. For the first time, I notice that unlike his clothes, it is shiny. Pristine. "Do you need me to find you somewhere to go where you'll be safe?"

"We have someplace," I say. I leave it at that. I imagine Ben knows exactly what I'm thinking. P.F. doesn't need to know. He doesn't need to know because I still don't know who he is or why he seems to care so much about us. A part of me still thinks he may be the one who took my Dad in the first place. Maybe he's so sweaty because he's jonesing for a cigarette.

"What are you thinking, Zoey?" he asks.

"Do you smoke?"

He offers that sad, jowly, endearing smile. "I tried it once. Didn't take." With that, he opens the driver's side door and tosses his copy of Ben's dream diary into the backseat. "Be safe. Promise me that you'll be safe, and speedy."

"It's not up to us," Ben says again, as if P.F. is really fucking dumb.

"Try," P.F. says. He wipes his coat sleeve across his forehead. Then he closes the door and drives off. We stare until the taillights have vanished and the motor has faded into the rhythm of the crickets.

Back at the house, my brother hurries upstairs for some

"decompression time," as Mom used to put it. Pete is on the couch. He still seems antsy, not that I can blame him. I sit beside him. If he's looking for an excuse to say goodbye in a way that won't make him look like a total dick, he's wasting his time. He could storm out and slam the door without a word, and I still wouldn't think he was a total dick. I would think the opposite. I would think, *Thank you for sticking it out as long as you did.*

We turn on the TV. We watch the last half of a medical procedural. I check my cell phone and find that it's not working. It's charged, but it's not working. Dad probably forgot to pay the bill. The company wouldn't shut it off this quickly. Except Dad probably forgot to pay the bill for a few *months.* So now we're stuck. Really stuck. Really fucked.

"I never get to watch TV," Pete says. He rests his head on my shoulder. "They don't let the boarders."

I'd like not to panic, and I'd like to ask Pete two questions: Would he want to kiss me and protect me from all the bad things? And would he want ditch school for a few days to drive me and Ben to Rhode Island?

I only work up the nerve to ask him the latter.

MINDING
THE METAPHOR

Chapter Ten

"Rhode Island?" Pete asks.

"My aunt and uncle are there. Ben will be safe there until we figure this thing out."

"What *thing*," he says. It's the first exasperation he's shown. I've assumed he wasn't very curious about what was going on with this P.F. fellow and whatnot, and that's why he hasn't asked questions. But maybe . . . maybe he's just waiting for me to feel comfortable enough to open up to him. Which I'm not, not yet.

I sigh. Then again, even more loudly. "You're better off not knowing," I say to him. "Please, trust me." I'm mimicking P.F.'s language, I realize after I've said this. What does this Political Consultant know that he's not telling me?

Pete stands up from the couch and heads out to the foyer, fumbling for his cell phone. When the front door closes behind him, a big part of me wonders if that's the last I'll ever see of Pete Ashburn. I wouldn't blame him for bolting. I would more than understand. What would his parents say about all this? What would his twin sister, Abby? Or maybe he's calling that Anne girl right now. If I were her, I'd tell him: "Dude, what are you even there for to start with when I have such nice hair?"

The seconds tick by. I mute the TV. Pete, finally, reappears. He shifts on his feet and runs his hands through his hair.

"I can go," he says. "But I won't. Not until you explain to me what in the hell is going on here, Zoey."

Oh, would it were that I had an answer, that I had the guts, even, to tell him what it is I do know. Or what I think I know. I take a deep breath, then start coughing. That lasts about a minute. Pete gets up, goes into the kitchen, comes back with a glass of water. I drink it. Then I have to pee. I go pee, come back, find Pete pacing around the living room. He gives me a look that seems to be imploring, and hostile, and expectant, and caring, and warm, and blank, all at once. His curly hair has grown just a tad too shaggy. I wish I could just go tug on it. I can't. I can't.

"Please don't make me," I say.

Pete says nothing. His face grows more blank. I imagine him leaving. I imagine me and Ben trying to manage this, *this*, alone. In even more danger. Pete is the closest thing I have to a friend here. I have no one. I have to try.

"This is going to sound crazy," I begin, watching Pete's face warily. His eyes brighten, just a touch. He wants me to go on. He has no idea what he's in store for.

"I should start by saying that I don't believe in ghosts," I say, trying again. This story needs too much preamble. This lunatic story. This dangerous, confusing, lunatic story.

"I do," Pete says.

"You do?" I say.

"Yes," he says.

The old me would have started calling him an imbecile, especially if Dad were around to hear and approve. The new me is just grateful.

"Mom's ghost has been visiting Ben at night," I say very quickly. Then I swallow and speak a little slower. "He says she has. He says she's been telling him these initials and dates, and telling him to write them down in a notebook. A 'J-File' or something, which it turns out is . . . I don't know. Valuable or something."

"To who?" Pete asks. "Like on eBay?"

I hesitate. I thought the ghost part of this conversation was going to be tough, but now that I've gotten to what comes next, I realize that talking about the mysterious and dubious circumstances relating to how the J-File has come into existence was comparatively easy.

"Dad's not just on a trip," I say. "He's been kidnapped. The kidnappers want the notebook, the J-File."

I take another breath. I can get away with not telling Pete this last part. But I want to tell him. I want to have someone to confide in. I wish Molly were here and that we were still friends, but she's not here and he is.

"It's worse than you think," I say. "I think Mom is telling Ben about people who Dad has killed. I think that's what's in the notebook. Records of Dad's . . . assassinations. It's so awful. Pete, it's so awful. I didn't know this is who my dad was. Who he is."

"Why aren't you giving them the notebook, then?" Pete asks. "Are you not sure if you actually want your dad back now?"

"No," I say quickly. "I want Dad back." I hadn't been sure until I said it, actually. But now I'm sure. I want Dad back. Assassin Dad. I'd laugh at the idea of it, if everything in the universe were back to how things were in December. Or even four days ago.

"That guy whose house we went to, who was here the other day," I begin.

"P.F.," Pete says. A look that I can't quite place comes over his face. Then it's gone.

"He's some kind of Political Consultant. He said that the kidnappers will kill Dad even if they get the notebook. He said that he has law enforcement sources who want the notebook, to help bring down the syndicate that Dad is involved with." Jesus Christ and a thousand *oy veys*, these are the words coming out of my mouth, describing the state of things in Zoey's world.

"Law enforcement sources?" Pete says. "Then why are we going to Rhode Island?"

He said we. We're going to Rhode Island. We. Maybe he's going to help, even if my dad is a kidnapped killer and my mom is a ghost and my brother is . . . where is my brother, anyway? I'm not worried; he's probably upstairs, inventing a new language, or reading up on *Star Wars* memorabilia prices, or sleeping, or sitting on the floor tying then untying knots in a piece of string.

"P.F. said that his law enforcement sources need the full J-File by the end of the week. P.F. thought we should get out of town while Ben gets the rest of the stuff from Mom," I say. I pause. There were, like, twenty or so entries in the notebook already. Sweet Ayn Rand, my dad has been an active assassin. The thought of this fills me with dread, and then of all twisted things, I feel a little bit of pride. My fuckup dad is a good killer, apparently.

I start to laugh even though I really couldn't for the life of me say what's funny. Pete starts to laugh, too. I have even less of an idea what he's laughing about, but boy howdy this is a better reaction than it could have been.

"So we're going to Rhode Island, then," Pete says. "Better go get ready."

"You're really going to come?" I say. "You can take off school?"

"Don't worry about that," he says. "I've never been to Rhode Island."

I realize that I'll need some way to get out of school. I lack Pete's casual confidence that I can just take off. I break back into the computer and send the headmaster an email from Dad's account:

"Dear Mr. Standiford," I begin, before pausing. Would Dad call the headmaster Mr. Standiford? Would he call him by his first name? What is his first name? I read various online etiquette websites for guidance. None addresses the issue of forging an email from one's kidnapped father to the headmaster.

I try again: "Hello there, We're having a bit of a family emergency. My daughter, Zoey, and son, Ben, will be staying with relatives in Rhode Island for the next couple of days. Please excuse their absence. They should be back by . . ."

I don't know how to end this sentence. I don't know when we should be back by. P.F. and his contacts (or friends? or enemies?) demand fast results. And it's impossible to say when Ben and ghost Mom will be done with their work.

"They should be back by early next week. I will contact you as soon as I can if their Rhode Island jaunt is to be extended."

And why not?

"I would be most grateful if you would ask their teachers to be gentle in grading, given the multiple family difficulties my children have encountered in recent months.

"Sincerely,
"Jacob Trask"

I pack a small suitcase of clothes for myself, which turns into a large suitcase as I discover that I don't know what to bring on this trip. Some jeans, but what if they're not the right jeans, some skirts in case we go somewhere fancy, but what if I don't feel like wearing them, some T-shirts, but I hate all my T-shirts, etc. In all that, I almost forget to pack undies, but then I remember to pack them, and as I'm doing it I notice that they are mostly of the "three for $5 from Target" variety, and I wonder if a girl my age should have nicer undies. I then oversee Ben's considerably simpler packing of a small suitcase of disgusting T-shirts, polyester pants, and books about Brazil's exploding economy for himself.

And then we go.

The drive is supposed to take about eight hours. We take some back roads, stop at a crab shack in Maryland that Pete says he's heard about.

"I can't wait to try this with you," he says. He sounds a little nervous, and a little excited. "I hope you like the crabs."

Pete and I pound crabs with hammers, eat vinegary coleslaw. I can't get much meat from the crabs but find smashing them with hammers to be rather cathartic. My brother, naturally, chimes in to say it's "barbaric" to eat like this. He picks at a grilled cheese the cook agrees to whip up for him. I eat half his grilled cheese because all the crab-pounding has me a little bit hungry.

Pete offers to pay for dinner, but I whip out some of P.F.'s cash.

Ben says, "You should let Pete pay."

Pete puts his hand on my arm and says, "Let me pay," but then his phone rings. As he's looking at it, not answering it, I lay down cash. I want to use my agency while I have it.

We get back in the car. My brother sits in the backseat. I monitor as he takes off his coat, ready to jump in and remind him to buckle his seatbelt, during which time I also have the opportunity to revisit his outfit: ratty brown dress slacks (Dad's word, but priceless) and a T-shirt from some corporate event Dad once participated in that raised money for charity, even though my dad does not believe in charity (but he had to participate in these events, back when he had a *job* as a *corporate auditor* even if said *job* was really just a *front* for a very nefarious *other job killing people* that is looking like it may result in me and my brother being *orphaned*).

No, but I take it back. Dad believes that if you want to help someone—to be charitable—you should. He says that charity is "not a moral virtue" and that one should not feel *obligated* to help others. Which raises the question: What the hell are we doing on this cockamamie scheme to rescue him from *kidnappers* when anyone looking at this situation can see he put himself in this situation, and we are only endangering ourselves trying to get him back? I can already hear his answer. He'd say it in that "I know everything" tone of voice. A tone that my brother has inherited well. He'd say that just because he cannot demand that we help him doesn't mean we shouldn't. We should if it's what *we* want to do. I'm pretty sure it's what we want to do.

When I turn back around to face forward, I kick off my shoes and put my feet on the dashboard. I wouldn't have done that before, but it feels like a wall has come down between me and Pete now. I've just seen him as a compellingly attractive, useful body before. But I feel like he is becoming more than that to me. I feel like I am seeing him as a real *person* for the first time, if that makes any sense. I'm ready for him to see my hole-y socks now.

He tells me about his dad dying, drowning while on vacation in South Carolina, when he was eleven. They were in the water together. His dad got caught in an undertow. There was nothing that could be done. It was lucky he was a couple of feet away, he says, not stuck in that same current.

I ask him if it was hard growing up without a dad.

"My mom works a lot," he says. "So Abby and I got sent to boarding school early on. But that's where I met my first guitar teacher, Mr. Brown, in seventh grade. Life is mysterious, young Zoey."

I tell him about my mom. My beautiful, infuriating, insouciantly dressed dead mom—and about my missing dog, and about Molly, my best friend who no longer speaks to me. His hand rests on top of mine while we drive. I stop talking and stare out the window at the nothingness, since it's dark out, and memories come into my head then leave, just little bits of mental ephemera from a life I don't have anymore. I don't feel as terrible as I might.

"What about you, Benny?" Pete asks Ben. "What do you want to be when you grow up?"

Ben looks up from his book, which he's been reading quietly in the backseat using a small flashlight. "Maybe an economist," he says. "Or a journalist."

This surprises me. I've never heard him say he wanted to be a journalist before. I suppose I put Ben in his Ben Box a long time ago. I've mostly only paid attention to his leafy green vegetable consumption and his propensity for not looking both ways when he crosses the street and his tendency to clam up and freak out when he's forced to participate in something that he especially does not like, like conversation with strangers, or the eating of leafy green vegetables. I've forgotten that he is also a person who thinks about his own future.

I start drifting off into a nap. Pete turns on the radio, scans the stations. He lands on "Crazy," by Patsy Cline, which I don't know why I know, but I do. Pete starts singing along with it. His singing voice is different from his talking voice; it's got a melancholy to it that I don't hear when he's talking. He taps my hand with his finger as he sings, "Crazy, I'm crazy for feeling so lonely. I'm crazy, crazy for feeling so blue."

His phone rings. I glance at him as he glances at the bright screen, then hits the DECLINE CALL button.

"There's no such thing as mental illness," my brother cuts in, "because there is no such thing as the 'mind,' per se, only the brain. And we can't locate these supposed 'illnesses' within the brain. Despite hundreds of years of looking for them there. The treatments for mental illness are barbaric. Always have been. And doctors, and politicians, just diagnose people who threaten their world order as mentally ill. They use that diagnosis to lock those people up. Cut their brains up."

"My sister's on antidepressants," says Pete.

Which I also didn't know. Not that it matters. Almost everyone's on anti-depressants from what I understand. I'm not, only because I've been too lazy to get to someone who could prescribe them for me. And I never wanted my parents to feel badly that I felt badly. And . . . I don't know. I just didn't.

"People should take whatever drugs or other elixirs they find useful," says my brother. "The mind is a metaphor but the brain is still susceptible to drugs and other forms of relief."

"I disagree," Pete says.

My brother chortles. "Don't tell me you believe in the mind/body divide, still," he says. "What else, that the world is flat?"

The next song comes on. It's that song that goes "Workin' nine to five, what a way to make a living." Mom loved the movie that song was the theme to. I think that movie was called *Nine to Five*, too. We watched it on TV one night when we still lived in Rhode Island. The women in the movie were all harassed by their male (and female) coworkers and had suits with big shoulders. Mom said that everyone wore big shoulders in the eighties and that many people were harassed by their coworkers.

"Why?" I'd asked her. She'd laughed. "Why to which?" she'd asked back. Then she probably force-fed me some carrot sticks while ignoring the fact that I wore the same T-shirt every day for a week.

I rest my eyes but can't sleep. I have a nagging question that keeps me up: "The mind may be just a metaphor, but then why does it hurt so much when I have a headache?"

"It's your brain that hurts. Your mind is the experience of that brain," says my brother, like I'm mentally infirm. Which maybe I am because I don't know what the hell he's talking about.

"How?" I say to my brother. "How does seeing Mom's ghost fit in with the idea that there is no mind?"

"I don't see the contradiction," he says, again with the unpleasant *tone*.

Pete's still singing, but softer, still tapping my hand with his finger. But he's leaving the finger on my hand a little longer with each tap. Then he just rests his hand on my hand. I pretend to fall asleep just so that I can keep my eyes closed, savoring the feeling of this unexpected and unusual peace, for the last hour of our drive.

AWFUL AWFUL

Chapter Eleven

We cross the Rhode Island border just after 10 P.M. Drive up Route 95, past where I went to nature camp when I was a kid, past the beach exits, past the 24-hour diner where I worked for a few weeks as a waitress one summer when I was about fifteen, until the owners discovered that I was never going to stop being a terrible waitress and asked me not to come back.

"I can't wait to show you the beach here," I say. "Maybe we can to go Newport and see the mansions. And I really want to eat some Del's lemonade. That's just frozen lemonade with chunks of lemon in it, but it's a real Rhode Island speciality. And we'll go for clam cakes. Those are the best. And get some Awful Awfuls."

"What are those?" Pete asks.

"Milkshakes," says Ben. "All they are are milkshakes."

"You get them from this place called Newport Creamery," I say. "They only come in chocolate, strawberry, coffee, and vanilla. I think I've only ever had chocolate, actually. Who gets strawberry? We used to go to Newport Creamery on Friday nights and get grilled cheese and Awful Awfuls."

"They're just milkshakes," says Ben again from the back-seat. "And they're not even originally from Rhode Island. A New Jersey company had them first. Newport Creamery bought the name when that company went out of business."

"I can't wait to try one," says Pete. "Maybe I'll get strawberry." I smile at him. He's still doing things to my hand with his hand. Nice things. Things that make me feel squishy inside.

I know we're not on vacation here. But it feels like a respite. I also have this crazy feeling like maybe Molly and I could reconcile while I'm back. She'd have to forgive me if she saw me. We were best friends for almost twelve years, since we met in kindergarten. Our *mothers* were best friends. Our dads went bike riding every weekend. If I stop by her house, and she sees me, we'll be friends again. I know it. Things have to improve, to be improving. I try to psychically connect with her brain, so my brain can ask her brain if my theory has legs. (Needless to say, it doesn't work.)

Twenty minutes or so later, we get off at the North Kingstown exit, drive along Route 1, and finally pull into Uncle Henry and Aunt Lisa's funny little "newfangled development" (as Mom put it) in which all the houses, Mom liked to show me, are gigantic and come in one of three models: faux Tudor-meets-Italian castle; faux Victorian-meets-White House; and then a third model that combines all four styles. I can feel myself starting to relax as we turn the corner to their house—it's the second model, Victorian-meets-White-House, wide with multiple decorative columns and also a spindly turret, all covered in vinyl siding that Mom used to call "tacky" and Dad liked to recommend as "practical." (I liked the turret, personally, until I learned that it is not a functional turret. What sick architect would put a non-functional turret on a house?)

Concerns about the house's architectural quirks aside, I'm glad to be here. I'm thinking that at last we'll have proper adult supervision, people to take responsibility, people to make sure we eat properly, even if we can't come to a consensus about the house's exterior. Then I see a police car pulling out of the driveway.

We park on the other side of the street, in front of a neighbor's house—they've got the faux Tudor-meets-Italian-castle style; it's covered in fake stone and has several gold statues of frolicking naked women and boys on the lawn. Mom had *many* unkind words about the golden naked boys, back when she was alive.

"What's going on?" Pete asks. I feel like my heart is going to explode.

"I don't know," I say.

"The police were here," my brother observes. "And now they are leaving."

"Thanks, Ben," I say to him as we traverse the flagstones that keep the grass from being trampled, then walk up the portico, flanked by one American flag and one flag with the Boston Red Sox logo on it, to the front door. I ring the bell.

Aunt Lisa opens the door.

"Oh, Zoey," she says. She grabs me into a hug and kisses the top of my head. I lean into the hug for a moment. I miss my aunt and uncle. I miss having a grown-up around.

"And *you*," she says, reaching out for my little brother. She knows better than to envelop him but just puts her hands near Ben without touching any Ben proper.

"Hi, Aunt Lisa," he says.

"I'm Pete," says Pete, sticking out his hand. Aunt Lisa folds him into her arms.

"I'm Aunt Lisa," she says. Letting go, she smiles at us. "Come in, come in."

We go inside, through the tiled foyer and into the living room, which has a blue canvas couch, a dark green rug, a big TV, and no books. Uncle Henry is sitting on the couch, on the phone. He's wearing a pair of blue jeans that look as if they were designed to give off the appearance of belonging to a person who works in construction. Uncle Henry is a lawyer, mostly handling divorces and drunk driving-type stuff.

Dad, who sometimes encourages me to consider law school, one day, in the future, says it's an "honest way to earn a living," though he always sounds a little sarcastic when he says it. Mom always said that being this kind of lawyer, living in a subdivision filled with vinyl siding, is boring and beneath her little brother, who "had so much potential." Mom really liked saying to Aunt Lisa, "Don't you think he has so much potential?" to which Uncle Henry would reply, "You're talking about *my* lost potential, Julia? Really? How's being a housewife working for you?"

Aunt Lisa has a PhD herself, which she isn't exactly making the most of—she sometimes teaches a couple of classes at some local community colleges. This sounds cool, but she always says, surprisingly cheerfully, that she'd get paid more to work at McDonald's. There's no way to get a higher-paying academic job in this part of the country. And that would be the moment she'd change the subject to the Boston Red Sox, or kiss me on the head and say that I was looking more and more beautiful every day. Or at least that's what used to happen.

"It took us more than ten hours to drive here," Ben says to Aunt Lisa.

"That's a long time," she says.

"Why were the police here?" I ask.

"We had a break-in tonight," she says. She strokes my hair.

"What happened?" I ask. I can feel my stomach doing flips, my hands clenching again. I reach out for another hug.

Aunt Lisa kisses the top of my head. "We're okay, baby," she says. "It doesn't look like anything was stolen. Your uncle and I weren't hurt. Someone came into the house while we were out at dinner and . . . I don't know what they did. Nothing seems to have been touched. They left a cigarette in the toilet is all. You know how I feel about smoking. But it could have been worse. It's unnerving is all." She points at Uncle Henry, who drinks beer from a bottle as he listens to whatever is being said on the other end of the line, and explains he's on the phone with the alarm company to find out why the warning sirens didn't go off.

Warning sirens are going off in my head. Oh no. No no no no no.

"But how are you?" she says. "Why are you coming to visit now? Don't you have school?"

"Shit," I say in a panic. I look toward Pete. His face looks frozen.

"It's not that big of a deal, I don't think," Aunt Lisa says. "Nothing got stolen. We're just a little shaken. It's strange to come home and discover that somebody has been rummaging through your things."

"Hey, kids," says Uncle Henry, getting off the phone. He looks just a little bit like my mom. Enough to make me feel her presence, but not enough for it to be overwhelming. He taps my brother on the arm and gives me a slightly beery-smelling hug. He holds out his hand to Pete.

"Henry Booth," he says to him.

"Pete Ashburn," Pete says.

"You kids hungry?" Uncle Henry asks.

"Can I talk to you?" Pete says to me.

"We'll go out to the car and get our bags," I say to Aunt Lisa and Uncle Henry. "Just be a sec."

"I'll help you," says Uncle Henry, who laughs when he sees Pete's old Volvo.

"Do you get twelve miles to the gallon in this boat?" he asks.

"Fifteen," says Pete.

"I used to have a Chevy Nova," says Uncle Henry. "Teal. That got, like, six and a half. It also got me a whole buncha girlfriends."

We carry the bags into the house. My bag, made of a ballistic-grade and extremely unattractive mauve synthetic material, is heavy. Why did I pack as if I were never coming home again?

Uncle Henry takes my bag up the stairs and into the room I always stay in. It's a little guest room where Aunt Lisa also does crafts like scrapbooking. This should have been a kid's room. I don't know why they don't have kids. Aunt Lisa would be a great mom. Maybe it's not too late. I don't really know how old Aunt Lisa and Uncle Henry are. They are grown-up age. I believe they are in their early or mid-thirties. I don't think that is too old to have kids.

There is some religious-looking, through not actually *religious*, artwork purchased from T.J. Maxx on the walls. It's a pair of large pictures, orangey-brown, showing a sunset over the water. You can see some black-silhouetted birds flying, too. Mom, predictably, hated this artwork as much as she hated everything about this house. She said that you should not get artwork from the same place where you buy discount underpants. My unattractive suitcase is also from T.J. Maxx, incidentally.

Ben's bag goes into Uncle Henry's study. He'll sleep on an air mattress in there, amidst the golf clubs and the dusty boxes with printers and other computer equipment that never gets set up. I don't know where Pete will sleep. I wonder if Aunt Lisa will have him sleep in my room. That seems improbable, but exciting. But improbable. And also inappropriate, considering that Pete and I haven't even really kissed. I blush even thinking about the various sleeping possibilities.

"Why don't you leave your bag here," I suggest to him, pointing next to Ben's bag.

"Okay," he says. He seems to have bigger things on his mind than our sleeping arrangement. I blush again.

We go back downstairs. Ben is drinking milk at the kitchen table, which is a kind of blond wood, with a vase of pretty flowers in the middle of it. Aunt Lisa is cooking eggs.

Pete, Uncle Henry, and I take seats at the table. Uncle Henry asks me about school. I make up answers. He asks Ben about the economy. Ben says some technical-sounding things about the S&P 500 (which I believe relates to stocks, or maybe bonds, but definitely not horsies) to which Uncle Henry says, "Very interesting. I'll have to talk to my financial advisor about this."

We all look up at Aunt Lisa as she comes over with the pan of eggs, spooning them out onto our plates. Aunt Lisa says she's keeping chickens at the house now, on top of the alpacas.

"Fresh eggs every day," Aunt Lisa says. "Wait till you taste the yolks. They're so thick and rich and *yellow*. You'll never want to go back to supermarket eggs."

"How are the alpacas?" I ask Aunt Lisa.

"We're trying to sell them," she says. "But the market's kind of bottomed out. You know it's against the law to eat your own alpacas?" She shakes her head. "I don't agree with your father's politics about much, but I am concerned about the nanny state sometimes. Telling me what to do with my own investment animals!"

"Where is your father?" says Uncle Henry. "Don't you have school? Do you think he'd want to buy the alpacas?"

"We have the week off," I say tersely, before Ben can say something truthful or factual.

"Why didn't your father come with you?" he asks. He drinks some more beer. I feel like he's putting weird emphasis on the word father.

"Aren't the eggs delicious?" says Aunt Lisa. "And the best part is that once the hens are too old to stop laying, then we can eat *them*. It's a 'use the whole animal' philosophy. Very Native American."

"It's way past my bedtime," says Ben.

The eggs really are delicious. It really is way past Ben's bedtime. I'm fading, too.

"Where should I sleep, Mrs. Booth?" Pete asks.

"Lisa," says Aunt Lisa. "I'll make up the couch." As we eat and she scoots off to procure bedding, Uncle Henry asks, "And why did you just decide yesterday to come visit?"

"We just haven't seen you for a while," I say.

"Why didn't your father come?" he asks.

"Oh, you know Dad," I say.

Uncle Henry drinks some more beer. "How is your father?" he asks. "Still wacky?"

"Um. I guess," I say.

"Yeah?" says Uncle Henry. "Do you kids need money? I know your dad isn't working."

Oh boy. This again. This used to be a fun little thing, back when we lived in Rhode Island. Uncle Henry would get tipsy and then, haha jokingly, harangue my dad for not earning enough money to keep my mom in a well-enough-appointed manner. He'd harass my dad about what Uncle Henry called his "increasingly asinine and cockamamie political views, no, I'm kidding, you know I love you, Jacob." Dad would tell him to butt out. Mom would then tell Dad to butt out, though she seemed to enjoy the kerfuffle a little, as did Uncle Henry. Aunt Lisa would cook eggs. This is even less fun now.

"I've got to get Ben to bed," I say.

"Okay," says Uncle Henry. He drinks the rest of his beer and looks like he wants to say something. He doesn't say anything.

"Thank you for letting us stay," I say.

"Kid, you're always welcome here," he says. "Your dad and I may not always see eye to eye, but you're family."

Pete follows Ben and me upstairs. "I really think we should leave tonight," he says to me, quietly, when we get upstairs.

"No," I say, surprising myself with my adamance. "Why?"

"It's not safe," he says. "Not for us. And not for your aunt and uncle."

"The cigarette was obviously just to scare us. We're scared! They win! But they aren't going to *hurt* us. Not while we're still got the unfinished J-File," I say, probably too loudly.

I don't especially believe any of what I'm saying. I just don't want to leave. But then Ben chimes in.

"I think we should stay as well," he says. "It seems statistically unlikely that the person who left the cigarette in the toilet would return to the house tonight, knowing that we are likely to be under increased police surveillance. At least seventy-nine percent unlikely."

"Good point," I say. "Yeah."

"Plus my back hurts," Ben says. "That backseat is terrible."

Pete looks wary, and weary, and very nearly furious, and says, "Okay. But we are leaving first thing in the morning."

"Okay," I say to him. "Okay?" I say to Ben.

"I'd really like to stay and finish the notebook," Ben says. "I think our odds of getting Dad home safely vastly increase with a complete notebook."

I look at Pete. "I don't think so," he says. "Morning." He turns and heads back downstairs. His hunched shoulders convey unhappiness.

I put Ben to bed on the blow-up mattress and come downstairs to say goodnight to Uncle Henry and Aunt Lisa. Pete lays on the couch, watching the big television and looking . . . stony.

"It'll be okay," I say to him.

He looks at me with an almost bewildered expression on his face. I don't know what to say or do. I sit on the couch for a second. The covers are pulled up to his neck. He looks younger than he is. I say, "Thank you, Pete."

"You're welcome," he says, reaching out to grab my arm. His hand rests there for a long moment. He lets go.

I go up to my room and get into bed. I feel so frustrated and nervous and scared and disappointed. We won't be drinking Del's frozen lemonade. We won't be going to the beach. We're not going to drink Awful Awfuls. It's just the one real-life, confusing, and hellish kind of awful, not the chocolate-flavored, delicious double awful I'd been so looking forward to.

I'm trying not to cry from disappointment, not to regret too much the things we won't have. Because I have to stay focused on the one thing that I can do, and have to do, while we're here.

IT'S
HAPPENING

Chapter Twelve

Molly told me, a while ago, she never wanted to see me again. I'd had sex with her ex-boyfriend. It was my first and only time having sex. And I honestly didn't think she'd care that much, seeing as she was, disposition-wise, pretty bohemian for a teenager. Plus, she just never seemed *that* into him.

As it turns out, I guess she was into him enough.

Her stupid boyfriend. His name was Donald. Donald! Can you imagine splitting with your best friend over some guy named Donald? I would have answered that question in the negative not so long ago.

Donald is good at drawing. He is a year older than we are, is sweet, and, since he turned sixteen, will come pick a person up in his Jeep if it is snowing out and the person wants to get out of the house. He knows how to do some tricks on a skateboard. We've known him since elementary school, when he used give us the good parts of his lunch (homemade cookies; my lunches had mini carrots for dessert) and let us use his bike when we wanted it. Then toward the end of junior high school, he and Molly started to date. It seemed sort of half-hearted while they were dating, at least to me. He drove her places and bought her things.

But he'd always done that. She seemed . . . I don't know. Not in love. Just in like. They liked a lot of the same subtitled movies. And many of the same artists, whose works featured things like decaying animals and full bosoms. But apparently these shared interests, plus hanging out all the time, was not enough to sustain their relationship. They broke up after about two years.

So, that was a long time to be halfheartedly together, I will admit. But neither of them seemed really *upset* after the breakup. They stayed pals. So did Donald and I. We'd always liked each other. Before and even during the time that he and Molly were together, sometimes we'd sit on the couch together, under a blanket, and talk. Sometimes we'd hug. It probably wasn't appropriate. After they broke up last summer, when I turned sixteen, it seemed less inappropriate. Still not *perfectly* appropriate. But less inappropriate.

We went to the movies together one time after he and Molly broke up, just Donald and me. The movies up the street from my parents' old house. It was supposed to be a funny movie. It wasn't a funny movie. We stayed through the whole thing, though, and shared a popcorn mixed with peanut M&Ms that he bought, of course. We held hands. He drove me home. Came inside to hang out some more. My parents were already in bed. We decided to have some schnapps from their dusty, rarely used liquor cabinet. Make that *I* decided. Donald was up for anything. Schnapps, no schnapps. It tasted like sweet, peachy fire. My brother wandered downstairs while we were drinking the schnapps. He saw the bottle on the table.

"You're drinking Mom and Dad's liquor?" he asked, sleepily. "What is that?"

"A little schnapps," I said. I giggled. This all seemed hysterical.

"It's funny that Jews drink an alcohol originated by German monks," said Ben. "They thought it had medicinal purposes."

"I'm feeling very healthy," Donald said. He laughed.

My brother smelled the liquor. "Peach," he said. "Peaches originated in China, though the name suggests that the fruit originally comes from Persia. Peaches have been cultivated in China for thousands of years. About four thousand years, in fact." And as he did most nights, Ben poured a glass of milk, drank it, scratched himself in the crotch, and went back to bed.

It got to be one in the morning, two in the morning, two thirty. Donald started off on Dad's leather reading chair while I lounged on the somewhat severe wool couch, shoes off, feet akimbo, hair spilled over the throw pillows. But over time our seating arrangement shifted. I invited him to sit with me on the couch. Then Donald and I sat on the severe couch together under a blanket, watching infomercials. And cuddling. He smoothed my hair with his hands.

It was easy, once we were tucked in, for me to kiss him. And at that point, I seized an opportunity, by way of seizing my best friend's ex-boyfriend's pants zipper. I was tired of being a virgin. No one I knew was a virgin anymore. (Note: it's possible I didn't know that many people.)

Donald, not a virgin, had a condom. We used it. The experience itself was not especially loving, or exciting, or painful. It lasted a little while, long enough to get through part of an ad for something called the ShamWow!, and I felt a little bit embarrassed as it was happening, plus a little curious how one cloth could do so *many* different things. But I was glad to do it.

And then, sweet relief, it was done.

Afterwards, I said to Donald, my new lover (ew gross), "I need to go up to my room so my parents don't catch us here."

"Good idea," he said. He stroked my hair again. And then I fell asleep.

My father found us in the morning. He shrieked. Donald jumped up. The condom was now stuck to a part of him that my parents—and, arguably, me—should never have seen. I covered myself tightly with the blanket, willing all this not to be happening. As with all the things I tried to control mentally, this trick did not work. It was happening.

My mother heard the commotion. More Trasks then saw Donald in his most private of ways. Mom also saw me, on the couch, wrapped in blankets, trying to die on the spot.

"Jacob, let's go get a new couch today," Mom said to my dad. Then she left the room. Dad followed. He busied himself with some project in the backyard. Mom went into the kitchen for breakfast. Donald got dressed and went home. He'd always gotten along so well with my parents before this.

I suspected he wouldn't join us on the back deck for grilling on hot summer nights anymore. He and Molly used to both come over for that. Dad would cook steaks on the grill. Mom would ask my friends if they thought she needed a facelift, and that sort of thing. She'd dole out what seemed like really misguided advice about love. Dad would rail against the government. Ben would recite facts about whatever obscure subject was catching his attention. All the weirdness, and there was a lot of it, these evenings were really fun and cozy, and they're over.

Later in the day that Donald and I were caught in our delicate state, as I tried to hide in my bedroom, Mom made me come downstairs and eat breakfast and talk. Were Donald and I a couple? Was I concerned that I might be pregnant? If I were pregnant, would I get an abortion? I'd have to get an abortion, she said. She cried, as if *she* were a teen mother being kicked out of her parents' house in the dead of winter. (It was, I repeat, summer. We'd had Donald and Molly over for dinner just a couple of nights earlier.)

"I'm not pregnant," I whispered.

"How do you know he doesn't have AIDS?" Mom asked.

"He doesn't have AIDS," I said.

"He might," she said. She started crying again. Now she's being kicked out of her parents' house, and she has just discovered that she has AIDS.

"Mom," I begged. "Please, please can we not talk about this?"

She then told me that she'd always hoped I would tell her about the first time I was going to have sex, so that she and I could celebrate with champagne afterwards. She told me that she'd imagined I'd be in my last years of college, and it would be with someone who'd repeatedly asked me to marry him, but who I'd rejected because I was too young and had too much work to do on my career before I could get married.

"Should we get out champagne?" she asked me, sniffling.

"Please stop," I said. The only thing I could imagine being more mortifying than the actual story of how my mother learned that I'd had sex for the first time was this idea she was now proposing.

"We should make an appointment with Planned Parenthood for your abortion," she then said.

"I'm not pregnant," I said again. I guess I could have been pregnant. But it seemed unlikely, since we'd used a condom, as Mom unfortunately knew.

Mom then made me take prenatal vitamins, just in case I was pregnant, and just in case I decided not to have an abortion. Later in the week, she sat me down on the gold velvet couch she and Dad went out and bought from an upscale consignment shop—because *nobody's* had sex on a used couch, of course—and told me that she was not ready to be a grandmother. But that if I had a baby, she would, of course, love it very much. I said I was sure she would. She hugged me. She slipped a package of condoms into my tote bag. Then she asked me which of several handsome movie stars I would have sex with, given the opportunity. I did not answer. She told me about her carnal feelings toward a surprisingly broad group of famous men, none of whom resembled my father in any way. This was Mom being her most motherly.

And still, Molly didn't have to know. I could have kept it from her. Donald had no reason to tell her, either. I wanted to tell her, because she was my best friend, and you tend to tell your best friend when you've done "it"—or, really, anything—for the first time. But, given the circumstances, I decided to stay mum.

Mom did not stay mum. She was the one who brought it up. When Molly came over to get me for something a week or two after the devirginizing of *moi*. Mom said to Molly that kids these days are so much more progressive than they were when she was young.

"You could never have made it with your best friend's ex-boyfriend so soon after they'd broken up in my day and age!" Mom said to Molly, who was missing some necessary context. Which I provided when we got outside. Provided while expressing a lot of regret. Then, when that seemed not to be eliciting friendship, full of chortles, like, "Isn't it hilarious that Donald and I drank schnapps and then my parents caught him with a condom stuck to his most Donaldy parts in the morning?" Then begging: "Molly, I didn't mean to upset you. I didn't know you'd even care. I honestly didn't. You didn't seem to miss him at all. And I just wanted to be *done* with this."

"That's the most pathetic thing I've ever heard," Molly said to me as she left. She was crying. I don't think it was about Donald. She didn't love him. I don't know what it was about. She could be irrationally emotional sometimes. Occasionally explosive. But usually pretty mild and unbothered by things that would, like, really get *my* goat. For example, if I think that my parents are going to send me to summer camp to learn how to horseback ride, but then they decide not to send me to summer camp to learn how to horseback ride, then I will become furious. Hysterical. Angry beyond belief, seized by emotions that take me over like some kind of a demon.

When something similar happened to Molly—because we were going to go to camp *together* the summer we turned fifteen, but both had camp taken away when we got caught doing something really stupid (sneaking out in the middle of the night to play video games, in our pajamas, at the local 7-Eleven)—she just took it in stride.

"We'll get jobs then," she said, shrugging, while I was sobbing and red-faced like a baby. And indeed, she got us both jobs at Howie's, a local fried chicken fast-food restaurant, for that summer. And let me offer some advice: if you ever go to Howie's, just off Route 2 in West Warwick, do not eat the coleslaw, because I know what the fifteen-year-old employees do to it when Howie is not around, and you would not consider these things to enhance the dish's appeal.

But Molly did not take this whole Donald thing in stride,

such as by going out and getting us jobs together, which might have been a lot of fun and pleasantly constructive. (She was already working at a different restaurant, where they did not have an opening for me; I was spending the summer doing nothing you'd want anyone to know about.) No, she kicked me to the curb is what she did. Hasn't been to Alexandria to visit, except for my mom's funeral, even though she's got relatives somewhere in the Maryland suburbs. Before I moved to Alexandria, we'd made plans to go see them in Maryland and have them take us out jousting, that being the state sport and all. Like all my horseback-related plans, this one failed to make it out of the gate.

Yeah. The last time Molly and I hung out was when Mom told her about me and Donald. "Making it." It might be the last time we ever hang out, if she never forgives me.

Except that tonight, tonight I am determined to make sure she forgives me.

Around midnight, I get up out of bed. I figure I'll get dressed, find the keys to one of Aunt Lisa's and Uncle Henry's cars, and drive over to Molly's house. Where I'll . . . I'm not sure. I can't really ring the doorbell at this time of night. Maybe I'll bring my cell and call her when I get there. And if she won't take my call, I'll . . . figure something out. She's my best friend, even if she won't talk to me, and I need her back in what has become the mustered-up fustercluck of my life.

I don't turn on the light to get dressed in order to be as inconspicuous as possible, which leads to lots of knocking over lamps and stubbing my toe and shout-whispering "HOLY MOTHER THAT HURTS" and that sort of thing. When I open the door of my room, Pete is standing there in the hallway.

"Hey!" I say to him, more loudly than I'd meant to.

"I wanted to talk to you," he says quietly.

"About what?" I say back as quietly as I can.

"Can I come in?" he asks, edging back into the bedroom.

"Okay," I say. I walk back into the room. Pete reaches to switch on the light, but I say, again in the loud whisper, "Leave it off. Don't want to wake anyone." I'm not sure why I think that banging into every piece of furniture is unobtrusive, but turning the lights on would wake everyone. This is midnight logic.

"Zoey," he says to me. "I really think we need to leave here. I think we should wake Ben up and go."

"I can't," I say.

"Why?" he asks. "I'll do the driving."

"There's someone else I have to go see," I say.

"When?" he asks. "We have to leave early in the morning."

"Now," I say. "I'm going to go now."

"Go where?"

"Warwick."

Warwick is the town where I used to live. It's where Molly still lives, at least I assume, at her parents' house. I lived in that house, practically, back before everything. I tell Pete my plan. Some of it, anyway. I say I'm going to try to win back an old friend.

"I'll drive you," he says.

"I don't need you to," I say.

"I'll drive you," he says.

But I don't want him to. I feel like I need to see my friend, my ex-friend, without an audience.

"I have to go alone," I say to Pete. "But do you mind if I use your car?"

We go downstairs, tiptoeing in a way that is surely much louder than mere walking would have been. His keys are in the pocket of his coat. I pull on my coat. It's colder in Rhode Island than it is in Virginia. I'm feeling sleepy and energized at the same time. Terrified and calmly facing my crap. Pete hands me the one big black key that looks like it's been chewed on, and touches my hand in the process.

"Please be careful, Zoey," he says. Then he touches my arm. "Are you going to see an old boyfriend?" he asks.

"No!" I say, realizing that he doesn't know my old life, my old friends. My old screwups. Only the new ones. "Oh, no. No. It's not that at all, Pete."

"Be safe," he says. Then he kisses me on the cheek. He holds his lips there. His lips are so soft. I feel . . . lost. But also present. And also like if I don't move, I am not going to see Molly. Like I could just give up everything that I thought I had to do and just keep my cheek raised to these lips.

But I can't. I get too easily distracted. I always have. I pull back and look at that face, that wide-eyed face, those brownish curls falling over the forehead.

"I'm just going to Warwick," I say. "It's the suburbs." I pause. "Thank you for being worried," I say.

"Don't thank me." He stops. If I don't leave, I won't leave.

"Thank you," I say again. "For being worried. And for lending me the Volvo. For asking if it's an ex-boyfriend." I smile at Pete. He has a weird mix of expressions over his face, all at the same time.

I can't parse them all. Mostly, Pete looks tired and concerned, and angry. And I think I see a glimmer of something affectionate. But I'm probably wrong about that. He only kissed my cheek, not my lips. He's probably just being familiar. And if I'm wrong about that then I'm probably wrong about all of what I think I'm seeing on him, in him. I don't even know him. I don't know why he's here with me in

Rhode Island, or why he wants to leave. I keep asking, but I still don't know. My mood darkens, my anxiety rises again. What *is* going on here? How come Pete could just take off from school? Why is he helping me? He doesn't even know me. He's got a much prettier and more attractively dressed girl at Shenandoah who loves him.

I leave Pete in the vestibule and go out to the car. Get in the driver's seat, adjust the seat forward so I can reach the pedals, adjust the mirrors, try to remember what else one is supposed to do when driving in the wee hours of the morning. I've never driven a lot, and never driven this car. I turn the car on and turn on the radio because that's what you're supposed to do, listen to music. It's a song I haven't heard in a while, one of those melancholy songs that sounds like it should be cheerful but hits you right in the gut. I listen and I start to cry.

For a few minutes, I sit in the driver's seat, singing along with the radio and crying over some dumb song about a fisherman who's got the blues and feels better with an unnamed "you" in his arms. Dad loves this song. Present tense; can't fathom that the present tense might no longer be applicable. Dad says the song was popular when he was in college, which was a hundred million years ago. I've only heard it a few times, when it's randomly been playing in some ice cream parlor or something. It's not a song I could pick out by title or band or anything. But here it is.

Then there's a tap on the window. I see it's Pete.

"Okay?" he mouths.

I give him a thumbs-up, then shake my head because, thumbs-up? Really, Zoey? Then I start the car again, even though it's started, cringing as I hear something bad happening in the engine. At least I think it's the engine. And then

I drive off toward Warwick, remembering partway down the road to turn on the headlights, the flash of brightness coming just in time to see a small fox dash from in front of the car and into one of the neighbor's yards—that neighbor also has faux turrets; I didn't even know there were foxes in this neighborhood—and run run run away, off on some mission of its own, probably just as important to it as mine is to me.

CALL A
SPADE A SPADE

Chapter Thirteen

When I get to Molly's house, the lights are all off. Of course they are. It's almost one in the morning. I sit outside in the car for a few minutes, looking at the two-story house. A split-level in a neighborhood of modest split-levels and old pine and maple trees. I spent so many nights here for so many years.

I get out of the car. My legs are shaking a little bit in my jeans. Bad jeans. They're too dark. I thought I wanted dark jeans when I got these, but now I think they seem too severe. I wish I had new jeans. Walk up the driveway and then the gravel path to the front door. The door's locked, obviously. I can't exactly ring the bell. I pull out my cell phone, call Molly. No response. I text. Nothing. Shit.

Walk around back. No lights. Not even in the basement. Molly's older sister has been living there since her divorce. Or *had* been living there, last I knew; moved back from New Jersey, where her husband's family worked in the trash hauling business. We thought that was hilarious when Shira married into the trash-hauling business. Imagine having to travel all the way to New Jersey to marry into mafia, when you can't throw a recyclable bottle without hitting Casa Nostre in the Biggest Little! What, we used to say with exaggerated made-up accents, Rhode Island mobsters aren't good enough for you, Shira? Shira seemed to find this funny, too, up until her actual divorce. (It was sad. Turned out he wanted kids, she wasn't ready. You'd have thought they'd have sorted through that before getting married, but I guess the ring finger and the womb don't always have compatible wants.)

But that was a year ago. Before I moved to Virginia. Maybe Shira has a new made man who's gotten her out of the basement. Or maybe she just goes to sleep at a reasonable hour now.

I check the back door. Locked. Jiggle the sliding glass door, which we used to leave unlocked when we rambled away from the house in the middle of the night, back when we used to do that sort of thing. Locked. I could turn around and go back to Aunt Lisa and Uncle Henry's now. I tried. But the thought of that makes me so sad. Like, unbelievably sad. Despairingly sad. But what to do?

I circle the house one more time, looking for some entryway that somehow I've never before known about in the decade-plus since I first started spending time in this house. Nothing. Except . . . There's that maple tree on the side of the house where Molly's room is. The one Molly and I tried to play Lone Ranger on when we were about nine— she hung on the lowest branch; I pretended to be a horse and was supposed to run under her so she could drop onto my shoulders. The branch broke before I got there. Once she got back from the hospital (minor concussion, plus poison ivy from the unfortunate thicket she landed on), her parents said if we ever went anywhere near that tree again there would be certain unnamed Serious Consequences.

It is time to try again.

I skulk over to the tree, around the side of the house. It is so dark it's hard to make out much of anything about it, except that it's still there. I walk to the trunk and reach for the first branch. If I stretch, I can just get my hands around it. Will it hold? THAT is a good question. I'd rather not find out the answer with a concussion. Or poison ivy.

There is some sort of shovel in the back of the house, I recall. A spade, I think it's called? I'm not so familiar with gardening implements, or much of anything relating to the useful arts. I go back and fetch it from its spot leaning against the house. It's heavier than I thought a shovel would be; hope I can lift it high enough to hit the branch and test its strength.

And I can! These small victories. I bang the branch two or three times. I'm getting a little bit winded lifting the shovel so high, then heaving it at the branch, but I do it, and the branch holds. Hi-ho Silver at last.

Dropping the shovel with a bit more of a clang than might be ideal, I hoist myself onto the branch by holding on, then walking myself up the trunk. I'm nimbler than I thought I'd be. It's possible that the loathsome lacrosse has got me into a little bit of an athletic way. I start feeling more confident, jaunty even, as I reach for the next branch up. Which, I realize, I can't test, since the shovel is down on the ground. Hm. I just grab at it and tug. It should fall if it won't hold me, I think. It holds. I climb up and sit on it, my legs splayed on either side. I've got one more branch to go, I think, then I should be at Molly's window, at which point . . . I have no idea. Like usual. *Oy vey*.

Up I go to the next branch. A fall from this height would

produce, I think, quite a bad concussion. Some broken bones. The worst case of poison ivy *ever*. But no, my luck, like the tree, holds. And here I am, close to the branch, a couple of feet away from Molly's window, assuming she hasn't switched rooms. Now how to get in?

I shimmy along the branch, smelling the earthy, barky smell, feeling bugs fall into my hair (real bugs, imaginary ones, I don't know), praying to a higher power I don't believe in to keep me safe as I attempt this profoundly stupid feat to win back my old friend. And more than that, within reaching distance of the window, I am making all kinds of unenforceable negotiations with that great nonexistent being in the sky about how good I'll be if somehow this works out. I'll be better than good. I'll get up on time. I'll make sure Ben eats real food. I'll get Dad back. I'll make sure Dad is punished for what he's done. I'll make sure no one else in our family is killed, or kills. I'll thank Pete. I'll do my homework. The thing that doesn't exist comes through; the branch doesn't fall to the ground, and neither do I.

I'm about a foot from the window, about to reach out to it to try to open it from the outside, like some sort of cat burglar, when I suddenly see Molly's face in the window, looking right at me.

She screams. I scream. I almost fall from the branch but hold on and don't fall. Molly holds up her index finger, looking shaken and stern. She leaves the window. I keep holding on. She comes back, opens the window.

"Where did you go?" I ask.

"I had to turn off the alarm," she says.

"When did you get an alarm?" I ask.

"This winter," she says. She doesn't say, "After your mother was killed and everyone freaked out." I assume, narcissistically, but also kind of really reasonably, that that was the impetus. She does say, "What are you doing here on a tree outside my window, you psycho?"

I start to defend myself. Then I start to laugh. Then I start to talk. "I wanted to apologize," I say. "Please take me back." I reach out my arms, then think *concussion*, and grab the tree again, clutching myself to it. "Why were you at the window?" I ask. "I'm sorry if I woke you up."

"You didn't," she says. "I was just having a bad dream. I get insomnia and then nightmares. This one . . . it was about your mom, actually. She was telling me that you were in trouble."

"Holy lord," I'm about to say, when I hear an extremely distressing, extremely scary *bang!* like a car is backfiring. But I think, *It's just a car backfiring.*

But then there's another *bang!*, then another.

These *bangs* are feeling awfully personal. I hear something hit the tree, *thwap*, a violent moment that shakes the tree a little bit. It's a violent scary moment. Another *bang*. I grab the branch even tighter, hugging it to me. Wishing myself back to somewhere safe, but there is nowhere safe. There is nowhere safe. Bits of bark crumble. I can still feel so many bugs on me.

"Get down!" I shout at Molly. "Get away from the window and get down!"

Looking terrified, quite understandably, she moves back from the window. I can picture her going to the far side of the bed. Crouching next to it. I hope she's crouching next to it.

My heart is pounding. My mind is racing. Am I close enough to the window to get inside? I don't think I am. Not without some acrobatic maneuvering that would leave me quite vulnerable. Can I stay where I am? The bullets whizzing around me would suggest not. How many bullets does this shooter have? And *why* are they directed at me? A *plan*, Zoey. Think. Think.

I start climbing back down the tree. The shooter can't see me very well. I'm sure of it. I'm happy for the dark jeans. I'm glad for the camouflaging qualities of my dad's beat-up army jacket I stole from him a couple of years ago. (No, Dad wasn't ever in the Army. He got it from Gap. I think he did. That's the story he's always told, anyway.) This is not a graceful egress from the tree. But I get down, and I get down without being shot.

The *bang-bang-bang*s stop for a second. Christ. I try to suck in my stomach and hide behind the tree. I can't tell if this is effective, but since I'm not being shot, it must be at least moderately effective. I should probably also try to lose five or six pounds so that I don't have to suck in my stomach like this next time I need cover from arboreal sources. I can hear my mom's voice in my head saying that it's unseemly to be concerned about five pounds. She thought I was vain whenever I worried about my weight. This from a woman who claimed to be thirty-seven three years in a row; was still making that claim up until the day she was killed.

Then I hear footsteps. Crunches on gravel. Padding on the grass. I wonder if Molly has called the police. I wonder if she has, if that is a good idea or a bad idea. I wonder if it was Mom's ghost that came to her in the dream, or if this was just the coincidental moment her subconscious was telling her to forgive me. I hear a man's voice say "OW!"

I peer out from behind the tree and see a lumpy-looking man lifting up his left foot, which has been injured in some way; maybe stubbed on a tree root, in which case, thanks, trees. He's got the gun clutched in his right hand. I remember that Molly's yard is littered with rocks. I have an idea. It might even be a decent idea.

Reaching out, I grab the shovel. Then I look around me for a rock, a good-sized one, but not too big. I reach down with the shovel and scoop up the rock. C'mon, Zoey, I think. You can do this. You can. My heart is pounding, but I also feel like I'm slipping into warrior mode or something. In principle, this should work. My heart pounding, my arms not quite up to the task, I use the shovel like a lacrosse stick, like a catapult, to heave the rock at the man, who I still can't quite make out in the dark.

The rock goes *near* the man, I think; it at least goes somewhere within his ambit, I surmise, because I can see him stop as he seems to be examining his environs, to see what has just happened. And while he is distracted, I look for another rock but then have a different idea, and run straight to him, shouting "aaaaaarrrrrrrr" as I do it, and finally thwack him on the left side of the head with the shovel. The man lets out an "umph" and looks at me, then rather melts to the ground.

Finally, I can see his face. And what I can see is it's the lobbyist. It's the *goddamn* lobbyist. The one from the Postal Museum. From the night this all began. Now he's splayed out on Molly's lawn, wearing more wrinkled khakis and a navy blue windbreaker. Why? Why? Why?

I bend down, and, like before, I take his gun. This one looks different. It's sleeker, somehow. A little lighter than the other one. I put it into the pocket of my Gap army coat, then, again like before, feel around in his pockets. He's lying on his right side. He hasn't lost weight; I still can't reach into the pockets that he's fallen on top of. But in the left pocket, he's got a wallet, which I open. There's his driver's license at the front, and there's his name: Peter Francis Greenawalt.

HI HO

Chapter Fourteen

I'm standing over this *man*, this P.F., holding a gun, when Molly comes dashing out of the house.

"WHAT IN THE NAME OF ALL THAT IS GOOD IS GOING ON?" she shouts.

"Molly, be quiet," I say. When I see the startled expression on her face, I realize that I am pointing the gun on her. "Help me move him," I say.

"To *where*?" she asks. It's a good question.

"Is your sister still in the basement?" I ask.

"Are you out of your *mind*?" Molly says back. "You are, aren't you. You are out of your mind. I should have known you'd go crazy for real eventually when I let you convince me to break into that stable and go horseback riding in the middle of the night that time."

"That was *your* idea!" I say. It was, too! Molly was the one taking horseback riding lessons, not me, when we were fourteen. She was the one who knew how to put saddles on horses and how to get them to go where you wanted them to and whatnot. But this is no time for dickering over ancient history. This is the time for dragging a big, fat, passed-out lobbyist . . . somewhere.

"How about the trunk of the car?" I suggest, nodding toward Pete's Volvo.

"Oh, Jesus Christ," says Molly. She bends down and tries to lift P.F.—yes, this is P.F., another P.F. or *the* P.F., or who knows—by the armpits. It doesn't work. Molly's huffing a little. "He's fat," she says. I now realize Molly's had an underlying anti-fat bias as long as I've known her. I'm feeling less pro-Molly the longer this whole *thing* is happening.

"Can you try again?" I ask. "Can we try dragging?"

Molly bends down again. She tries to pull him from under the armpits while I shove against his feet, holding the gun in my hand as I'm doing it and pretty durn afraid I might accidentally pull the trigger. You can guess how successfully this goes.

"I'm going to call the police," Molly says. She's out of breath, bent over with her hands on her knees.

"Please don't," I say.

"Why?" Molly says.

"It's a long story," I say. I'm huffing, too. I wave my hand with the gun in it around in a careless gesture meant to indicate, "You know, too many details to get into right now." Then I realize I'm carelessly waving a gun around in the air. I put my gun hand down. I'm coming down from the adrenaline high. I'm starting to realize where I am again, who I'm with, what I'm doing here.

"Things are awful, Molly," I say, slipping the gun into my jacket pocket. "You won't be able to get your mind around it."

"I bet I could," Molly says. "It's been no picnic around here, either."

• • •

We end up leaving P.F. on the lawn. We don't know what else to do with him, since we can't carry him and we can't call the police. I drive the Volvo back to Aunt Lisa and Uncle Henry's house. Molly stays behind. She's going back to sleep, she says, if she can, with this fat guy passed out on the front lawn. Hopefully, she says, he'll have picked himself up and gone home, or gone *somewhere*, by the time her parents wake up.

"This is so so *profoundly* messed up, Zoey," she says. "And I'm saying this as someone who was recently kicked out of high school for buying some other kid's Adderall."

"I know," I say. Then, "Wait, you got thrown out of school?" I ask.

"Yeah," she says. "Ugh. I don't want to talk about it. I tried to tell Donald about it and he just said that he couldn't deal with me having more problems."

"You didn't tell me," I say. I feel hurt. Molly didn't tell me. "Why were you buying another kid's Adderall?"

"For the SATs," she says. "My doctor said she wouldn't give me any more."

"I'm sorry," I say.

"Yeah," she says again. "Yeah. It's time for things to stop being so *stupidly* messed up. Hey, does your brother have any Ritalin?"

"He went off his meds a while ago," I say. He did, too. Just decided one day about a year ago that he didn't need/ want them anymore. Had developed enough self-coping techniques and was focused enough without needing to resort, in his words, "to the machinations of Big Pharmaceutical and its disturbing crony relationship with the government and all so-called mental health doctors." I think he got that exact phrasing from Dad.

I also think that probably Ben was a little smarter, now that I think of it, when he was taking his Ritalin. I feel like the old, medicated Ben probably would have been more useful during this whole "Dad kidnapped" stage of things. He may have seen useful connections and patterns I'm not seeing. Like, say, figuring out that there is more than one P.F. Greenawalt. And why. And what to make of it. Like if we're being played by the one in Georgetown. And why this one here is trying to kill us. (Seriously, why is he trying to kill us????)

But no. At least he showed "Big Pharmaceutical" a thing or two, right?

So while I don't have access to the pills, or my brother's now only sometimes super-powerful weirdo brain, or any answers AT ALL about what in the HELL is going on with these P.F.s, the friendly one, supposedly, who I do not trust one iota, and the most definitely unfriendly one now passed out on the lawn, who I trust even less, I do share the sense it's time for things to get better.

When I get back to the house, I'm ready to go wake up Pete and Ben to explain to them that we aren't safe here in Rhode Island, that Aunt Lisa and Uncle Henry are in danger with us here, too, I think—I think?—but I find them already up, packed, and waiting for me to get home, ready with the same lecture.

I'm so tired. I'm so scared. I'm repacking my bag—how did my jeans and tops and lotions and other things explode around the room before we'd even spent one night at the house?—when I hear another alarming sound. It's a crash. A house-shaking crash. An earth-crashing shake. A nerve-demolisher.

I run to look out the window and can't see what's happened, but I can see lights going on in the neighbors' houses. So this isn't just in my head. Which is a relief.

I rush to the front door. Pete and Ben are already there. Aunt Lisa and Uncle Henry are coming down the stairs. This woke them up, too. Look outside, and holy shit. Holy shit. It would appear that something big and powerful has crashed through Pete's car. It's smoking up through the trunk.

We go outside to inspect. Indeed, there is a big smoking hole in the car. The neighbors are coming outside. Jesus. What if P.F. had been in there? I mean, what if he *had*?

"Meteorite," says Ben. He picks up a hunk of rock from the road. "Warm," he says. "This has been traveling for millions of years. And now it's here."

"It hit my car," says Pete. "I can't drive this. I can't drive this!" He looks around, as if he might have forgotten that he had another car there that we could use.

"We have to leave," I say. I can hear the anxiety in my voice. I want to hug Ben close, but that'll make it worse for him. I want to hug Pete, but I don't know if we have that kind of relationship.

"I know," Pete says. He sounds angry. He sounds so tired. "I know. This ends *today*. I just don't know how we're going to get back."

Just then, Molly pulls into the driveway, in that old Toyota her sister's ex-boyfriend gave her back in high school.

"Your mother," she says, getting out of the car. "She won't leave me alone."

We go back inside the house, then walk out the back door. Uncle Henry is standing in the backyard, dazedly holding a smooshed tomato. Aunt Lisa is checking on the alpacas.

From the smoke coming off their shed, their prospects are not fabulous. The house seems okay. The turret wasn't knocked off or anything.

I walk back to the alpaca shed. The two alpacas are lying dead in the shed, with blood on their llama-like, grey furry heads. There are two holes in the roof of the shed.

"Jesus Christ," I say.

Aunt Linda shoots me a look. She's stroking the heads of one of the alpacas, the grey one, who's lying on the hay as if he's napping. Then she shoots Uncle Henry, who's also come in, a somewhat different look.

"They were insured, right?" she asks. He nods. She appears to suppress a smile. I can almost hear her brain devising artisanal alpaca sausage recipes. Maybe she'll sell them at farmers markets or something.

I hug my aunt. "We have to go," I say.

"Stay, I'll cook you some breakfast," she says. I want to. I want to stay. I'm even a little curious what those gorgeous camelids taste like. Did they have a moment of insight, when the meteoroid hit them in the heads? Did they suddenly know they were going to die? Or know *why* they were about to die? Or why they lived? (To produce yarn and babies for yuppies who didn't understand the notion of an alpaca bubble, is why they lived, so far as I can tell. But what did their own lives mean to them?)

I hope it wasn't scary for them, when the meteorite came through the roof. I wonder if they sensed danger was coming. They might have better-developed instincts like that than I've got. Hell, it's turning out that a *tomato* might have better-developed instincts.

I suck at this, it's turning out. I suck at figuring out what is wrong and what to do about it. But I can at least try to follow the plan, which changes every fifteen minutes or thereabouts for reasons that don't seem entirely, sometimes even at all, obvious to me.

"We can't," I say, because this time I can see why we're committed to leaving, having been recently shot at by P.F.—*who the hell is P.F.???? Who are any of the P.F.s????*—and all. I can see Pete making his way to the shed, stepping around the bits of meteorite that are now scattered in holes around the yard. I'm no economist, but it seems obvious this won't be good for property values.

We go back out front. Pete and Ben have already put their bags into Molly's car; Ben's already settled into the cramped, filthy backseat of the car. Pete is in the driver's seat. Molly in the passenger's seat. She looks awful. Of course, she did just see me with a gun, help me try to drag a passed-out homicidal lobbyist across her front lawn, and find herself haunted, I guess, by good old dead Mom.

"What?" she says, when she notices me noticing her. "Stop looking at me like that."

I run upstairs, grab my bag, bring it down, toss it in the trunk. Molly has to get out to let me in. She and Pete are already Mom and Dad. I wonder if she'd sleep with him to make up for Donald. I get in the car, and then we go.

Ben has studied the maps—the road maps, the traffic maps, the traffic camera maps, and several other relevant maps—and devised the quickest possible route. Perhaps he's still able to see patterns after all, even without the drugs. In which case, why isn't he seeing kidnapping patterns, not just traffic patterns? Anyway, it'll take five hours, they claim.

"To where?" I ask.

Ben rattles off an address. Something something something

Chain Bridge Road, McLean, Virginia. He even gives me the zip code.

"What is that the address *for*?" I ask.

Ben shrugs. He's still not interested in personal details. Never was. You'd try to tell him about your day, and he'd glaze over. You could see him working out math problems in his head as you were complaining about, say, lacrosse practice. One got used to not sharing one's life with this robot brother. Figures he'd calculate how to get someplace we are fleeing to or racing toward or doing something involving an adverb and a verb regarding without him even asking what the place is or why we're going there.

"What is this place, Pete?" I ask anxiously, which is my most frequently applicable personal adverb.

Pete just keeps driving. Ben turns on his reading light and goes back to reading some sort of economics treatise. *The Road to Serfdom*, by Friedrich Hayek, I see when he shows me the cover. The definitive edition. It's libertarians' favorite book, next to *Atlas Shrugged*. Dad tried to get me to read it when I was younger. Because younger kids should definitely be reading libertarian economics treatises. But there's my brother. There's my brother. I guess this is his way of missing Dad. Or being, like, a genius. But if he's such a genius, why doesn't he know how to get us out of this?

I fall asleep, like I always fall asleep on car rides, but this time I'm listening to Molly, who is my friend again—I think, I think? I hope?—hold forth on her favorite experimental noise-rock bands. She used to make me mixes of them, back before Donald. I wished I was avant-garde enough, or whatever, to like the mixes.

When I wake up, it's light out, and we're parked in front of a monster-sized mansion.

"This is my mother's house," Pete says. He seems tired but certain. "We're going inside."

"Okay," I say, anxiously, because always.

We park in the driveway. Sleepily drift up the cobbled path to the gold-painted front door. It's an ornate house. It's surprisingly hot outside. We moved to Virginia in late August, and it was ninety degrees for thirty days in a row, halfway through September. I wonder when that starts. Maybe soon.

Pete rings the bell. I hear a dog barking. I smile. I'll get to play with a dog here. And a person with a dog is likely to be someone I like.

The door opens. Standing in front of us is P.F. Greenawalt. The first P.F. Greenawalt. P.F. Greenawalt, Political Consultant. Then a husky comes dashing past him, pushing its way out the door. Not just any husky. It's Roscoe.

LET MY
ROSCOE GO
Chapter Fifteen

Roscoe. All those weeks of looking. All those doors I knocked
on. All that crying. And here's my dog, my dog, sitting in
front of me, licking his lips. I bend down and hug him, bury
my face in his fur. He smells unusually clean.

"I missed you, baby dog," I say to him. "What are you
doing here? How did you get here?"

I look up. "How did he get here?" I ask, looking at Pete,
then at P.F., then at Pete again. "Pete?" I look at Molly.
Maybe she knows. She's nodding her head, eyes half-closed,
as if she's listening to music. Oh, Molly.

A woman appears at the doorway. A tall, blonde woman,
with what Mom used to call "Republican hair"—hair that's
an oddly unnatural and uniform shade of yellow, that's got
this little bit of wave to it in a couple of places. Precise hair.
Women in Rhode Island do not have such hair unless they
host evening news programs. It's mostly DC hair, and most
prevalent, Mom liked to say, during certain more unfortunate
presidencies.

I stand up. Roscoe leans against my legs. My dog. Things might be okay. My dog is back.

"Are you going to introduce me to your friends, Peter?" the precisely-coiffed woman asks.

"Don't do this, Mom," Pete says. "No more. It's over, Mom. No more games."

"What's over?" I ask.

The woman's perfect, blankly interested look matches her perfectly still blonde hair.

"I'm Madeleine Severy," she says. "Call me Mrs. Severy." She holds out her hand. I take it, damply. I regret, like usual, my own disheveled appearance. I look poor, I think. Molly, too. Molly looked so cute in the Biggest Little. Now she, like me, looks out of place.

Maybe not poor, exactly. I guess my standard about what poor is has changed since I moved to Virginia. But certainly out of our league, with Molly's bangs sprayed up like some shrubbery, as is often the way in Rhode Island, and a purple silk shirt tied up into a knot at the waist; me in my Gap army coat and shitty jeans and bangs that I've been meaning to get cut for quite a while, if only I hadn't been so busy trying to save my stupid father and run away from murderous lobbyists, etc.

This is Pete's mom, apparently? *Peter*'s mom? She looks very rich. "Here, come in." She steps aside. P.F. also steps aside. Then she calls to my dog. "Come in, Adolfo." Roscoe glances up at me, then trots into the house. I feel a stab in my heart. This isn't right. This is very not right.

"His name is Roscoe," I say. "Where did you find him?"

No one says anything.

"What's going on, Pete?" I ask. "*Peter*. Why is my dog here? Why are *we* here? And my dog."

"What is P.F. doing here?" Ben asks me. "That is P.F., isn't it?" Ben is not always great at recognizing faces, but I think he's on the money here. He's surprisingly unmoved by seeing Roscoe. I thought he liked Roscoe. I thought he loved him. I feel hurt that Ben isn't more excited to see our dog. Our family isn't what I thought it was, at all.

"Pete?" I say. Then I call out, hit my hands to my knee. "Roscoe!" If I can hug Roscoe again, then I will feel better. I can handle whatever it is going on here. I see Roscoe sitting next to Mrs. Severy. He looks up at her. He's waiting for her to tell him what to do. She doesn't let him come over to me.

I start to walk inside. Mrs. Severy is the one in control.

"Don't go in there," Pete says.

"Why?" I ask. "I don't understand what's happening, Pete."

"Come in," says Mrs. Severy again. Her voice is melodious and authoritative. I can see why Roscoe lets her tell him what to do.

"No," says Pete. "Mom. Stop this. Stop it now. I came here to tell you that it's over."

"Come in, Peter Francis," she says.

"Mom, I said no," Pete says.

Ben turns to me. "They're upset, right?"

"I think so," I say back to him. I look up, try to make eye contact with someone, anyone, looking for a hint. Peter Francis. P.F. I feel my head getting more buzzy. My thoughts are going even more scattered. I'm tired. Maybe I'm dreaming. Is this all just a highly realistic nightmare? It's got the elements of a dream. The confusion. The anxiety. The somewhat abstract and yet very authentic-feeling sense of danger involving snippets and images of things I know from the actual world, but combined into horrific new situations.

Maybe this is like what's been happening inside Ben's head when he goes to sleep at night and Mom details for him the times, dates, and places of Dad's murders. Except that Mom's not here and I don't seem to be asleep.

Molly stops nodding her head. The music, or whatever the hell was going on in her brain, has apparently stopped. "Are we going in?" she says. "I really have to pee."

She starts walking through the door.

Pete puts his hand on her arm. "No," he says. He looks up at his mother again. "No!" he shouts at her. "No, Mom. No. I did everything you asked. But I came here today to tell you that it's over. This is over. I'm not like you, Mom. I'm not. Let me go. Let them go."

"Roscoe," I say.

In my head, all of a sudden and not super appropriately, I have this song that we used to sing at our yearly, highly secular Passover seders, that springtime celebration of the Jews escaping enslavement in Egypt: "When Galt was in Egypt's land, let my Galt go." Next verse: "Tell old Julia, let my Galt go."

It was a take on that old anti-slavery song "Go Down Moses":

> *When Israel was in Egypt's land,*
> *Let my people go.*
> *Oppressed so hard they could not stand,*
> *Let my people go.*
> *Go down, Moses,*
> *Way down in Egypt's land.*
> *Tell old Pharaoh,*
> *Let my people go.*

Except Dad's version gave him the opportunity to bring up the beloved dog Mom had dispatched to Scituate. It also gave him the opportunity to talk about property rights and how Mom had violated them when she dispatched Galt to Scituate. He also liked to get into one of his lectures about states' rights and animal slavery, around this song.

Ben would top all this off with a flat statement about how most serious historians agree the Jews were never actually slaves in Egypt, and certainly did not, as the Passover story has it, wander in the desert for forty years after the escape was to have taken place.

"The boy is correct," Dad would bellow. "I'm proud of you, son!"

The Seder participants are also supposed to sing a song called "*Dayenu.*" The song is about how "it would have been enough" and is supposed to thank the great magical man in the sky for helping the Jews above and beyond what was really necessary. It says, it would have been enough if the lord had simply killed off the Egyptian families' firstborn sons. Then you say the word "*Dayenu.*" Then, it would have been enough if the Jews had simply been allowed to escape from slavery. *Dayenu.* It would have been enough if our enemies hadn't been drowned in the Red Sea as the Jews were fleeing from Egypt. *Dayenu.*

This song, for some reason, would always get tipsy old Dad talking about the things that weren't enough. It wasn't enough that Mom gave away his dog. "No *Dayenu!*" he'd say. Not enough that he had to keep working as a corporate auditor, even though he really wanted to, like, *write* or do something more important than being a glorified bookkeeper. "No *Dayenu!*"

"And where's my dog? My precious dog?" he'd say. Per the Passover meal's requirements, Dad would have had three glasses of wine by this part of the ceremony on top of the previous drinks. He's really not a good drinker. "And why do we even do this ceremony? You don't care about it, Julia. And it's not based in any sort of actual factual history. Why do we do this?"

Then he'd launch into "Let My Galt Go," at which point Mom would usually get up from the table and ask me and Ben if we'd like to go out for some ice cream cones. You're not supposed to eat breaded things, like cones, during the whole Passover week.

Ben would go for ice cream. He'd always go for ice cream. I'd stay home with Dad, and we'd eat some of the tinned flourless macaroons that taste good if you've had three glasses of wine, I suppose, and not so good otherwise. Dad would usually abstain from bread for three days of the week, saying that he liked the discipline of it, and that it was good for losing a few pounds, before giving in and eating some pizza or a peanut butter and jelly sandwich. I'd hold out as long as he did. It was one of our things that he'd do and I'd follow.

I'm not sure if now is the time to request divine intervention. Do we need any *Dayenu* moments here? Which ones? Locusts? The killing of the firstborn son? The parting of the . . . the what?

But even if the Passover story was made up, like Ben and Dad said it was, I was okay with that, too. That means that our people never had to suffer the actual hardships. We're just inspired storytellers. I didn't mind having that in my DNA, either. It's a convenient escape. I could use one of those about now.

Mrs. Severy comes back outside. Why does she have a different last name from Pete? Why does Pete have the same name as these other men, the one who tried to kill me, the one who says he tried to save me. Who is now here with Pete's mom. Who is Pete's mom? Why are we here? WHY ARE WE HERE? Let's *go*, I think. Please, let's go. Let my Roscoe go, and let's all go while we're at it.

Pete's mom, Mrs. Severy, looks quietly, elegantly furious. She says, "I should never have put you on this, Pete. You're over your head. You're just a musician. This should have been your sister's job."

"What job, Pete?" I ask.

"You work?" asks Ben. "But your family is rich. Look at this house. In this real estate market, this house must have cost . . . eighteen million. Maybe twenty."

"Whoa. Really?" Molly asks. She turns to Pete. "Why did you drive such a shitty car?" She chuckles. "Meteoroid."

Mrs. Severy smiles. "Kids, you must be thirsty after your long drive. Come in, have some water."

"NO," Pete says again. "Don't go in."

Molly says, "Dude, I have to *urinate*." She draws out each syllable: your-eee-nate. Mrs. Severy, who cannot be used to hearing people draw out the syllables of the word urinate, doesn't flinch.

Molly heads in, curtsying as she walks past a smiling Mrs. Severy. Molly, I realize all of a sudden, doesn't spend a lot of time with people who live in castles. I look at Ben and Pete, then walk inside, too. My dog is in there. Ben follows. Pete comes in after Ben. My stomach feels exactly like it's felt almost all the time since this whole business began. Tight. Pinched. Unpleasantly acidic. Full. I can't breathe too well. Oh, now it's a little different from how it's been for most of this adventure. And I really could use the bathroom. It's awful, but I think that I might have diarrhea. No, no, no no no nonononono. No. I can't have diarrhea now. Let my *bowels* go? No, please don't let them go, at least not until . . .

"Where's the bathroom?" I ask P.F.

I slink into the expansive marble foyer, which is flanked by two grand staircases, themselves flanked by golden handrails, up to a sweeping upstairs landing on which I can see a life-sized elephant statue, trunk erect. What the hell is this house?

"I'll walk you," he says. He and I head between the staircases toward what I can see is an absolutely gigantic tan-marbled kitchen. Molly follows.

"I'm going to piss in my pants," she says.

"What are you doing here?" I ask P.F., when we're away from the others (except Molly, who seems bizarrely uninterested, or maybe just doesn't realize, that something is seriously amiss here). "What's going on?"

"Do you trust me?" he asks.

"Are you out of your mind?" I'm bent over at the waist a little. "No. I don't. What the hell are you doing here? What's going on? You know Pete's *mom?*"

"Here's the bathroom," P.F. says.

Molly goes in. "Whoa, this is really fancy," she says, her voice echoey from behind the closed door.

"I met someone else named P.F. Greenawalt. Peter Francis Greenawalt. Met might not be the right word. He tried to kill me. I hit him in the side of the head with a shovel. A spade. Do you know him?" I ask. I hear the noise of Molly peeing, then the sound of the sink. My tummy's making unfeminine sounds. Distressingly unfeminine sounds.

"You coming out, Moll?" I ask.

"Hang on," she says. I hear some more noises. Shufflings, squeaks. I imagine she's opening the medicine cabinet, looking for something interesting. Wonder if she'll find anything. What she'll find.

"You okay?" I call in, after a few minutes.

"Fine," she says, a funny tone in her voice. A tone that makes it sound like she's straining to do something. Maybe she had to pee, then realized she had to poop? Or maybe . . .

"Drug problem," I mouth to P.F., who nods. "But she's paid the price. She's on the road to wellness," I whisper loudly, having no idea whatsoever what I'm talking about but feeling that words like these would be appropriate. Then I whisper: "So, who the hell are you anyway?"

"I'm P.F. Greenawalt," he says.

"Yeah, right," I say, as quietly as I can. Suddenly tears spring to my eyes. Yay emotional rollercoaster. "You and that other guy. The one who tried to kill me. Why did he try to kill me?"

"I . . ." He pauses. "Things are very complicated, Zoey."

"No shit," I say. My nose is running, and I feel in my pockets for a tissue. No tissue, but yes gun. Somehow I'd forgotten the gun. I wipe my nose on my sleeve, all classy-like.

"Everything I told you before was true," he says.

"Yeah? Yeah? Well, maybe. But even if so, I feel there were some serious omissions," I say, emboldened by the gun. "Yes, that's my feeling. I'd like some explanation of. Jesus, P.F. Everything. Why is my dog here? Why are *you* here? Why am *I* here! Where *is* my dog?"

"Be quiet," P.F. hisses. "This isn't a joke."

"I'm not laughing," I say, though I am laughing a little, but not a funny haha laugh, just a HEY I'M CONFUSED AND SCARED sort of laugh.

Then P.F. starts laughing. Which makes me laugh harder. And suddenly the two of us are standing in front of the bathroom cracking up. Totally inappropriately. The laughing bout stops all of a sudden. There's nothing funny going on here. And Molly has been quiet for a long goddamn time.

I call through the door, "Moll? You okay? Do you need more toilet paper or something?"

No answer.

P.F. knocks on the door. He looks *uncomfortable*. "Ahem. Pardon. Can I help with anything? Well, not help with anything going on in there. But with anything in *general*?"

"You could get my dad," I say. He doesn't respond. Neither does Molly.

P.F. tries the handle. Nothing. He pounds on the door. Nothing.

I think, for a moment, that I could offer to shoot the door open. I don't. P.F. goes out to retrieve a screwdriver. He comes back, unscrews the door handle. Pushes the door. Wind wafts over our tense faces. The bathroom window is open. Molly is gone.

"This is bad," P.F. says. "Where is she?"

"I don't know," I say. I genuinely don't. I still really have to use the bathroom, too.

"You can wait in here if you want while I go," I say, bobbing up and down, hoping P.F. doesn't take me up on this.

"I'll wait right here," he says. "DON'T try anything funny. Shit."

Well, yes. I close the knob-less door. Compose myself. Hope no one can see/is looking in through the hole in the door. Gaze out the open window. It opens out to a yard so big I can't see its boundaries. I can see what looks like a swimming pool, a ways away, which I guess could work as a Red Sea stand-in if we needed the great man upstairs to drown some enemies. And maybe a guest house past that? Is Molly in the guest house? Going for a swim?

After making an orchestra of humiliating noises, after which I do feel a little better in the tummy, though nowhere else, I wash up, using the pleasant-smelling soaps, and the single-use hand towels in this big marble bathroom.

"MOLLY!" I call out the window. No response. "MOOOOLLLLLLLYYYYYY," I try again, like she's a dog who's run off after a squirrel. My dog. I need to go find my dog again. My brother. Pete. Find Pete. Find out what our plans are. I'm certainly not the one making the plans. Just following. As best I can.

"They've sent someone after her," P.F. says to me when I come out of the bathroom. "You have to hope she's good at hiding now. That's the only hope."

I gaze at him. I feel my mouth hanging open, my eyes blinking too slowly.

"Pull yourself together, Zoey," he says in his nasal voice. "I told you this is serious."

"Who's gone after her?" I ask.

"Another of the P.F.s," he says. "We don't have time now. Just trust me, Zoey. You have to if you're going to get through this."

I don't trust him, *obviously*, but I have to follow when he guides me through a massive granite and stainless kitchen to a screened-in room at the back of the house. It's blocked off with a sliding glass door. It seems like such a cozy addition to this kind of cold, impressive living space. I think I can see a fire burning in a fireplace. I can definitely see Pete, standing, gesticulating. He looks furious. I can hear him, sort of. Moving closer, I can hear more.

"I *know* you think I'm incompetent and I *know* you think

you should have sent Abby instead of me. I don't *care*. I'm *tired* of trying to impress you. I *know* you think I'm a fuckup, Mom, and you always will. Well, so who cares. At least I'm not *evil*, Mom. At least I'm not evil."

Roscoe barks. I then see that Mrs. Severy is sitting on a floral couch. Roscoe is sitting at her feet. She's elegant, in the middle of this, and still has my dog.

Ben is sitting on a matching floral loveseat, kitty corner to Mrs. Severy's.

P.F. slides the door open. We come into the room.

"What's going on?" I ask, looking from person to person.

Mrs. Severy takes a deep, exasperated breath. "My son is explaining to me that I find him a disappointment and always have," she says. "It's ridiculous."

"It's *true*, Mom!" he shouts.

"Keep your voice down," she says. "You're not a disappointment. You're my son. However, you promised you could take care of things. You haven't. Now I'll have to pick up the pieces. Tie up the loose ends."

"Zoey isn't a loose end, Mother," he says.

Well, what?

"In fact she is, Peter," says Mrs. Severy. "Both these children are."

"I thought you'd be reasonable," Pete says. He sounds desperate. His voice has a little squeak to it.

I'm hovering near the door. I'd like to collect my dog and my brother and get *out of here*, but I'm just hovering. Timid. Always so timid. I wasn't raised to be timid, I just turned out that way. Can't play lacrosse. Can't collect my dog and save my brother and my father and my friend and Jesus, there are a lot of people who need saving right now.

"I thought you'd be mature enough to fulfill your

responsibilities," says Mrs. Severy. She uncrosses her legs at the ankles. Shifts in the sofa. P.F. starts to move as well. He turns his head to look at Ben. He pulls out a gun.

Without realizing I'm going to do it, or else probably the timidity would hold me back, I run at him. I can hear my dad's voice in my head: "Use your shoulder, aim for the soft middle, but high enough that you will make your opponent unsteady." I don't even know if Dad was *right*, but this is the best I can do. I aim for P.F.'s padded middle. I make contact. I hear a gunshot, then Ben's quiet voice, which says, so simply, so devastatingly, "Zoey, I'm hurt."

INSURANCE

Chapter Sixteen

I run to my brother. He's lying on the couch, not moving. There's blood on his jacket. I'm looking at his head, his chest, his stomach, his neck, trying not to touch or jostle him too much or upset him more.

"Where are you hurt, honey?" I say to Ben. He doesn't respond. "Why did you do this to him?" I cry out to P.F.

"We have to *run*," Pete says. "Zoey, we have to run right now."

"I don't know where he's hurt," I say to Pete. I look at Mrs. Severy, who continues to sit on the couch, somewhat imperviously, imperiously. Roscoe's nose is in the air. He is staring in our direction. He must want to come over to us. He must. He doesn't come.

P.F. is back on his feet, one hand holding the small of his back, which I suppose hurts since he's old and old people's backs always hurt when they fall. With his other hand, he's pointing the gun at Pete still.

"I'm going to need you to come with me," P.F. is saying, wincing at the same time.

"Shut up," I say. Then I scream it. "SHUT UP."

I turn back to my brother. I can tell he's disassociating. He used to do this a lot when he was younger, before they got the meds right. It's part of why he needed so many doctors, so many diagnoses. When a situation would get stressful, he'd react either by becoming madly destructive—breaking plates, throwing things, pulling his own hair out, punching whatever was around—or by disassociating. Becoming comatose, basically. Losing track of the world.

Sometimes those two states would work in tandem. He'd go into a dissociative lapse and be destructive while he'd be like that, then not remember it afterwards. Dad described it as a sort of "fugue state." He liked to add that many geniuses went into such "fugue states" while they were at their most productive. Which didn't seem too applicable in our case, unless you considered smashing every water glass in the house as being Ben's "most productive."

He doesn't do either much anymore. Meds helped. Then through some cognitive therapy, Ben learned self-calming techniques like deep breathing and self-analysis, and a bit of chilling the hell out, which got him off the meds. That's how we've gotten away with this irregular schedule during Dad's disappearance, and our search for Dad, and all the new people, and none of his regular diet. I guess being shot at Pete's mom's house while we're madly trying to find Dad has been a step beyond what self-calming can really take care of.

P.F. starts talking again, as I'm still trying to go over my brother, find out where he's hurt, find out how hurt he is. I've got the buzzy feeling in my head, but I'm also focusing, focusing on Ben, focusing on solving this *one problem* because

I can't handle more than one shot-brother-sized problem at a time.

"You're going to have to come with me," he's saying.

I pull the gun out of my jacket pocket and point it back at him. "I don't think that's the case," I say. "I think that isn't the case at all."

I've never used a gun before, but from having watched a terrific amount of police procedurals on television, I have some sense of how the contraption works—in addition to all those years of other, as it's turning out somewhat surprisingly useful, self-defense training exercises Dad put me through.

Like I've seen (fictional) cops and murderers do count-less times, I cock the trigger—at least I think that's what it's called, what I do, when you jiggle the gun in various ways and prepare to shoot it. I could pull the trigger. I could kill P.F. right now. Kill Mrs. Severy. Pete's mother. I could kill Pete's mother. I could kill myself. I could cry for even having that thought.

"We have to *leave*, Zoey," Pete says. He takes the gun from my hand. Keeps aiming it at P.F., then turning it toward his mother. "We're leaving," he says. His face looks strangely exhilarated, that lovely round face with a veneer of sweat on it, beneath that springy hair.

He puts on a pair of sunglasses pulled from his pocket, thick, plastic, ironic rich-kid ones, then nudges my brother. "Buddy, can you walk?" Ben doesn't answer. "Buddy?"

"You're going to have to carry him," I say. Pete hands me back the gun. "You okay with this?" he asks me. I nod. But I'm not okay with this. Really, really not okay with this. What choice do I have, though? I keep the gun aimed at the adults in the room while Pete scoops up my lumpy brother, still catatonic, still bleeding. I see, as he's lifting him, a tear in his jacket toward the upper arm, blood emanating from that tear. I heave a sigh of relief. *It's just the upper arm where Ben's been shot.* These are the thoughts of my life, right at this moment, with my dad missing and Pete's mom trying to . . . to what? I don't know. I don't know anything.

"Come on, Roscoe," I say to the dog as we're walking out of the room, my brother comatose, Pete having what seems an inappropriate smile on that lovely face, me carrying a gun.

Roscoe looks up at Mrs. Severy. He's waiting for her permission to leave with me. Oh, god, this, *this*, is too much. I start to cry. "Come on, Roscoe," I say again. Mrs. Severy doesn't say a word.

"Adolfo, you're a very good boy," she says calmly.

I walk over to Adolfo. Roscoe. Mrs. Severy's on the couch. I look her in the eye as I grab Roscoe's collar and start to drag him.

"Please, Roscoe," I say. I'm sobbing. "*Please.*"

I point the gun at the ceiling. Mrs. Severy reaches out and starts to take it from my hand. I pull the trigger. The trigger is looser, I guess is the word for it, than I'd have expected. It shoots easily. Smoothly. A bullet shoots up into the ceiling. I'm surprised how much kickback there is. So much I can feel it in my bicep. I flinch, but feel some power in me as well. I have agency. I have a *gun.*

"Come with me *now*, Roscoe," I shout. I point the gun at Mrs. Severy now, again, looking her in the eye. Her eyes look so much like Pete's. Those hazel eyes. I'd have thought she would have ice-blue eyes, but no, soft hazel, with some lines and wrinkles around them that make her seem even more elegant and powerful and some makeup stuck in those lines and wrinkles that undoes some of her elegance and power, but not by a lot.

I grab Roscoe's collar again and drag, and drag, and finally he starts to walk, reluctantly; I don't know what this woman has done to my dog, but he's my dog, and goddamnit it, he's coming with me. I think about pointing the gun at him to make him move faster, then I cry even harder when I realize I'm having this thought.

P.F. follows us to the front door. I'm dragging Roscoe with one hand, holding the gun in P.F.'s direction with the other hand, trying not to hook that loose trigger again, because I am scared and I am confused but I am not, no I am not, a nihilist. (It goes without saying that I know *this* because Dad sat me down, at age ten or eleven, over ice cream to tell me about the nihilists, who believe, in essence, that life is objectively pointless. "Libertarians don't necessarily think that life is without objective truths or morals. Our point is that the government shouldn't be telling people what to do except under a few extremely limited circumstances. And they certainly shouldn't be able to take forty percent of my income to pay for wars we shouldn't be involved with. Or public schools," I recall him saying. "But if you decide later, when you're older, that you are a nihilist, then that's your choice.")

Pete, ahead of me, carries a still-comatose Ben, dripping blood on that lovely white marble in the foyer, with that big elephant looking out from the second-story landing. It might be a real elephant, killed and stuffed and exhibited now, forever, to look out on this marble expanse that leads to the outdoors, the wilds of DC's wealthiest suburbs.

When we walk through the front door, P.F. says to me, "I can help you still."

"HOW?" I yell.

"We have to leave," Pete says, urgently.

"Where is Roscoe's leash?" I ask P.F. I'm sobbing again. "Please get me his leash."

P.F. disappears for a moment. He might not come back, I think, but he does, carrying a heavy leather leash with some sort of harness attached to it. We walked Roscoe on a hot pink piece of webbing Dad had picked up from a discount pet emporium, attached to a fake leather collar that he is no longer wearing.

"What is this?" I ask.

"Madeleine had this custom-made," says P.F.

I try to attach it to the dog. I don't know how it works. This is like what I imagine creepier adults use when they are enjoying naked time with other creepy adults.

"Here," P.F. says. He bends down and, with a few motions, wraps Roscoe in the leather in a way that makes him walkable. He looks at me. "I can still help you," he says. "I could have killed your dog. Or your brother. Or you. I didn't."

"You didn't kill Mrs. Severy, either," I say.

"Come on," says Pete.

I take the leather leash and walk out the door. P.F. stands there watching. I'm not sure where Mrs. Severy is. Pete keeps looking back, like he's making sure she's not following. Or like he's hoping to see her.

We get outside into the bright day. It's spring. It feels like real spring now. The trees have pink buds on them. I'm told cherry blossom season is DC's nicest time of year. The air is warm, not hot. The air smells delicious. I shield my eyes with my hand.

"Where's the car?" I ask Pete.

"Oh no," he says, still with my limp, large brother slung over his shoulder. "Molly had the keys."

We stand on that path, just outside the house. I'm holding

a gun in one hand, Roscoe's S&M-style leash in the other. Molly is missing. Where she's gone to, I don't know. I hope she's okay. It was probably smart to flee when she did, except she took our only mode of transportation with her. I don't *think* Mom would have told her to do that.

"We could . . . what's it called? We could carjack a car," I suggest.

"I don't think that's a great idea," Pete says. "If the people whose car we take call the police, we could end up . . ."

"In jail?" I say.

P.F. is still lingering—you might even say malingering—in the doorway.

"Point the gun at me," he says quietly.

"What?" I ask.

"Point it," he whispers.

I lift my arm, point the gun at him.

"Shoot into the foyer," he says. "Make sure you don't hit anyone."

I aim at the elephant and shoot. My bicep hurts again. Maybe more this time; it's still sore from the last shot. But I hit the elephant. I'm okay with the gun.

"Demand my car keys now," he says.

"Give me your keys," I hear myself saying.

"Louder," he says.

I say it louder. "Give me the keys! GIVE ME THE KEYS, GODDAMNIT!"

He reaches into the pocket of his rumpled pleated khaki pants. I notice that the hems are frayed, like he's been walking on them, dragging them on the ground. He hands me a black key.

We go into the long, long driveway, covered in crushed white shells. P.F.'s Lincoln is parked close to the big garage. Pete lays Ben into the backseat.

"He needs his seatbelt," I say. My parents always make us wear our seatbelts. Made us wear our seatbelts.

"It'll hurt him," Pete says. "It'll touch him where he's been shot."

"Uh huh," I say. Where he's been shot. Where Ben's been shot. "So we'll go to the hospital now."

"We can't," Pete says.

"Why not?" I ask. "Why not? He's been shot." That sounds reasonable. Get shot, go to the doctor. Brother is shot, brother needs doctor.

Pete slams his hands on the steering wheel several times. "That's *not* what I thought would happen," he says. "Once she saw you in person, I thought she'd be reasonable. That she'd understand."

"Understand *what*?" I ask.

He hits his hands on the steering wheel again, but more softly. He breathes out several times, loudly. "I want to come clean," he says. "I really do."

"I need you to take my brother to the hospital," I say. I can feel the rage boiling up inside of me again. And the power that comes with holding the gun. "Because that *man* who was with your *mother* shot him."

"If we do that, we may not get to your father in time," Pete says.

And then I shut up and start listening.

Pete explains to me what I must have known since we got to his mother's house, maybe longer, if I'd been paying attention. The P.F.s work for his mother. He doesn't know exactly what his mother does for a living, but he does know that she has a number of P.F.s working for her. He doesn't know if P.F. is their real name. It's the only name he's ever known any of them by. Maybe for exactly this reason, so they can't be identified by name.

Most of the P.F.s are, as far as he knows, widowers— *"They're widowers, Zoey,"* Pete says, the implication hanging in the air that they are widowers because of his mother, somehow. The implication being that my father is another of the P.F.s, maybe, when he is on the job. That Dad is a widower, and I am motherless, because of his mother.

She'd asked him to keep close watch on Zoey and Ben. To try to find the J-File. Which is in Molly's car. Which is somewhere. Hopefully somewhere safe.

"Why?" I ask, again, always.

"I wanted to impress her," he says, not answering the question I really wanted answered, which is why does she want the J-File? What *is* all of this?

But now he's crying. I can see the tears streaming down that face that I'm still amazed by, with its eyes I can't see behind the thick sunglasses, which is good, probably, seeing as how much those eyes look like someone who is the enemy of my family, I think.

"She didn't think I was up for it. For keeping track of you and Ben. Or looking for the J-File. She thought my sister should do this, but I wanted to do it. To show her that I'm not such a fuckup," Pete says. "But, I guess I am a fuckup, Zoey. Because I fell . . . for you. And I thought if we went there, I could convince her to leave us be . . ."

"Leave us be?" I say. "And my dad? And you and I are just supposed to . . . to what? To date? To go to the prom?" And as much as I hate to admit it, there's a part of me that still thinks I would like to go to the prom with Pete.

"We don't have proms at Shenandoah," Pete says.

"Seriously?"

"My arm hurts. I'm bleeding. It hurts," says my brother from the backseat, with that changing, warbly voice of his. "Why am I bleeding? What's *Roscoe* doing here?" I turn around in my seat and see Ben petting our dog. Giving the dog an awkward, joyful little hug. "Roscoe! Welcome home, Roscoe!" Roscoe's mouth lolls open. His tail thumps a little bit. At least Roscoe is happy! "Ow," Ben says. "It hurts. Are we going to a doctor?"

"We don't have time," Pete says.

"Don't have time to get my *shot brother* looked at?" I say.

Pete fumbles in his jacket pocket, pulls out his phone. Hands it to me. "Dial nine-one-one," he says.

"An ambulance?" I ask.

"Dial it!" Pete says.

I dial. "Now what?"

Pete takes the phone back from me. Holds it shoulder to ear while driving too fast. "I'd like to report a break-in," he says. He gives his mother's address. "Please hurry." He hangs up the phone. Searches for something on the car door. "How do you get the window down?" he mutters before finding the button. He opens the window, throws the phone out. The cool air feels good. I close my eyes, smell the blossoming trees.

Pete says, "That'll buy us a little time. Hopefully enough. We'll take you to get checked."

"Time for what?" Ben asks. "Did I miss something? I remember pulling into the driveway . . ."

Pete pulls into a strip mall parking lot, up to one of those drop-in clinics.

"We can get out," he says. "But if we do, we might not get to your father in time. But we might. It might not be too late, so long as they don't take a long time here. It's up to you."

I look at Ben. "How's your arm, honey?" I ask.

"It hurts," he says. He takes off his coat. He's wearing a Doctor Who T-shirt underneath. I can see the wound in full, now. It looks red and sore and, well, *angry and dangerous*, and like the sort of thing that under ordinary circumstances would one hundred percent require the attention of a medical professional.

"Let me see?" I ask him. The wound is getting my very unprofessional attention; Ben turns, shows me his upper arm. It's still bleeding. I can't tell if there's a bullet inside or if his arm's just been grazed. It doesn't look like he's going to die, thank you, higher power, thank you, if you exist, which you don't, but if you do, thank you.

"Can you wait to see the doctor?" I ask him. "Can you wait? Do you need to go now?"

"Buddy, your father is in trouble," Pete says. "If we go in here now, it's going to take a long time. The doctors might call the police . . ."

"You want to avoid the police," I say. "Like the kidnappers. And P.F. *P.F.s.* Your name is Pete. What's your middle name? What's your middle name, Pete? Is it Francis? Or . . . Frankie?"

"That's the same name," Ben says.

"Felonious?" I say. I don't know more male F names. I'm losing my authority here.

"Francis," Pete says. "That is my middle name. I am, no, I *was*, my mother's child. But I don't think you understand, Zoey," he says. "They are going to kill your father. We have to get to him first."

"Give me your shirt," I say to him.

"What for?" he asks.

"Tourniquet," I say.

Pete unbuckles his seatbelt. He takes off his coat, then

takes off his button-down shirt, a soft green and blue plaid he's wearing over a plain white V-necked T-shirt. He hands me the button-down. I rip off an arm. It takes a while to get through the seams, and my biceps are aching a little from the gun, but, using my teeth, I tear it off.

"C'mere, babe," I say to Ben, who leans forward. I tie the shirt above Ben's gunshot wound, his gunshot wound!, and say, mostly to myself, hopefully not loud enough to alarm my bleeding brother, "I hope this works."

Ben doesn't cry. He doesn't complain about the bloody injury, about me touching him. He just asks, "Can we try to get to the hospital soon enough that I won't lose my arm to gangrene from the loss of blood flow?"

Pete rebuckles his seatbelt. I'm crying again, trying not to let Ben see. It's my job to protect him. I think maybe I've failed, I'm failing, at this job.

"Where are we going?" I ask Pete.

"To get your father," Pete says.

"Where is he? How do I know this isn't a trap?" I say, feeling panicky again.

"I'm *going* to make this right," Pete says. "Please, Zoey." He keeps one hand on the steering wheel. Wipes my cheek with his right hand. Then puts it in my lap, picks up my left hand. "Zoey, I have to make this right," he says again. "Buddy, we'll do our best to get you to the doctor in time. We'll do our best."

I feel that melting feeling in my head, in my stomach. My heart is pounding. I feel confusion, panic, fear, *mistrust*. "Where is my dad?" I say, still leaving my left hand in his right one. I still have the gun in my pocket. I feel it with my right-hand index finger. I could remove it from the pocket. Could point it at Pete. Maybe I should. Maybe I need to. "Why should I trust you?" I say, pulling out the gun, touching its nose to Pete's fingers. Hoping Ben can't see.

Pete keeps his hand in mine. He stares straight ahead, says, "I'm pretty sure they're in a town in Virginia. A town called Lorton."

Ben perks up. "Is it . . ." He rattles off an address.

"How did you know?" Pete asks.

"Mom told me," Ben says. "There is a former prison in Lorton that is now an artists' colony. Norman Mailer, the writer, was held at that prison for two days in nineteen sixty-seven, after a Vietnam War protest. That was the protest when some people tried to make the Pentagon levitate. I don't think it's possible to make any big building levitate. It doesn't seem scientifically realistic."

"I don't think ghosts seem scientifically realistic," I say.

"That's true," says Ben. "But it doesn't directly bear on the Pentagon levitation issue."

He then settles back into the seat and, tugging on Roscoe's tail three times, looks down at his bloody, bound arm, picks up his economics book, and starts to read.

MOM'S
MODEL HOME

Chapter Seventeen

We're on the Beltway, stuck in traffic. One is always stuck in traffic on the highway that encircles DC. Usually it's annoying. You have to pee, or something, and you're inching along this massive ugly road while your brother's spouting off facts about *whatever* the hell is on his mind and your dad is talking about how private roads would relieve congestion, and, back before she was killed, your mother would be singing along with the radio in her terrible voice.

Right now, mid-afternoon on Saturday—two or three days after the original deadline to get the kidnappers the J-File, I realize, depending on which day the kidnappers considered to be day one—in P.F.'s bizarre old-man car that he told us to steal from him, it's worse. Yes, I have to pee. I always have to pee. And yes, my brother is talking about some odd, obscure thing that's on his mind. (I can't concentrate enough even to grasp what he's on about this time. I keep hearing him say the word "platelets," but I'm not getting more than that.) What I can't hold in is my anxiety over where we are, what we're doing, what's to come, what's happened.

"Can you imagine if DC had to be evacuated?" asks Ben, moving on from platelets and other blood-related matters for the moment. "If, say, a nuclear bomb were headed for the White House?" He's looking up from his economics book, petting Roscoe. Did I not notice that he had the book with him at Mrs. Severy's house? Why didn't he keep the whole briefcase, then, with the J-File in it?

Color has come back to his face. The tourniquet worked. I allow myself a small sigh of relief. Roscoe's tongue is lolling; I believe that is the technical word for it.

"We'd be incinerated while stuck in traffic," Ben continues. "There have been proposals to expand the highway. I'm not convinced that they would actually move the cars any more quickly."

"No?" Pete asks, absently.

I watch Ben watch Pete.

"You're not really interested," Ben says. "I'll stop talking."

Ben, I realize, is getting better at reading faces. Which means I should probably get better at hiding my feelings.

"How much longer?" I ask Pete.

"Not too far," Pete says.

"That could mean anything on the Beltway," Ben observes. "Look at all the cars. The first section of the Beltway opened in nineteen fifty-seven. There was heated debate about whether to call it the Capitol Beltway or the Capital Beltway."

"What do you mean debate? You just said the same thing twice," I say.

"No, Capitol with an *o* or Capital with an *a*," Ben says. "With an *o* it means the capitol building. With an *a* it means

the capital city. They are homophones." Pete chuckles. "Two
words that sound the same but have different meanings," Ben
says. "Capitol and capital. Why is that funny?"

I can hear Dad's joke in my head: "Homophonia is when
people are afraid that they don't know the difference between
capitol and capital." I can hear Mom's correction in my head:
"Capitol and capital don't actually sound the same," with
her emphasizing the *o* in the one and the *a* in the other.

"I don't know what you're talking about," I finally say.
I'm just not up for this conversation.

"But I just told you," Ben says. "This is information. So
you *do* know."

"Are we almost there?" I ask again. I'm dozing off, still
with one hand in Pete's, the other around the gun on my
right side. I put the gun back in my jacket pocket. It's probably not safe to have it in my lap with my hand around
it if I'm unconscious. Among other problems, Pete might
take it from me. I can smell myself as I'm moving; I need a
shower. I need this to be over. I really need this to be over.

"Almost," Pete says. He starts inching into the right lane.
A black Ford with darkened windows and a dent in its side
almost hits him, speeding up in the lane he's shifting into.

"Pete!" I shout.

He blares the horn of the Lincoln. "Goddamn Maryland
drivers," he says. "Maniacs."

"You don't think . . ." I say. "That's not P.F.? Or *a* P.F.?"

"I think it's just a bad driver," Pete says.

"Okay," I say. "Okay." I pat Pete's leg. Then: "Pete, who
is your mother?"

"She's my mother," he says. "What do you mean who is
she?"

Now is not the time to be cagey. Unless he thinks I know

more than I do. My hackles go back up. The car eases forward, foot by foot, toward the Lorton exit. I can see the sign for it just up ahead. It might as well be on the moon, as fast as we're going to get there.

"I mean what's her deal," I say. "I mean why's she involved with my life. Why did she send you to spy on me and Ben?" Then I sort of lose it. My voice cracks. "What do you think I mean who is she? What would you want to know if you were in my shoes?" My shoes, incidentally, are a pair of well-worn clogs that are not hiding my footly odor very well right now.

"I'd want to know everything," Pete says.

"Yeah," I say. I let go of his leg with a gesture to show that it wasn't intimate. It was protective. "Or even just *something.*"

Pete puts on his turn signal. He sighs. I look back at my brother.

"How's your arm doing, honey?" I call back to him.

"My arm hurts," he says.

"I don't want to tell you," Pete says. "I don't want you to know." He's looking at me. He's staring at me. I can see something happening in my peripheral vision.

"Pete," I say. I point forward. It's the black Ford again, swerving into our lane.

"Goddamn Maryland drivers," he says again, slamming on the brakes.

"Are they trying to hurt us?" I ask.

"They'd hurt us if they were trying to hurt us," Pete says. "They wouldn't count on a five-mile-an-hour traffic accident."

"Who are they, Pete?" I ask.

"In the car? I don't know—"

"Who is your mother?"

He hesitates. "She's . . . complicated," he says.

"All men think their mothers are complicated," says Ben from the backseat. "So says Freud. Who has largely been discredited by mainstream psychoanalytic thinking."

"Madeleine Severy is unusually complicated," says Pete. He sighs. He looks at me. I've never seen him look so frightened. "Will you still like me after I tell you this?" he asks.

My stomach turns. It's that flippy feeling of romance and it's that flippy feeling of dread. "I don't know what I feel about you now," I say.

"Is he your boyfriend?" Ben asks from the backseat. I don't answer. Neither does Pete.

We reach the exit. Drive down a stretch of prettier-than-usual strip-malled road, then take a left to a bridge that goes over a narrow river and into the world's most charming gingerbread town. We pass a place called "Mom's" advertising fresh pie.

"How about this?" Pete says. "I tell you the truth from now on. And the truth is: I love this place. They have the best blueberry pie I've ever had in my whole life. I wrote a song about it called 'Mom's Blueberry Pie.' The joke of the song is that my own mom would never make pie."

I get what Pete is trying to do. I wish like anything we were just on a friendly road trip, too: me and Pete and my brother and my (possibly drugged? brainwashed?) dog, off to this neighborhood of Victorian houses painted bright colors for pie and a picnic by the river. Like normal kids get to do. Then we'd go from here to prom because I'm not letting that one go in this fantasy version of our time together. But Pete's mom, who'd never bake pie, and my dad . . . enough.

Pete pulls the car into a complex of new townhouses done up in the Victorian style the rest of the town seems to have come by more organically. He stops in front of a row of townhouses with an OPEN HOUSE sign out front. He parks. Sighs again. Gets out of the car. I follow, as does Ben, holding Roscoe's scary leather leash with the arm that isn't hours away from having to be cut off. Not hours. Hour. A person has about two hours without blood flow before their limb becomes permanently useless, I remember from my childhood lectures on health and safety. We've been out and about for about an hour now. But Ben's bad arm isn't bleeding; he isn't delirious; except for an occasional wince, he doesn't even seem all that hurt. Dad's tourniquet worked the magic it promised. Very nice. Good for Dad.

Pete fiddles with one of those key-holding lock boxes attached to the rail leading up to the brightly painted, three-story townhouse. It opens; he gets out a key.

"What is this place?" I ask.

"Model home," he says. "Mom's a realtor."

"A *realtor*?" I ask. I hadn't figured on the DC metro area's competitive real estate market underlying any of our recent goddamn adventures.

"It's her cover," he says. "Well, not just a cover. She actually makes a lot of money selling houses."

"Oh yeah?" I say.

"Ssh," he says, opening the door. We walk into a perfect and yet strangely generic home. It's got hardwood floors that look like they are made of plastic. The kitchen, right off to the right, has granite countertops, stainless appliances. A bowl of green apples sit on top of a lacquered dark brown table.

"What are we . . . ?" I start asking.

"SSSSHHHH," Pete says again. He gestures to follow him. First we go upstairs, tiptoeing, except Roscoe, whose nails go *clip-clip-clip* on the wood. We peek inside one upstairs bedroom. There's a big platform bed in there, covered in an apple-green duvet, with nice fluffy pillows on top, and an attached bathroom, with gleaming white accoutrements. There's no sticky dried-up pee in front of the toilet, like there always is in our house. Mom complained bitterly that she was down on her hands and knees five, six, seven times a day cleaning up the piss that Dad and Ben would leave for her. She begged them to clean it up themselves. Dad asked why we couldn't just get one of those absorbent rugs.

"Because those urine-soaked rugs are the most disgusting objects known to man," Mom said.

"You're supposed to wash them a lot," Dad replied.

"Yes, *I'm* supposed to wash your piss-filled rug a lot," Mom said. "I can see that's your plan, Jacob, to get out of learning how to urinate into the toilet instead of all over my floor. And nice job teaching Ben to do the same. I should get you penis-people a litterbox to use. It would be cleaner."

After Mom was killed, Dad brought home one of those rugs that go in front of the toilet. I don't think he's washed it once. I always make sure to wear shoes in the bathroom. That's my solution to living with gross penis-people.

But if I lived here, I could probably use the bathroom barefoot and not have to worry about what I'm stepping in. If I lived here, I suppose I'd be in an even weirder world than the one I'm already in, which is plenty weird.

Pete leads us into another bedroom. This one has a crib in it.

"A baby lives here?" I ask.

"SHHHH," he says. "Jesus, Zoey. Keep quiet."

Ben says, "That wasn't very quiet, Pete."

Pete rubs his head with his hands. He takes off his sunglasses. His eyes have dark circles under them.

"I don't think they're here," he says. "I . . . I must have been wrong."

"Who was here?" I ask.

Pete walks to the crib and looks inside it. There's a teddy bear. It looks unused. Unloved. He hugs it.

"This was my bear," he says. "Mom kept it on a shelf in my room when I was a kid."

"It's cute," I say. "Did you love it?"

"No," Pete says. He gives it to Roscoe, who starts chewing on it.

"Did you think my dad was here?" I ask, losing whatever was left of my patience. "Is this where we were rushing to?"

"Yes," Pete says. "This is where we were rushing to. My mom is a real estate agent, because it gives her . . . a good cover story. Access to properties all over Virginia and Maryland and DC. She's used this house to . . . hide certain things before. I think. I thought. I thought it was where your dad would be."

"Cover story for what?" I ask.

"Oh, Zoey," Pete says.

I decide to ignore him. "Let me see your arm," I say to Ben. "Maybe we'll just go to the hospital now. We didn't find Dad. We can at least save your arm."

"No," Ben says. "No. We have to save Dad. This isn't his fault. I know it's not. Mom told me. Mom told me!" He might start disassociating again. Or getting violent and angry. Which might be cathartic for me, to see him destroy this model house.

Pete heads downstairs. Roscoe tugs, so Ben follows. I follow, too. I feel that we've been defeated. Maybe this was the plan, to defeat us. Maybe Pete's disclosures and promises were just subterfuge, for what? It's not like we were inches away from finding Dad before. We've been defeated from the beginning. Even if we'd known what the J-File was that first night, back at the Postal Museum, when my cell phone still worked and the kidnappers were getting in touch with me, what?

We get back down to the first floor. I wish I knew what to do next.

I walk to the back window in the dining room with the green apples on the table. I reach for an apple to eat. I'm hungry. Starving. It's fake. Nothing to eat. Nothing is real. Across that lovely river I can see a tiny little shack, nearly hidden underneath the bridge we crossed to get to this town. Looks like a nice place to be a hermit. Seems like there's smoke coming out of a chimney. Nice day for that. Spring fires are a comfort, a treat.

I can see someone on the yard by the river, with binoculars. I squint, try to make him out. Can't see much. Just a dark-haired guy observing the water. Maybe he's a scientist. Or a fisherman. Or libertarian scientist fisherman. I should learn how to fish. Really be self-sufficient.

Ben goes to the first-floor bathroom, leaving Roscoe with Pete. The two of them walk to me, by the window. Roscoe still has the bear in his mouth.

"Cover story for what?" I ask Pete again. I'm staring at his face, hoping to get some clue if I should trust him. If he's trying to help me or trying to hurt me.

"My mom isn't an ordinary assassin," he begins.

"Not an *ordinary* assassin," I repeat. "That's like saying, 'This person is an *unusual* . . .' I don't know. Psychopath. Monster." My analogies are failing me. "What is an 'ordinary assassin,' Pete?" I make scare quotes with my fingers, trying to regain some pull.

"You're not stupid, Zoey," he says. "We live in Washington. Ordinary assassins work for the Department of Defense, other agencies. They're assassins by proxy, like the lawyers who give the okay to the CIA so that they can go kill terrorists in, like, Pakistan. Or they're the actual CIA people who go kill the terrorists in Pakistan. Who do you think, like, does this in the real world?"

I feel a burning in my cheeks. Embarrassed at my own sheltered world, my own naïveté. The greater DC area is full of assassins. Of course it is! Pete's mom is one of them. My dad is one of them? But he *hates* the government! And if it's all so ordinary, then . . .

"What's not ordinary about your mom?" I ask.

"She's involved with a private enterprise. Finds clever people who are bored with regular life," he says, his face growing harder. "They think they are getting into something easy. Exciting. They may travel to do a job. But if they try to get out—"

"What?" I say, dreading the answer, needing the answer.

"I told you, Zoey," Pete says. "The P.F.s are mostly widowers."

"Like my dad," I say. I hate my dad. I hate him more than I've ever hated anything. Even lacrosse, and I really hate lacrosse. I hate everything. I hate *everything*.

"I guess that's that then," I say. "I guess let's just get Ben to the hospital, so, you know, he won't lose his arm. I'm sorry to have to ask you this, but can I borrow money to pay for it? After that we'll get out of your life. I promise."

I'm beginning to concoct plans for post-all-of-*this*. Ben and I and Roscoe will maybe go back to Rhode Island. Hopefully Molly made it back home. Hopefully this will all be over, the P.F.s trying to kill us, Pete and people like him introducing me to feelings and worlds and confusions that I can't really do anything with or about. I'll resume my martial arts training. No, screw that; I'll take up guns. Maybe I can take a gun class at a local range, I think it's called. So in case this isn't over, I'll be prepared to answer the question: Is Mrs. Severy going to kill me and Ben?

"Zoey, don't," Pete says. He puts his hand on my hand again. He leans in, then leans back. He's crying. "Please don't."

"Don't what?" I say coldly.

"Don't blame me," he says.

"I don't blame you," I say. The truth, is I don't blame anyone at this point except Dad.

"I wish I knew where else to look," Pete says.

"Did we check the basement?" Ben asks. He's out of the bathroom. I have no doubt he's left behind biological samples of many varieties. It's not only gross, but it'll be proof we were here, if that comes to matter. Which it may or may not. We rushed here only to find nothing, no evidence of humanity, no one on our tail. No Dad. Just a forgotten stuffed animal.

"Not yet," Pete says. He walks us through the open first floor, past the severe-looking suede couch, the glass coffee table with sharp edges that I think someone who has any use for the upstairs crib probably should not responsibly own. There's a door I'd taken as leading to a closet that he now opens. He reaches in, like he's looking for a light switch. Then there's light.

Oh, gahd. Is Dad in the basement of this cold, severe, perfect model home, here in this town with a river and good pie? Pete starts walking down the stairs. I start racing after him, then stop when I have this thought: I could push him. Push him down, then run down the stairs myself, see if Dad is there, if he is, then rescue him. Pete seems to be out of ideas anyway, if he ever had any that were useful to our cause. It would be easy to do.

But I don't. I follow him to the bottom of the stairs, into the small basement. Which is empty, it looks, on first glance. A washer and dryer, another small bathroom with just another clean toilet and sink in it, and nothing else. I stand in the middle of the room. Roscoe and my brother stay upstairs, looking down at us. Roscoe's making whimpering noises. My brother just keeps muttering about Norman Mailer levitating the Pentagon. Pete walks along the walls of the room. Bends down. Picks something up. Holds it up to the light.

"Do you recognize this?" he asks me.

I do. It's Dad's cell phone. Stubborn Dad, who wouldn't upgrade because "planned obsolescence is a travesty and a conspiracy and I'm not falling for that bullshit of having to buy a new device every six months just because Apple computers wants to make more money."

The phone never worked well, even when it was new. Now it doesn't work at all; I take it in my hand, push buttons. It's dead. Dad was here, this probably means. Oh, Dad, please don't be like the phone. Please, Dad, don't be discarded and inert. Dead.

"Where is he?" I ask. "Where is my dad? Pete, where is he? He was here. This is his phone. Where is he now?"

"I don't know," Pete says. "I don't know. I thought he was here. The only houses I know my mom uses for business are this one and the house in Georgetown."

The house in Georgetown. The house where we went after that party, with my brother, with the gun. When Pete and P.F. pretended not to know each other.

"You knew P.F. already that night," I say.

"Yes," Pete says. "I knew him already. I know some of my mother's associates. The most loyal ones."

"Most loyal," I say. I'm crushed. I'm devastated. By everything. But we're not done yet, because Dad isn't here, and either Pete has been lying about thinking that he might be here, or Pete really doesn't know where he is. And either way, I'm in rough shape; hopefully my dad isn't in dead shape.

We go back upstairs, find Ben by the window looking out over the river. My brain is racing. My heart is racing. Dad was HERE. In Pete's mom's model home. His cell phone is still here. Is he still alive? If so, where is he? If he's dead, where is he? Are *they*, whoever they are, still after the J-File? Is it still with Molly? Is Molly okay? Where is Dad? How can I find him? What has he done?

"That house is on fire," Ben says, pointing at the shack.

The shack is indeed in flames. This isn't smoke coming out of a smokestack. Black smoke rises in a vertical plume. Angry orange licks at the roof. The man with the binoculars is gone.

I have a terrible feeling, but I also have a feeling of finally fixing on something that might get me to the end of *all this*. It might not be the end that I've hoped for, when I've even had the temerity to hope for *anything* other than making it through another day without seeing a cigarette in my toilet, without any family member dying or being kidnapped. Or losing an arm.

"No wonder she chose this house," Pete says, almost to himself.

He's out the door before I am.

WHEN THERE'S SMOKE

Chapter Eighteen

The car is in front of the house, away from the river, across which the shack is on fire. I have a terrible feeling that my terrible father is inside that house.

"You guys drive. I'm going to swim across," I tell Pete and Ben and Roscoe.

"Swim?" Pete says.

"I don't think there's time to get there by car," I say. I'm in okay shape. I'm reasonably fit. I've got a lot of adrenaline running through me.

"I think there's a dinghy you can use," Pete says. Which sounds better than swimming.

When I turn to leave them, to go make my way across, to try to save my father, if he's there in the burning house, if he can be saved, if he even should be saved, I hesitate. What if Pete is not our friend? What if he is still under the spell of his mother? Always was. My brother holds the J-File in his head. To the extent anyone wants the J-File destroyed, killing my brother would be an obvious move. To the extent anyone wants to know what's in the J-File, stealing my brother and making him write it out for them is also an obvious move.

"Trust me," Pete says to me, repeating the same line I've heard so many times over the last days, from people who have turned out to be affiliated with murderers. It turns out I'm affiliated with a murderer, too, and he may be dying in a burning house across the river.

"Be safe," I say, before dashing away, down some gravel-covered steps until I reach a small, new-looking dock on the river's edge.

There's an orange, floating blow-up watercraft there with oars and a little motor hanging off the back. I look at it with curiosity and urgency, being unfamiliar with boats and motors, wondering if I need a key to get it started, how the oars are involved, etc. Finally, after awkwardly entering the blow-up boat, I see a cord hanging off the motor and tug it; I've seen other people, like people mowing lawns, tug on cords attached to motors, with the result of the motor revving up. After a few pulls, this one gets going, too, at which point I determine that I don't know how to steer this orange vehicle and that I am tied up to the dock.

I get the boat untied fairly quickly, which is when not being able to steer becomes more of a problem. I bump along the wrong way and into the dock; this I bump off of, propelling me the wrong way again, with some terrible black exhaust billowing up into my nose. And as this rather fraught excitement is progressing, I'm also getting sopping wet from this brown river and watching the house across the way burn, but not to the ground. It's happening slowly. I see that the shack is partially made of stone; the roof is on fire and causing an alarming amount of smoke, but the bottom seems to be holding, at least for now. Oh, please, please let it hold. Let

Dad be in that bottom part, so I can kill him myself, assuming he's there. It's possible that, should I ever manage to get this goddamn boat across the river, I am going to come across nothing but a hermit with faulty wiring. And my brother and Pete will be departed to places unknown.

Keep yourself together, Zoey, I tell myself, myself being Zoey. I play with the stick-type thing coming off the motor until by some miracle it starts going in the direction I want it to go in, which is across this murky body of water and toward the burning house.

It takes minutes to cross the river, I think. Tense minutes during which I am dive-bombed by several menacing birds, catch wind of my own stink when the wind blows the wrong way, and watch as the house grows more aflame. The boat putters and sputters. This isn't a zippy and sleek cigarette boat out of a movie. This is the kind of lumpy, lumbering boat an inept dummy would be stuck with in real life.

But I progress. Inch forward. Then get stuck. The river is so shallow that the boat seems to be caught on a rock. *SHIT.* I jump up and down, trying to wriggle free, which manages to make the dinghy more unsteady, and me more wet, and accomplishes nothing productive. *SHIT SHIT SHIT.* I guess I will be swimming after all.

Jump out of the dinghy. Realize it's still sputtering and stuck. Try for a moment to shut it off; remember that time is really *short* here and decide to let it burn itself out of gas. Screw the environment; more important things to worry about right now. Turns out I don't have to swim to shore. I'm walking to shore. The water only goes up to my knees. Jesus, I should have just walked from the beginning, could have avoided this whole ding dong dinghy mishap.

Birds are back to flying alarmingly close to my head as

I'm slugging through the last few feet of river. I'm shouting at them, "Go away!" then think, maybe don't shout right now, Zoey, maybe try to keep the tiniest element of surprise here. Then again, this is not Normandy. I'm hardly staging a surprise storming of the beach. I am pretty out there and in the open, coming ashore to this burning house to try to save the murderous Dad, and why why why why why why why why why any of this, I think for a moment, before I reach ground.

The grounding is both literal and metaphorical. There's no dock on this side of the river, just a rocky, muddy patch before the grass, before the shack. My stupid shoes slip off as I'm hiking up to the house. I try to put them back on. They fall off again, I leave them in the mud, start to run, hardly noticing the rocks embedding themselves into my feet.

I reach the shack; it's farther from the river than I'd thought. It's dark, no lights on that I can see. The windows are dusty, coated with a thick dirt. Under other circumstances I could see Dad liking this place, saying it has "character," Mom saying that he's a character, Ben saying that he feels like a character in a movie sometimes, asking if that's normal. It is now, Benny, I think to myself, as I make my way around, looking for an entrance, feeling some embers drop on me, glad that I'm all wet so hopefully I won't burn to death. Hopefully none of us will burn to death.

The front door is, predictably, in front. And locked. I jiggle the handle several times to see if maybe the door is only just reluctant to open, as opposed to being determined. It's determined. Feeling pressure to act from the heat of the fire, I take the gun from my pocket, hold it up to the door, and shoot. The kickback takes my breath away. The bullet goes through the door. No one screams. Apparently I haven't killed

anyone, Dad or a hermit, on the other side. But the bullet isn't a
key; the door still doesn't open.

"Dad?" I yell. "Dad?" Nothing.

I abandon my plan to shoot my way into the cabin; frankly,
I don't even know if I have more bullets left in this gun. Even
if I knew how many bullets I started with, I haven't been
counting how many bullets it's expelled so far, but it seems
like a lot, and I don't think it's got an endless supply, like an
extremely lethal clown car. So now I move over to the dusty
window.

I peer in, hoping to catch a glimpse of what's inside the
cabin. Can't see anything. The window's small and so dirty
I can't even tell if there's a curtain blocking my view. Okay,
okay, act fast, not much time. I take off the army coat and
wrap my fist with it, then punch the window. It does not
crack; my fist does. Goddamn that hurts. I punch it again and
cry out. I think I've broken the bones in my hand. This glass
is tougher than I'd have expected. Tougher than I am. I try
with my elbow this time and just feel a shooting pain up my
arm, but the glass doesn't give.

"Dad? Dad!" I'm still crying out, having fully given up on
the element of mystery, surprise. "Dad! I'm here, Dad! I'm
here!"

He might be upstairs, already dead of smoke inhalation or
flame, or he might not be here in this cabin at all. "Dad!" I
shout again. "Dad! Dad!"

I stare helplessly at the impenetrable cabin. How will I
get in? How will I get in? I point the gun at the window and,
hoping there is a bullet and hoping the glass isn't bulletproof
and hoping that, if it's not bulletproof, it won't penetrate
only to hit my father—because wouldn't that be the worst
irony; I'm shooting my way in to save him, and I kill the old

bastard—and, *Dayenu*, *Dayenu*, Dad, there is a bullet, and it pierces the glass.

Holding my eye to the hole, I don't see a dead father right inside. I don't see much of anything right inside. I think I can make out a brown couch, a brown table. I elbow the window again, near the bullethole. It feels like it's giving. Please, window, give, I'm thinking, elbowing it again, the pain tremendous, the need to get inside more tremendous.

I hear a car on gravel. I look up. It's the Lincoln. Pete at the wheel. He did not steal my brother. *Dayenu* again. *Dayenu* for so much. Yes, I'm using the word wrong if you're talking in the technical sense, but this is how Dad uses it, used it, and I'm his daughter, and *Dayenu Dayenu Dayenu*.

"Get out of the car," I say, rushing to Pete's window. "Ben, get out. Take Roscoe."

"Why?" Pete asks. He looks shocked, looking at my hand. I look down. It's bleeding, looks twisted.

"I need the car," I say. "Trust me."

Pete gets out, leaves the key in the ignition. Ben picks up his book and Roscoe's leash, and gets out, too.

"Go stand over there," I shout, pointing at a tree toward the road.

I get into the driver's seat. Move the seat forward, then put on my seatbelt. No time to think about this being a bad idea, or a failing idea. I adjust the steering wheel slightly and hit the gas.

BAM. I hit the house at the door. BAM. I go through the door. (*Dayenu. Dayenu*, Dad!) BAM. The airbag goes off in my face, feeling like a punch, covering me in a white powder that sticks because I'm still so wet. I take a deep breath, try to open the door. I'm stuck, the door won't open. I put the car in reverse, honk so that if Pete and Ben and Roscoe are nearby they'll get the hell away, look in the rearview mirror, then hit the gas again. Once I'm out a few feet, I stop the car, turn it off, get out, take one breath, shout "DON'T FOLLOW ME" to Pete, Ben, and Roscoe, then turn and run into the cabin.

I get inside and can smell the smoke everywhere. I look for Dad. Don't see him. This is a small cabin. Just a one-room box here on the first floor, with those stone walls, thank God, thank God, thank you, God.

"Dad?" I shout. "Dad! Dad!"

I can smell the smoke. How is it not coming down the stairs? How has it been burning for all these minutes without the whole cabin going up in flames? I don't know. Maybe it's too wet to burn quickly. Maybe it hasn't been going as long as it seems. This is just like that dream I sometimes have, only Mom isn't chasing me this time.

Pete calls my name from the hole in the front of the cabin. "Are you okay?" he yells in.

"Keep Ben away!" I shout back at him. "Get Ben and get Roscoe and get away from here!"

I go into the kitchen area of the cabin. Just a sink and two burners, and a small fridge. Find two dish towels. Wet them in the sink. Hold one over my nose and mouth and run to the stairs. Please don't let the stairs be on fire, I think. They aren't, *Dayenu.*

"Dad! Dad!" I shout again.

I run up the stairs, not sure what I'll find when I get there. Smoke. Lots of smoke. I get down on my hands and knees and crawl. It can't be big up here. The first floor is so small. I crawl to the left. It's hot. It's hot up here. My eyes burn. Tears are streaming out of them. My palms are picking up splinters on this wooden floor, and they hurt, but I don't stop. It's probably not smart to have a gun in a fire like this. Be fast, Zoey, I tell myself. Be fast. Be brave.

"Dad!" I shout when I enter the first room. I can't see much. "Dad! Where are you, Dad?"

I don't hear anything. I through as much of it as I can, but it's too hot and too smoky. I'm crawling out, down a small hall, into another room. There are no carpets on the floor, bad for my knees, good for limiting flammability. *Dayenu*, *Dayenu*. I hear something in this room. A scraping of some sort.

"Dad!" I shout again. "Dad, are you in here?" I start to get up onto my feet, but it's too smoky, and if I choke I won't be any use here. Ben needs me to live through this. I need me to live through this. I'd like to see Pete again. And Roscoe. I'd like to save Dad. I'd really like to save my dad.

Crawling, I examine the corners of the room and see nothing. I don't know where the fire is exactly; I know that it seems the amount of smoke around me is increasing. I hear the scraping again, crawl toward it. Not sure what I'm crawling toward.

In the middle of the room I feel a chair leg. I keep feeling. I feel a human leg. I peer at it as closely as I can. I think it's Dad. I think it's Dad! I shake the leg, tap it. "Dad, Dad," I say. "Dad."

The leg isn't moving. It's tied to the chair. I move in the direction of the head. Is Dad breathing? Is this Dad? I get to the head; it's Dad. Oh, lord, it's Dad. I put my hand on his chest to see if he's taking in air, if I can feel a heartbeat. And yes, yes, yes, there is breath. There is life. I take the second dish towel and put it on his face. Realize I can't see his hands.

Crawl around the other side of the chair. Arms tied. I try to untie the knots. They are tied too tight. Dad made me practice tying and untying knots when I was young, but I'm not young anymore, and that was a long time ago. Try to put myself back into being six, eight, a good student, diligent. Work the knots. My hands still hurt from punching the window. The rope is burning them. The smoke is choking. Where are the flames? My eyes are stinging. Dad's not moving, except for the tiniest bit of breath.

But I get the knots. I get them off his hands. I get them off his legs. I take his head and say, "Dad, we have to go. We have to get out of here."

He looks up at me and I can see his eyes open for the first time. Dad is looking at me. He lifts his hand and brushes my face. He looks exhausted.

"Leave me here," he whispers.

FEET DOWN, ROLL FORWARD

Chapter Nineteen

Dad won't, or can't, move. The dish towel is sliding off his face onto the floor. I put it back, hold it there.

"We have to go, Dad," I say. "The house is on fire."

"Zoey, you shouldn't have come here," he says.

"Dad, we can talk about this when we get outside," I say. "We have to go."

"No," he says. I try to drag him, but I have to stand up to get any pull, at which point the smoke becomes too thick to breathe, even with the quickly drying cloth over my mouth and nose.

"Please, Dad," I say. "Please. After everything you've put us through. You can't do *this* to us now. Ben needs you. I need you. Roscoe."

"You found Roscoe?" Dad says, lifting his head just a little.

"Yeah," I say. "He's outside. He's waiting for you. So is Ben."

"Ben," Dad repeats. He lays his head back down and

begins to curl himself on the floor, like a dog fitting himself into a too-small dog bed. "No no no no," Dad says. "No no no no. Zoey, go. Go."

I slap him. "Get up," I say. "Stop this."

Dad stands up, seems immediately overcome by the smoke, or something, and falls back to the floor.

"Come on," I say, tugging on his arm. "Daddy. We have to crawl."

He gets on his knees. I lead him toward the doorway, checking every few inches to make sure he is still with me. He is. But when we get to the door, I see that there is now fire in the hall. My stupid hope that the cabin wasn't actually on fire—that this was merely some sort of staging, designed to give us an appearance of danger without any real danger—is gone.

We crawl back into the room. I close the door behind us.

"Is there a window in here?" I ask.

"I think so," Dad says.

"You *think* so?" I repeat. This is not how Dad taught eight-year-old me to survey a room, any room, from which one might need to execute an escape. "Follow me," I order him as I crawl toward an outer wall, where I hope I will find an openable window. He follows, I see, as I turn back repeatedly to make sure he's still there and that our room hasn't yet been engulfed with flames.

I get to the wall. Feel my way up it and along it, looking for a way out. It's hard to breathe, but I'm doing okay, I am, and I find a window and try to open it. It's locked. Or stuck in some way that makes it hard to open. I feel around it until I come to what seems like an old-fashioned window lock, which is hot because, I guess, of the *fire*. Using the towel to touch it, I try to get it unclasped. It doesn't work. It might be that the lock is stuck, or that the window is painted shut, or not even designed to open.

"Shit," I say. Then remember Dad. "Sorry," I say, not even sure if he can hear me. There's no time to find another way. I pull out the gun, hoping there's a bullet left, and that it's an effective bullet, and I shoot the window lock, with the same pain as always, then try the window again. *Dayenu*—it opens. It opens! I put the gun back in my pocket and look out the window. We're on the side of the cabin facing the river. Looking up, I see fire. Looking down, pretty far down, I see rocks and mud, my shoes still where I left them, and no other options.

I pull my father up by his collar. Say to him, "Keep your feet down and roll forward when you hit the ground," like he isn't the one who taught *me* how to survive a long jump.

He hesitates at the window.

"Go," I say to him, giving him a shove. He jumps. I get my head out the window just in time to see him land on his ass and scream in pain, then scoot off to the side. It's my turn. My turn to try out my dad's theory of survival: feet down, roll forward. I climb up into the window. Say a quick "*Dayenu*" to myself and jump.

It's over in a heartbeat. My body does the right thing, for once. My knees bend, followed by a little tumble forward through the mud, stopping right by my clogs. I put them on. Walk to Dad. He's moaning in pain.

"I think I broke my tailbone," he says. He sneezes. "And there's a high pollen count today. This is awful for my allergies. I haven't had my decongestants in a *week*."

"Not now, Dad," I say, trying to help this broken man stand. "Let's get to Ben and Roscoe." And Pete, I think. "He's a musician," I tell Dad, without identifying who I am talking about. "He writes songs. He wrote a song about me."

"You should have left me," Dad says quietly, climbing onto his knees and leaning forward.

"Why?" I shout. "So you can make us orphans? And get off scot-goddamn-free with all the things in that *J-File* that we've been hearing so much about? The Jacob File of very terrible murders? Jacob's list of assassinations?"

"It's not a Jacob File," Dad says, looking surprised. "Did somebody tell you that? Why do you think it's a Jacob File?"

"Why do you think?" I shout, waving my arms around at EVERYTHING. I look at Dad again, exasperated, furious. And maybe it is just allergies, but I don't think so; I think he's weeping, his cheek on the muddy ground. He reaches out to grab my ankle and holds on. "Zoey, it's not the Jacob File. It's the Julia File."

We sit in the mud, and Dad, between sniffles and sneezes, tells me that it was Mom, not him, who worked for Mrs. Severy. That he'd spent my whole life trying to protect me from the consequences of her little freelance killing job.

"She specialized in slow-acting poisons," he says. I really didn't know Mom at all.

"Why didn't you stop her?" I ask.

"I believe in private militias," Dad says. He sits up. Winces. Sneezes. "We were so young when this started," he says. "We just didn't know what would happen. We didn't know. And when your mother tried to get out . . ."

"I thought it's the spouses who get killed," I say, all world-weary and wise to the ways of freelance assassins. "Not the killers themselves."

"Oh, Zoey," Dad says. He looks more sad than I have ever

seen him. Sadder than when he learned John Galt had been given away. Sadder than at Mom's funeral. "Your mother was trying to get out. P.F.—do you know P.F.?"

"More than one," I say.

Dad nods. "The short one. He said he could help us. He told Mom to bring him the J-File. That he had friends in law enforcement who'd use it to stop Mrs. Severy. We didn't know if we could trust him. But we also didn't know what other choice we had. Then Mom . . ."

"Was killed," I say.

Dad nods again. "But even before then. She, she couldn't find the J-File the night she was going to bring it to P.F. She was going to tell him. To figure out another way to make Mrs. Severy stop. To make her pay. That's what she told me her plan was. Then you'd go to college. Your mother and brother and I would go to California, too, maybe. For a fresh start."

"Ben doesn't like changes to his routine," I say.

"Right, right," Dad says. I don't say anything to modify my earlier observation, even though, thinking about it, Ben has actually proven shockingly adaptable. My brother may be as much a mystery as my dead, killer mother. *Killer mother.* I'm appalled. I'm aghast. I'm shocked. And I wish she were here so I could ask her about it. How did she learn about slow-acting poisons? How many people did she kill? Was it hard to do? Did they know she was there to kill them? Were they bad people? Was she bad?

"But how did you get kidnapped?" I ask. "And why were your kidnappers asking *me* for the J-File?"

Dad's quiet. "Dad?"

"I'm so embarrassed, Zoey," he says. "I've made so many mistakes. When your mother was killed, I . . . I did my best. But I was a mess. An irrational mess."

"How did *you* get kidnapped?" I ask again.

"I tried to blackmail Mrs. Severy," Dad says. He's shaking his head. "I told her that I was going to leak the J-File if she didn't pay me one million. I thought a million dollars was reasonable. It would last us a long time, but it's not so much that she couldn't spare it. And she'd have to swear to me that she would never come near you and your brother."

"But you didn't have the J-File," I say. "I don't understand."

"I don't know what I was thinking," Dad says. "No, I do. I know what I was thinking. It made so much sense to me at the time. I thought if Mom didn't have the J-File, that meant either it had truly gone missing or else Mrs. Severy's *goons* had already gotten their hands on it somehow. Mrs. Severy wouldn't know if the J-File really was missing. For all she'd know, I really had it. Either that, or she'd know I didn't, and wouldn't take my threat seriously. My thought was that either way there was unlikely to be a negative outcome if I embarked on this path."

"I'd say you got that pretty wrong," I say, extending my arms to highlight various truly terrible facets of our environment.

"It would seem so," Dad says. He's quiet, then says, "I'd take it all back if I could, Zoey. All of it. I can't bear to think about . . . I kept trying to tell them that you didn't have the J-File. To leave you alone. That you couldn't do anything. That the file had just . . . disappeared altogether."

"Oh," I say. "You don't know about Ben."

"What about Ben?" Dad asks.

I don't answer. Now might not be the time to bring up Mom's ghost. Or Ben's dream diary. "We should go get him and get out of here," I say.

I stand up, help a grimacing Dad to his feet. Dad puts his hands on his tailbone and says, "It really hurts. But I don't think doctors can fix a broken tailbone."

"I don't know either," I say. We take tiny steps, Dad seeming old and feeble.

"Is that my jacket?" he asks me.

"Yeah," I say.

"It looks nice," Dad says.

When we get around the house, I expect that we will reunite, get in the Lincoln, if it still drives, and go home. And after that? I don't know. I'll get my cell phone turned back on, I guess. Go back to lacrosse practice. Take some shooting lessons. Do some research about slow-acting poisons. Make sure Ben eats kale, and Dad doesn't blackmail anyone.

Turning the corner, I see another car pulling up to the cabin. It's a big black SUV. It stops next to our smashed up Lincoln. Both P.F.s get out, followed by Mrs. Severy.

Pete steps forward first. "Mom, what are you doing here?" he says.

"Putting an end to this nonsense," says Mrs. Severy. It is getting to be dusk, but she still wears a pair of expensive-looking, surprisingly fashionable sunglasses over her eyes. She peers over them at the scene before her: my brother holding a book in one hand and Roscoe's leash in the other; Roscoe, whose tail is slowly wagging; the still-slowly-burning cabin; Pete, chest out, confrontational. She seems only just to be noticing me and my wrecked father hobbling toward the others when I pull the gun out of my pocket again, old hat. Aim it toward Mrs. Severy. She wants this over? Me, too. I cock, then pull, the trigger.

Nothing. The gun is empty. No *Dayenu*.

P.F.—the first one, from the first night—pulls out his gun.

He aims it at me. I guess after all these tackles and tumbles, I am the one he hates the most. I wrack my brain, trying to think of the self-defense move one would employ in this situation. I can only think of one.

"Roscoe!" I shout, hoping that my big husky knows that he should bite P.F. on the arm, make him drop the gun. He's a husky, he's a wolf, he has to have this killer instinct somewhere in him even if we spend so much time reassuring nervous children that no, he'd never hurt a fly. "Roscoe, help me! Ben, let him go. Please, Roscoe!"

Ben drops the leash. Roscoe comes running toward me. *Roscoe, bite him, bite P.F.*, I think. Roscoe doesn't bite him. He just runs toward me and Dad, wagging that fluffy, banner-like tail of his. Mrs. Severy cries out, "Don't shoot Adolfo!"

Roscoe stops, standing in the middle of our pack. His tail is still wagging, but slowly, and he is looking between us, and Mrs. Severy, and the P.F.s, and Ben and Pete. I'm trying again to think of exactly how we can all live through this. There's no jiu-Dadsu move that comes to mind. No physical one. There's always the mental-jitsu, of trying to get someone to help you. I'm trying to send brain signals to the P.F. who isn't directly aiming to kill us, and trying to make some eye contact.

"Where is the J-File?" Mrs. Severy says louder than I've heard her say anything before. "If you tell me, I may let you leave."

I consider saying that it is with Molly, then think that this information is unlikely to help us stay alive; and I don't need to get Molly killed because of the idiot, evil Trasks, too.

"We don't have it," I say, completely depleted. "It's gone. It's gone! Gone! Even if you shoot me and my dog and everyone I love, it's still gone!"

"You are your father's daughter," Mrs. Severy says. "I don't mean that as a compliment." She sighs. "I suppose we are at an impasse." She nods to P.F. again. He pulls out his gun once more. I think of running to him, to tackle him again. But my body is done, after everything. And I won't be able to surprise him. I could try to reach the car, use it to run him over. But there's no time to get there. He's walking toward me and Dad and Roscoe.

This may be it, I think. I've played my last hand. My brain signals, my eye contact, are ineffective.

P.F. lifts his hand. Aims. I hold Dad's hand with my left hand and touch Roscoe's head with my right, thinking, toward Dad and Roscoe and Ben and even Pete, I think, *I love you. I love you. I love you. And Ben, honey, I'm sorry I didn't protect you enough.* I don't know how much kale it would have taken to have kept him safe from *this.*

I hear a gunshot. But a moment later, the world still exists. I still exist.

Look up to see if Dad is still standing. He is. Roscoe isn't hit, either.

"Ben!" I call out. He calls back to me, "I'm right here."

"Are you okay?" I ask.

"My arm still hurts from before," he says.

"Are you hurt in any *new* way?" I yell.

"No," he says. "Not in any new way."

"Pete?" I say. "I'm here," he yells back.

Who is missing? Who's been shot?

Short P.F. is standing next to Mrs. Severy, holding the gun to her head. Fat lobbyist P.F. is on the ground. His forehead is bleeding.

"Get out of here," still-alive P.F. says to me.

WE REGRET
TO INFORM YOU

Chapter Twenty

The keys are already in the ignition of the black SUV. Pete gets behind the wheel. I sit next to him. Dad and Ben and Roscoe sit in the backseat.

The last thing I see, as we drive away, is P.F. walking Mrs. Severy toward the cabin.

No one talks as we head back onto the crowded highway into Old Town. Pete says nothing about his mother being marched into a fire. About the possibility that he will be an orphan after this, or the possibility that he won't be. I steal glances at Dad in the rearview mirror. He looks awful, as you might expect after having been kidnapped, tied to a chair, and left in a burning cabin. I can't imagine he ate very well in the last week, and he has a more gaunt look to him, though you can still see his belly extending under a T-shirt with a picture of a heroic superhero on it. That shirt seems richly ironic right now. And, belonging to a "hirsute people" as he is wont to put it—it's his fancy way of saying that he has a lot of *hair* and I don't know why he can't just say it like that—this week without shaving has left his face covered in thick and uneven bristle. He's got dark rings under his eyes. Darker than usual.

He also just looks worn out. Done. I think about him asking me to leave him in the cabin and try to stop thinking about it. That was the most terrifying moment of my life. And especially of late, I'm not wanting for terrifying moments. But it's really scary seeing Dad sitting quietly like this, too.

Ben, who is looking a little more oily than usual, could also use a shave—evidently he is a hirsute Trask as well. He doesn't ask what happened in the cabin, nor if we'll get to see the jail where Norman Mailer stayed when he tried to levitate the Pentagon. He just keeps petting and hugging Roscoe, who looks healthier than ever. (Roscoe's thick black and white coat is glossy. If I didn't know better, I'd say he appears to have had a pedicure. Certainly, if nothing else, his nails, and his whole being, look better-groomed than any other Trask. His eyes are bright and calm, and closing, slowly, as he settles in for a nap.)

Did it work, when Mailer tried to levitate the Pentagon? Does it work when anyone tries to make anything levitate, or are we all just stuck in a confusing but unmagical world after all? I used to think—to believe—that we had either reason, or magic, in this world, but not both. And probably just reason. Picking wood shards out of my hands and brushing off my knees, I'm worried we don't have either. In which case, what do we have?

We have a brother with a shot arm, is what we have, and to tend to this we stop at a drop-in medical clinic on the way home. When we pull up, Dad starts to get out of the car.

"Medical reporting laws might cause some problems

here," Ben says. "If we go in with an adult, I'm concerned that the police will be notified. It might be safer if only the kids go inside, and we don't use our real names."

Dad looks stunned and hurt, settling back into the car. Pete and I take Ben inside, give the receptionist a fake name. Smith. Hank Smith. Because *that's* not suspicious. The doctor asks what happened to young Hank's arm. Nearly crying, again, I explain that one of his careless cousins, Bob Smith (??!!), was shooting BB guns in the backyard. The doctor says that the wound does not look like a BB gun wound—it's not "arrayed" in the way, she explains, a BB gun wound would be—but I just shrug, and, counting on Ben's enhanced facial expression-reading skills, give my brother a stern look that tells him now is not the time to be concerned about the *truth* or *facts*.

And he does something that nearly makes me fall over in surprise. "I know hospitals are legally mandated to report to law enforcement in cases of gunshot sounds. And in child endangerment cases," he says, "I can see why you'd be confused about the nature of my injury. But I assure you that high-caliber BB guns array identically to youth-marketed .22 caliber rifles. I would be quite pleased to put you in touch with my friends at the National Rifle Association to give you more information if you'd like."

"That's okay, Hank," she says.

The doctor cleans and wraps Ben's arm. Gives us a bottle of antibiotics and instructions to use Neosporin and fresh bandages twice a day for two weeks, then asks one more time if there are "problems at home" that we "need to tell an adult about."

I can see the doctor, in her clean white jacket, looking all of us over. I'm filthy. Covered in mud, smelling like a house fire, which I can only hope covers up the smell of a person who hasn't showered or changed clothes in quite a while. I haven't slept a full night in over a week. Haven't eaten a real meal in days, I don't think; I can't even remember. My brother is shot in the arm and we've got an unbelievable story about how this came to be, that I guess we're going to get away with?

Then Pete . . . well, he looks great, somehow, his hair still curled attractively over his forehead, his skin with a healthy sheen to it. His clothes are rumpled, but appealingly so. I do not detect any stench on his person. Is he as pulled-together as he looks? If so, how can this be? Did he not just go through what we went through? I'm gazing at him, trying to know this boy, and I don't. I know that I'm drawn to him, almost chemically so. And I know, or I think I know, that he helped us after trying to hurt us. But I don't know *him*.

"We're fine," I say to the doctor.

You have to love the American medical system and its respect for privacy. Pete pays the receptionist with $200 in cash from his wallet and we walk out the door.

"How did you do that?" I ask my brother when the door is shut behind us.

"I used bits and pieces of facts that I know to be true and wove them together in untrue ways," Ben says.

"You lie now?" I ask.

"Not *right* now," he says. "I'm going to run back to the car so I can see Roscoe again."

Pete holds my hand for a moment in the parking lot as my brother runs off, and we're walking more slowly back to the car.

"I know this is crazy," he says. "I, I wish I could take you to prom."

"Shenandoah doesn't have a prom," I reply.

"I said it was crazy," he says.

• • •

We get back in the car and make our way through quiet,
quaint Old Town. It's Sunday and spring in the early evening.
Tourists are walking up and down our peaceful, shop-lined
streets.

"It's strange but good being back," Dad says as we're
driving down King Street.

"We ate there," Ben says, pointing at Lee's as we drive by.

"She's from Guam," I explain to Dad, which I assume he'll
understand means that she's not still hoping slavery starts up
again. Or actively working toward making that happen. I'm
trying to please him again, I realize. I stop talking.

"Did you like it?" Dad asks.

"Yeah, it's good," I say. "Lee said she'd give me a job if I
need one. She gave me a tarot reading."

"Your mother believed that horseshit," Dad says.

"Yeah," I say. "It was really helpful, actually." I stare
down at my lap, then turn around to look at him, and Benny,
and Roscoe. Ben is reading. Dad is watching out the window,
with one hand on Roscoe, and tears running down his face.

"Why didn't you leave her, Dad?" I ask.

"Over the tarot?" he asks. He laughs, wipes his eyes on
his shoulder. I laugh. No one asks why Dad would have left
Mom. I suppose Pete probably knows the context already.
Ben is just lost in his book. And Roscoe doesn't speak English
that well.

The sky is turning a kind of burnt orange; the cherry trees
are in full pink bloom. Both sides of King Street are silly with
those trees, covered in the delightful, glorious, deliciously
scented blossoms. They will last only a couple of days, I
understand, before falling to the ground and becoming so

much pink trash. But for now, just briefly, they are beautiful and perfect.

I look at Pete. I want to say something to him. More like I want to want to say something to him. I'm out of words. I'm filled with a longing for him to stay with me, but I don't think it's going to happen.

Pete stops in front of our house. Uncle Henry is sitting on the front stoop. He's smoking a cigarette, which he stubs out on the step as soon as he sees us. "Sorry. A bad habit. Just an occasional cancer stick when I'm out of town."

"What are you doing here?" I ask him, getting out of the car.

"Your aunt and I got worried when you left the way you did," he says, eyeing my father, holding out his hand to shake my father's hand. "Jacob," he says, his voice lowering a register or two. "How're things?"

"Not at the house, Henry," dad says. "Never at the house. Julia's allergic. You know that."

"She's dead," Uncle Henry says.

"Yes, I'm aware," my dad says. Then: "Still, not here."

"Are you okay?" I ask.

"Same as always," says Uncle Henry. "Aunt Lisa is inside. We used the key that your mom gave us when we first helped you move in."

"Great," says my father. "Really, great. You all hungry? I'm starved."

"I am not literally starved, but I am very hungry," says my brother.

He goes inside the house. My father and Uncle Henry follow. I call Roscoe out of the car, say to Pete, "Want to stay for dinner? We can get takeout from Lee's."

"I do. I want to," Pete says, touching my hand, then

touching my arm, then pulling away. "I'm going to find Ben's notebook. Get it back for him."

"Oh," I say. "Are we still in danger, Pete?"

"Molly might be if I don't find that notebook," he says.

"Oh," I say, startled. "I thought this was over."

"Wouldn't that be great?" Pete says.

"Do you want me to come with you?" I ask.

He smiles. He kisses my forehead. "Of course I do, nervous girl," he says.

"But I can't," I say.

"I'll come back," he says. "I'll have your brother's notebook. I'll make sure your friend is safe. And isn't taking too much Ritalin. I'll come back. Please promise me that you believe that."

"Okay," I say, trying to let down my guard, trying to be vulnerable, which is harder and scarier than trying to be invulnerable, after all this. I don't really know Pete.

He's been holding Roscoe's leash. He hands it to me. Bends down to pet my dog, then says, "You're like a brother to me." Roscoe licks Pete on his cheek. "Thanks, dog," he says before standing up, kissing me on the cheek.

"Does that make us related?" I ask.

"Luckily not," says Pete, who then gets a serious look on his face. "We have a lot more to do, Zoey," he says, and I don't know if he means a lot more to do vis-a-vis our parents or each other or what.

"See you soon, I hope," I say.

"I promise," he says.

I stand on my tiptoes and kiss him, one soft kiss on the lips that I swear to myself I will never lose the feeling of. I try to record it in my brain and on my skin, in that moment. Then Roscoe starts fidgeting, and a mosquito bites me on the cheek, and I step back down onto my heels. The kiss is already just a memory, even while Pete is still standing in front of me.

When he drives away, I turn to come inside. My aunt and uncle are sitting on the gold couch, eating pieces of what looks like pepperoni.

"Alpaca sausage," says Aunt Lisa, holding out a piece for me. "S'good."

"Thanks," I say, handing it to Roscoe, who gobbles it down. I'm composing a list in my head of the normal-life things that need doing now that we are home: wash my school uniform, Ben's school uniform; put my floral dress in the dry cleaning pile; get dog food; get human food; get cell phone turned back on; get bills paid. Prepare, mentally, for lacrosse practices and seeing Muffies and Annes with bright futures and bright presents before them. I wonder if Pete will be in school, and if he is, what we will be to each other.

I walk to the kitchen counter to examine the pile of mail splayed on the granite. Bills, bills, magazine offers. A slim envelope from Berkeley. I open it. "We regret to inform you . . ." I put the letter down. No California. No escape. Maybe I will go to the University of Rhode Island and become a marine biologist after all. I can keep an eye on Molly there, if she's speaking with me.

That is if URI will even have me. If we'd even have the money to pay for it, without Dad's job or Mom's freelance income, or bribes having been paid. I wish I had money and could just drift off to Europe. I would like to see the Stonehenge of Sweden, I think. I will have to stop by Lee's tomorrow to ask her if I can still come work for her. I hope I am okay as a waitress. But will we even get to stay here? Will we have to move? Are we still in danger? If we are, then who is trying to hurt us?

Dad comes out of the bathroom wiping his hands on his pants. His eyes meet mine.

"Why?" I ask him.

He gives me a sad half-smile, opens his arms. I step in for a hug. Dad kisses the top of my head. He stopped being really affectionate when I was younger. Maybe I'm the one who stopped it. I've missed him.

"You smell like smoke," he says.

"I know, I need to shower," I say.

"You were brave," he says. "You should be proud. You are strong. I knew you would be. Don't let yourself get bored, baby girl. Don't trap yourself too young, with babies and mortgages. Husbands."

"But you think I should go to college so I can meet a husband," I say. "I saw your email to your Individualists."

"Well, okay. But I didn't mean it like that," he says. "I just . . . I don't want you to be unfulfilled. Mundanity isn't good for people like you. Or your mother. You understand, Zoey, your mother didn't do what she did because she needed the money. Not at first. Okay? Do you understand?"

And suddenly I do understand. All my life, I thought I was like Dad. Weird, quiet, awkward, short, messy, disorganized, into peanut butter sandwiches with the crusts cut off, and having a strong dislike for organized activities.

But maybe it's not Dad who I'm like. Maybe it's Mom. My insouciantly dressed, murdered mother who has left us like *this*. My interesting, slow-acting-poison specialist mother, who found our home life so wretched that she became a murderer just to be less bored. Who then got herself killed and

Dad kidnapped. And put me and Ben and Roscoe in danger. And left me to fix it.

But I did. I fixed it. I wish I could talk to my mom about fixing it. I wish I could talk to her about Pete. And about why she became a slow-acting poison specialist. I wonder if her ghost will visit me and explain. I hope it will. I'd like to know how all this happened. I'd like to know her. It seems unlikely. I haven't dreamed of her much at all, and when I have, she and I haven't been chatty.

And I still haven't seen any solid evidence that would lead me to believe ghosts actually exist, besides, you know, my brother being visited by hers on a regular basis. But also, I might just be past being surprised by anything. Ben told me it was statistically impossible we'd find Roscoe again. And now look at us. Anything could happen next. I mean, it really could.

"You want takeout, sweetie?" Dad asks.

"Yeah," I say.

"Pizza?" says Dad. I'd been hungry for Lee's. But now pizza sounds fine. Pizza, shower, sleep. Then life, I guess. A life where I finish high school, get through a handful more lacrosse games without working up a sweat, maybe find out if Pete and I like each other when we aren't on the hunt for our criminally inclined parents, and then, who knows.

But first this. "So, we found something last night," says Aunt Lisa, putting down her bag of alpaca sausage on the table. Roscoe immediately hops over to sniff it. He's licking his lips. "Don't know if it's important or not. Found it in an air duct. Noticed when we turned the heat on last night. It burned a little. Brr, it gets colder in Virginia than you'd think, and I'm a New England girl!"

"Where is it?" I ask.

"Right here," she says, pulling a Ziploc out of her bag. I walk over to take it from her and instantly know what I'm looking at.

"Ben, come with me," I say, going upstairs to my room.

"I'm reading," he says.

"Come with me," I say.

"You're too bossy," he says, but follows this time.

When we get to my room, I turn on the light that makes the sea creatures swim across my walls. Take off the crusty, worn army jacket. Put the gun in my bedside table, then open the bag, which is filled with shreds of paper, charred and browned in places, with bits of my mother's handwriting on them. I forgot what terrible handwriting she had. She'd write notes and lists that only our family could read. Outsiders would look and say, "Julia, you should have been a doctor!" And she'd laugh, say, "I can't stand blood."

Thinking of her saying that brings quick tears to my eyes. Mom couldn't stand blood, but she was a killer and I want desperately to know where she got the idea to do this, and if it was *hard* to kill people. If they knew that she was killing them. How much she got paid to do it. If she liked doing it. If she loved me, and Dad, and Ben. If she was like me when she was my age. If she sees herself in me.

I pull out one scrap, with initials K.L. and a bit of an address. Another piece has 45 Neptune Drive, and the date 4/13 on it, but I can't make out the year.

"It's the J-File, Benny," I say, feeling agitated.

"It would appear to be," Ben says. "Though I would have to examine more of the papers to be able to say for certain. These papers definitely appear to have similarities with my dream diary."

"You've seen these before, right?" I ask. My voice gets

louder. "Mom never visited you in your dreams, right? You just made up this crazy story. I know you know how to lie now. Why would you have lied about *this*?" I have to take slow breaths, talk myself down. If I keep this up, Ben is going to have one of his class-A meltdowns. Or maybe I'm going to have one of Ben's class-A meltdowns. Like the nuclear reactor I'm named after (though I believe I've had more actual meltdowns than it's had; the name Zoe apparently was an acronym for "zero power," which makes a girl feel good and all). And there's a gun in my bedside table. (One with no bullets in it, I think, I think?)

But Ben stays calm. He's really changed, this little brother. This maddening little brother, the Trask bound for goodness if not greatness.

"If Mom hadn't visited me in my dreams, how would I have known that it wasn't Dad's fault?" he says. And maybe he's right.

The J-File. I don't know, obviously, how this turned up, torn, in the heating duct. Maybe Mom hid it there, having second thoughts about giving it to P.F. Maybe then she had second thoughts about the second thoughts and visited Ben in his dreams to complete what she started.

Or maybe Ben really had found it, and had some understanding of what he was looking at. He might have gotten upset, then destroyed it in one of his now-rare fits, and forgotten that part, holding on to the J-File part that he saw in that steel-trap brain. I don't know. I do know that I'm hungry. And tired of wondering, all the time, who is lying. And just tired. I put the Ziploc in my dresser and try to give Ben a hug. He squirms away, which is an odd relief. Not everything has changed.

• • •

"Where's your friend Pete, honey?" Aunt Lisa asks when we come back downstairs.

"He had to go," I say. "I think he'll be back."

"Good," says Aunt Lisa. "He seems very nice."

"Is he your boyfriend?" asks Uncle Henry. I shrug.

And here we all are, at home, waiting for our pizza. I pet Roscoe, toss his ball around, put off starting on laundry and homework. Ben sits on the floor reading a very thick book. Dad is in his ransacked office, ignoring the mess, catching up with the Internet. Uncle Henry and Aunt Lisa watch television, nibbling on the homemade sausage. Nothing's changed; everything's changed. I know these people as well as I know anything, and in some ways I know everything about them. I love them. They love me. I can predict what they'll do in almost any situation. Almost.

What I don't know yet is what I'll do. When I was little, between lectures about Ayn Rand's cats and the proper technique for executing a perfect kick and the reasons why bread crusts are disgusting, Dad would tell me that the most important thing is not to be tripped up by your own worst tendencies. To learn your own patterns, and learn how to defeat the bad ones. To stop yourself from making the mistakes that your body and your brain want you to make. To make sure you won't be your own fatal enemy. That I won't be *my* own fatal enemy.

Whenever I looked confused or annoyed at this sort of ranting—which was a lot—he'd repeat a quote from Abraham Lincoln, Dad's favorite "dead white powermonger." Maybe he figured Abraham Lincoln was someone a ten-year-old girl could relate to, or at least someone we'd both heard of outside our home, unlike Ayn Rand.

The quote: "Do I not destroy my enemies when I make them my friends?"

I would stare at him, bored and pissed off. He would then go on to describe in great detail his "quibbles" with Abraham Lincoln—namely, that our sixteenth president suspended *habeas corpus* and expanded the role of the federal government. (In the name of ending slavery. Yes, Dad *did* admit that ending slavery was a good thing to do. *"But at what cost?"*)

"What enemy should I make my friend, Dad?" I once asked. "What enemy do I want to destroy?"

"Your own weakness," he replied.

"That's the lamest thing I've ever heard. It doesn't even mean anything."

"It's a metaphor."

"What's a *metaphor*?" I asked.

Dad left and made a sandwich.

All these years, a few English classes, and a mother I never knew later, I think I might have a better idea what Dad was trying to say.

But I know what I need now. More metaphors. I'm serious. I need for my enemies not to be quite so goddamn *literal* for a while. I need to know what I like. Who I am. Maybe I can see what it is inside me that could turn me into a slow-acting poison specialist, and then dead.

I wish my mom were here to help me with that part. But in a way, I guess, she already has. And now that I know, I suppose I can think about the next move. Which is dinner. Which suddenly, very suddenly, feels much more important than it had.

"Dad," I call out. "Dad?"

"What, honey?" he shouts.

"C'mon, Roscoe," I say, tapping my thigh and walking into the office. The office is exactly how P.F. and I left it. A worse wreck than usual. Papers akimbo. Books all over the floor. Framed movie posters are hanging crookedly, but they might have been that way even before the great search of the J-File twisted through this place like a tornado on a mission. "I'm sorry it's such a mess in here," I say. "We were trying to find . . . Mom's list."

"I'll clean up tomorrow," says Dad, looking around like he's noticing the state of things for the first time. He definitely won't clean up tomorrow. He probably won't ever clean up. I'll do it one day when I don't want to work on a school project. Or when school is over and I have nothing else to do, and I'm drifting toward . . . I don't know what yet.

"I don't want pizza," I say suddenly. "I'm really hungry for Lee's."

I squeeze Roscoe's ball in my hand for what seems like minutes. It feels like my whole future depends on what Dad says next.

And what he says is, "Okay, baby girl. You can choose."

Acknowledgments

Thank you first and foremost to my dream of an editor, Dan Ehrenhaft, and to everyone at Soho Teen. It's almost impossible to imagine a better experience than I've had working with you. And a huge thank you to my agent, Emily Sylvan Kim at Prospect Agency, for your cheerleading and representation, and also for being a thoroughly terrific person.

My husband Ray is not only the most supportive, and brilliant, and hilarious partner I could ask for—his deep knowledge about Ayn Rand, and his Murray-the-dog walking skills, were also both essential to the completion of this project. Murray the dog and Derrick the cat's adorableness were also crucial in harder-to-define, but obviously still-very-important, ways.

And thank you Mom and Dad. I hope you know that none of the parent characters in this book are based on you. I love you very much, and I appreciate everything you've done for me—including all the times you didn't tell me, exasperatedly, to go use my law degree already. My brother Lee and sister-in-law Lori are also better cheerleaders than I could have asked for. Plus, their dog Kaya is by far the cutest husky mix I know.

I am lucky enough to have married into a family as warm and supportive as the one I was born into. Thank you, Lehmanns and Rosas, for making me feel like one of your own (and for not telling me exasperatedly to go use my law degree).

There aren't enough thanks in the world for the friends and family members who have helped in various critical ways through the years. In no particular order, but with lots and lots of appreciation, and apologies in advance for anyone who I have forgotten with this very forgetful brain: thank you to Jodi, Alex, Karen, Sharon, James, Dan, Theresa, Eli, Lucia and Sean, Vicki and David, Steve, San and Abs, Jamie, Dan and the kiddies, Aunt Sandi and Uncle Albert, cousin Ally, Mr. and Mrs. Sockol, cousins Kenny and Lisa and Bill—and Aunt Arleen and Uncle Larry, please know that I borrowed the dog story out of love.

Thank you to Back Porch Books for publishing my first novel, and to Rick and Jeff for everything it took for that to happen.

Finally, while it may not seem obvious, I don't think any of this would have happened had Columbia Law School not admitted me, educated me, and set me on a strange and unpredictable (and maybe a little impecunious) path that led from New York to Saipan to DC, with many stops along the way. Thank you especially, CLS, for not telling me too exasperatedly to go use my law degree already.